Crash into Me

Crash into Me

TAYLOR ROMAGNOLI

wattpad books
FRAYED PAGES

An imprint of Wattpad WEBTOON Book Group

Published in Canada and the United States by Wattpad WEBTOON Book Group, a division of WEBTOON Entertainment Inc.

36 Wellington Street E., Suite 200, Toronto, ON M5E 1C7 Canada
5700 Wilshire Boulevard, Suite 220, Los Angeles, CA 90036 USA

www.wattpad.com
www.frayedpagesmedia.com

First Frayed Pages x Wattpad Books edition: May 2026

ISBN 978-1-99834-169-6 (Trade Paper original)
ISBN 978-1-99834-170-2 (eBook edition)

Library and Archives Canada Cataloguing in Publication and U.S. Library of Congress Cataloging in Publication information is available upon request.

Printed and bound in Canada

1 3 5 7 9 10 8 6 4 2

Cover design by Lesley Worrell
Author photo by Christine Hamrick
Typesetting by Delaney Anderson

For my grandmother Renee, who was the first person to read the original draft of this novel. She passed before she could see this story published, but she'll always be my number one fan.

Playlist

cruel summer
The Maine

Saltwater
Geowulf

Deep End
Holly Humberstone

Serotonin
girl in red

Summer
Current Joys

Waiting on the Summer (Dave Edwards Remix)
VHS Collection

Disorder
Third Eye Blind

Close to You
Gracie Abrams

circle the drain
Soccer Mommy

New Shapes
Charli xcx, Christine and the Queens, Caroline Polachek

Colossal Youth
Moonpools & Caterpillars

New Religion
The Heydaze

Give It Up
KC & the Sunshine Band

Savior Complex
Phoebe Bridgers

I Wanna Get Better
Bleachers

mirrorball
Taylor Swift

Despicable Dogs (Washed Out Remix)
Small Black

Your Weather
Chief

Closer
Jack River

Don't Look Back in Anger
Oasis

Deep Inside of You
Third Eye Blind

Disarm
The Smashing Pumpkins

Not Strong Enough
boygenius

Take Me as You Please
The Story So Far

Me & My Dog
boygenius

Most Wanted Man
Lucy Dacus

Where Is Her Head
The National

Believe Me Natalie
The Killers

Playlist
CONTINUED

Huggin & Kissin
Big Black Delta

Just Pretend
Bad Omens

When I Say You Are Killing Me
Ten Kills the Pack

Punisher
Phoebe Bridgers

Summer (Acoustic Version)
Real Friends

cellophane
FKA twigs

Ritalin
Dexter and The Moonrocks

White Lie
The Lumineers

i'm worried it will always be you
Katie Gregson-MacLeod

LA in a Cop Car
The Dangerous Summer

Emergency
Paramore

Summer's End
Phoebe Bridgers

Sour Breath
Julien Baker

complex
Katie Gregson-MacLeod

white lies
Katie Gregson-MacLeod

Death Wish
Gracie Abrams

So Long, So Long
Dashboard Confessional

Will You Love Me Tomorrow
The Shirelles

this is me trying
Taylor Swift

Stop Making This Hurt
Bleachers

Even If She Falls
blink-182

Crash into Me
Stevie Nicks

Author's Note

This book contains depictions and descriptions of active drug addiction and eating disorders, but also recovery, therapy, and an understanding of how difficult it can be to get or ask for help. While the subject matter is based on real-life experiences, the content of this book is fictional. Any similarities to people and places is coincidental.

If you or someone you love is struggling with addiction, contact the Substance Abuse and Mental Health Services Administration's national hotline at 1-800-662-HELP (4357).

One

"The cure for anything is salt water: sweat, tears, or the sea."

Karen Blixen wrote that. We studied her *Seven Gothic Tales* short-story anthology in one of my last creative writing classes at Sky Valley, and maybe the quote had only stuck with me because I'd gone from having never in my life seen the beach to living at one just two weeks before classes started my final semester.

There had been so much going on at the time, I could barely process seeing the ocean for the first time, but I sort of understood what she meant. The smell of salt in the air carried with it something intangible and unrecognizable—almost hopeful. I'd told myself I'd find time to appreciate it later.

That was six months ago. Since then, I'd finished my last semester of college, submitted poetry and an anthology of short stories for various finals, and then skipped graduation because my mom had found my sister, Nikki, unconscious in the bathroom after dinner one night.

Nikki had always been slim, but this was nothing like when we were in high school, when she'd skip meals to fit into a pair of jeans she wanted to wear or stay late after soccer practice to run more. It had seemed so fine. So normal. But maybe we should have treated it like it *wasn't.* I tried not to let those thoughts scream like sirens in my head as I went at least twenty miles per hour over the speed limit the entire four-hour drive across South Carolina from Sky Valley to Dahlia Point.

So with all due respect to Karen Blixen, I'm not sure I buy into it. All the salt water in the world wouldn't have helped my sister. She was drowning out there, and I hadn't seen her flailing until it was too late.

I had gotten to the hospital downtown around 3 a.m. to see my sister asleep in bed, monitors beeping and tubes sticking out of her frail body like she was some kind of science experiment. Tears stung the backs of my eyes, but I kept it together for Mom, who held Nikki's limp hand in hers, her gray-streaked dirty-blond hair piled into a mess on top of her head and her old Carolina Panthers sweatshirt on inside out. I sat beside her, swallowed my salty tears, and decided I wasn't going to let this happen again.

Nobody prepares you for what to do when your sister has an eating disorder, but it didn't change how *aware* I was of my unpreparedness. After Nikki had been admitted to Otter House for rehab, I checked ten different books about eating disorders out from the local library, including memoirs, self-help books, and novels (and definitely was over the limit of books you could check out at once, but I could be persuasive when I wanted to be). I became an expert overnight, and I visited Nikki as often as I could (unfortunately, I couldn't persuade my way into being there outside the allotted visiting hours)—sometimes alone, and sometimes with our mom.

In the meantime, I tried to finally appreciate the ocean more during my morning runs. I'd only been in Dahlia Point full-time for two weeks, instead of the occasional weekend home to do laundry and have Mom's homemade lasagna, and it had taken me some time to carve out a new running route in my new home. We lived two blocks in from the beach, and at the end of every street was a pathway that led to a wooden boardwalk that took you over dunes dotted with colorful flowers and onto the plush beige expanse of beach. I wasn't enough of a sea-savvy local to pay attention to the tides, but usually in the mornings the tide was so low that there was close to a quarter of a mile between the boardwalk and where the waves kissed the sand.

I ran from the pathway on Sixth Street, past the pier that had supposedly been under construction since last year and one of the jetties that had SUCK LESS spray-painted in bright-blue graffiti. *Thanks, I'll try*, I usually said to myself when I passed it.

There was typically a middle-aged man running his golden retriever, which shot past me in flashes of blond fur. This time, we gave each other a friendly nod as I passed.

I looped around at a massive blue house—the classic Southern kind with three levels of wraparound porches, and which I had learned the locals of Dahlia Point called the Whale—and made my way back to the Sixth Street pathway.

It was easy to feel small at what felt like the edge of the world, watching the sea glint like diamonds as it melted into the vast horizon. My whole route was about two miles there and back, and for those two miles, I was okay with feeling small. It made everything feel so much less daunting than it really was.

Broken seashells crunched underneath me as I slowed to walking pace and made my way back up the beach and to the boardwalk, down to where the base of the stairs met the faded concrete of the street. I kicked around bits of sand that dusted the pavement the way stars would dot the sky on a clear night. As I trudged up the street, passing cute little bungalows in a myriad of vibrant colors, I realized how much our house stuck out. It somewhat resembled the others on the street, with the same raised foundation and screened-in front porch, but white paint peeled off the shutters and front stairs, exposing a layer of worn, splintering wood. Grass and weeds grew tall against the siding, and two palm trees brushed against the faded gray of the roof. The previous owner had been a shut-in, and now that school was out, Mom's priority was "getting the house to look like a home"—her words, not mine.

I made my way inside and winced as the screen door closed behind me with a loud creak.

"Nat?" My mom's voice carried from the kitchen to the front of the house, followed by the sound of clattering dishes. "You back?"

"No, it's Neal Caffrey come to steal your replica of *Saint George and the Dragon*." I chuckled as I kicked off my sneakers onto the welcome mat in front of the door. It was the first thing Mom had bought for the new house when we were getting ready to move—she had to have it when we saw it at HomeGoods because it said OH SHIT, NOT YOU AGAIN. She found that *hilarious*.

"Neal Caffrey would *know* it's fake," she called back.

"Good point," I said as I heaved out a sigh.

Gracie, our aging Borzoi, lifted her head off the old paisley couch in the front den by way of greeting me. That had become her new spot in the house since she could easily play security guard from the front window. I walked over and gave her a quick scratch on her long snout.

"Speaking of," Mom continued as I made my way into the kitchen, "we're overdue for a *White Collar* rewatch."

Mom and I binged a lot of older shows and movies, but *White Collar* was the one we kept going back to. There was something deeply comforting about watching a show where you already knew the ending—there were no surprises or tricks or unexpected scenes that made you emotional, and surprises and I were *not* natural cohabitants.

I sat down at a stained-glass bar stool at our tiny kitchen island and watched her lean forward on her toes to put a stack of bowls in the cabinet beside our aesthetically vintage baby-blue Smeg fridge. Mom treated our new house like her own canvas, doing things she never would have done back in that standard-issue townhouse we grew up in. Here, she insisted upon a retro theme for our new kitchen—we had half of the matching Smeg appliances, like a toaster and a coffee maker, and she was almost through painting the trim around the white cabinets the same blue as the appliances. Painter's tarp covered our kitchen table and the entire left side of the counters by the sink, so we'd been eating dinner on the couch and watching a variety of comfort shows.

"And deviate from our nightly *Bake Off* episodes?" I feigned offense, clapping my hands to my chest. "Blasphemous."

She finally spun around to face me, leaning back against the counter and pressing her hands onto it. The sleeves of her deep-green workman's shirt were rolled up, revealing her paint-speckled forearms, and she softened her gaze on me. When you're a child, your parents do their best to shield you from emotional turbulence, including their own. But as an adult, I'd grown to know that look. She was contemplating saying something about how I should be *taking it easy*, or that she was *worried about me*, or some combination of the two.

But instead she said, "When are you leaving?"

"As soon as I get sand out of uncomfortable places," I replied, plucking an apple from the ceramic bowl Mom had made a few years ago in the center of the island. Silence settled between us, and it was only then I realized she had all the windows open, and even from a block away the sound of the ocean could be heard faintly in the distance. Maybe one day I'd believe salt water could cure all things, but not today.

>> <<

I was halfway to Otter House when a text from Nikki's attending nurse appeared on my Jetta's dashboard screen.

BECK (OTTER HOUSE): Nikki's begging for a peanut butter and jelly cream cold brew from bad beans. She says "pls pls pls (sabrina carpenter voice)"

BECK (OTTER HOUSE): I'm okay with it—she's doing well

Bad Beans had quickly become our favorite coffee shop when we moved to Dahlia Point. It wasn't actually *in* Dahlia Point, but after scouring social media for the best coffee places in the area when I'd come home for spring break, Nikki had insisted upon trying it despite the twenty-minute car ride inland toward the airport. It was worth it, obviously, and she never let me hear the end of it, insisting we take the drive out there at least once a weekend. They had a menu about a mile long and constantly rotated seasonal drinks and specials—when Taylor Swift dropped her *The Tortured Poets Department* album, they had a special cookies and cream cold foam drink for that day only, or on Star Wars Day (May 4) they served some weird blue drink that was supposed to resemble what they drank on Tatooine. Nikki liked to experiment and get different drinks, but I stuck to my iced vanilla latte.

Some people associated vanilla anything with being boring, but I preferred to think of it as keeping to a routine. I knew what I liked, and there was no point in deviating. Routine kept me focused, especially during a time when my focus was desperately needed.

Bad Beans happened to be on the way to Otter House, so I usually stopped to get a latte for myself, but I didn't get one for my sister unless I'd gotten approval beforehand. Her meals were supervised, and typically, outside food and drink wasn't allowed. Repairing her relationship with food took priority over peanut butter and jelly cream cold brews. But with those three words, my mood lifted. *She's doing well.*

I rolled my windows down and blasted Holly Humberstone, sticking my hand out to feel the late-spring air breeze through my fingers. I'd finished almost a quarter of my latte by the time I made it to the palm tree–lined driveway of Otter House and pulled into a marked visitor's spot in the parking lot. It was clear a conscious effort had been made to not make it look like a recovery facility, with perfectly manicured landscaping and a big stone fountain with a pineapple at the top in front of the building. It was probably one of the reasons Nikki had felt comfortable with this place over the several others we'd looked at. It didn't feel so sterile and sad, and maybe it was somewhere she could actually see herself getting better.

After putting both of our drinks into a carrying tray, I trekked across the parking lot, balancing the tray in one hand while my tote bag hung half open off my shoulder as I tried to stick my keys into it. My phone buzzed in my pocket, and as I struggled to fish it out of my jeans, I collided shoulder to shoulder with another person going about a hundred miles per hour in the opposite direction.

"Oh shit." A guy's voice startled me, and before I could react, I toppled backward and fell down hard onto the concrete. A mess of ice cubes and coffee spilled down the front of my T-shirt, soaking me in sticky liquid. I groaned as I shakily got to my knees, feeling my whole lower body vibrate with pain.

"Goddamn it." I grimaced at the sight of our lattes, now a crime scene of cold brew, espresso, and oat milk in the parking lot. There was no salvaging them.

"Oh my god, I'm so sorry."

I was so distraught I'd almost forgotten about the latte assassin, but there he was, already on his feet and decidedly *not* covered in cold brew, extending a hand to me.

"Come on, let me help you up." There was an unexpected kindness to his voice—something foreign, like he might as well have been speaking another language.

My eyes were immediately drawn to a scar that trailed up from the base of his thumb and wrapped around his wrist, disappearing into the inside of his forearm. It was deep, but a soft, faded red color, which meant it had healed the best it could a long time ago. He wore a silver ring on his pointer finger that glinted in the late-morning sun.

"Are you gonna take my hand?" His deep voice pulled me out of my daze. "I look kind of ridiculous just standing here now."

I cautiously slipped my hand into his, feeling calloused skin on his palm.

"All right, now the other."

He motioned for me to take his other hand, crossed over the other arm, and with more force than I expected, hoisted me onto my feet. At five seven I liked to consider myself almost tall, but I barely came up to his chest, and with the sun backlighting him in a paradoxically angelic way, it felt like his shadow was swallowing me whole.

I finally got a good look at his face, and had to remind myself to breathe. I have never believed the sight of someone could literally *take your breath away*, but my lungs were struggling.

His jawline was angular and strong, and light freckles dusted his nose and cheeks. Another scar grazed the bottom of his chin, though not nearly as angry looking as the one on his wrist. His hair had probably been styled back at some point, but most of it had come undone, and chocolate-brown locks cascaded in messy waves onto his forehead. But it was his eyes that sucked me in—the deepest blue, dark and endless like the ocean in a storm.

Then he smiled at me, endearing and just a little guilty, and everything in me softened.

"I really am sorry. Are you all right?"

"I'm fine," I replied. "No use crying over spilled coffee."

He chuckled and rubbed the back of his neck, dropping his gaze to the now-empty plastic cups that gently rolled around on the pavement. He bent down to pick them up and stacked one into the other.

"There's a coffee shop down the street," he said, gesturing outward with the plastic cups. "I can get you something else, if you want."

I almost said yes to that enticing smile of his—the kind that I was sure got him whatever he wanted. But I was there for a reason, and the more I dillydallied with the latte assassin, the less time I had with my sister.

"Don't worry about it," I reassured him. My whole body still buzzed, but whether it was from the impact or something else, I wasn't sure. "I need to get going."

"Okay, well . . . see you around," he said with casual assuredness before sidestepping and letting me walk by, and I tried to convince my body not to betray me and look back at him.

"Morning, Nat." Beck was already at the check-in desk, and greeted me when I walked in with a puzzled look. "You're, uh . . ." She gestured to the front of my baby-pink T-shirt, where my spilled latte was on full display. "Guess your coffee run was unsuccessful."

"Don't ask." I fished my ID out of my wallet and handed it to her. "Thank god Nikki has enough clothes here to stock a boutique."

Beck grinned as she handed me my visitor's pass before walking me back to Nikki's room.

As I made my way through the halls, passing closed doors with all kinds of stories behind them, I couldn't help but think about the guy in the parking lot. Had he been visiting someone like I was, a family member or a close friend, so they didn't have to spend all their days here alone? Did he feel guilty, like I did?

The smell of acetone hit me as soon as I walked into Nikki's room, where she was crouched over on her bed, painting her toenails a vibrant pink. Like everything about my sister's entire existence, she'd found a way to be as maximalist as she could with her temporary room, from the pink-and-orange-checkered comforter on her bed to the strings of rainbow beads that hung in front of the window. As the sun streamed in, it sent a confetti of colors across the pale wooden floors.

As soon as Nikki looked up at me, she let out a snicker. "Are you *wearing* my cold brew?"

"Aren't you the one who's always telling me to be more risky with my fashion choices? Consider this a risk that did *not* pay off."

She laughed as I began digging through the college dorm–grade dresser in the corner of her room. The drawer was half empty, and I clocked about six shirts strewn across the itchy armchair in the other corner.

"Are these clean?" I picked up a tie-dyed crop top and folded it into a little square.

"Oh, yeah, I just did my laundry." She sounded bored, and turned her attention back to painting her toenails.

"Nik." I picked up another shirt to fold. "You have to put your clothes *away* after they're washed, otherwise they're going to be a wrinkled mess when you go to wear them."

"Well, I *did*." She let out a frustrated groan. "But then I couldn't decide what to wear to yoga this morning, and didn't have time to put it all back."

"You have time now." I tossed the rest of the shirts at her, and she yelped.

"Um, hello? Wet nail polish!"

There was a faded navy Sky Valley University crewneck in one of the dresser drawers (which upon further inspection was definitely *mine*), and I quickly changed. Nikki and I didn't share clothes too often, since we had decidedly *much* different styles, but when I became aware of some of the hallmark signs of certain eating disorders, I realized she'd been hiding her weight loss in oversized T-shirts and hoodies, including mine.

Hindsight was 20/20, but that didn't make the revelation suck any less.

"What compelled you to make these risky fashionable choices?" Nikki asked, nodding at the stained T-shirt in my hand.

I heaved out another sigh as I lowered myself onto her bed. "I was distracted getting out of my car and I tripped. Spilled everything all over me."

There wasn't really a point to telling Nikki the truth, mostly because there was a guy involved. I wasn't a *dater*, for no reason other than it wasn't currently worth the time or effort for me, but my overeager little sister didn't buy that excuse. She'd take one encounter with the latte assassin and escalate it to the point of setting up a wedding board on Pinterest. It was better for all of us to stay grounded and present.

"At least you smell good now." She shrugged.

I playfully shoved her arm. "Excuse me, are you implying I *didn't* smell good?"

"You said it, not me."

Nikki tied her platinum-blond hair up into a bun, her grown-out brunet roots a tangible indicator of the two weeks she'd been here already. But a healthy glow had returned to her cheeks, and her eyes weren't so glassy and sad.

Then again, she'd never really looked *sick* to me, but that was one of the first things I learned after her diagnosis. Sometimes it wasn't obvious, and that was what made finding out hurt that much more. She would still do her makeup and wear her loud outfits, and she'd go out every weekend with the friends she'd already made here. When I'd come home some weekends we'd bake slutty brownies and eat the whole tray while we binge-watched *Laguna Beach*.

But it should have been more obvious to *me*. I was her older sister, and if I couldn't see her struggling, then who could have?

"What?" She eyed me suspiciously.

"Nothing." I shook my head at her and smiled. "You look good, Nik."

She rolled her eyes and flopped back onto her bed. Even if she didn't believe me right now, it was still important she heard it from me.

"Can we watch *Legally Blonde*?" she asked.

"I thought you'd never ask."

Two

May 16

Hi Dad,

I went to see Nikki again yesterday, and she's starting to really seem like herself again, biting sarcastic wit and all.

But sometimes when I glance over at her, I can still see the tiredness in her eyes, like she's had enough of this already. I keep thinking I should have seen it sooner—that I should've noticed the skipped meals, the long showers, and all the things I learned a little too late. And then I think, what if it truly is too late? The world is full of a thousand little what-ifs, and I can't stop tripping over every single one.

They say recovery isn't linear. That's what the pamphlet says, anyway. But I wish it was. I wish there was a map with a clear path out of the dark, because right now everything feels like walking blindfolded with no one even holding my hand to guide me. I reach out sometimes and think maybe I'll find your hand. I hate that I can't fix this for her. I hate that all I can do is show up with lattes and a smile and pretend I'm not terrified every second of every day that one day the damage will be irreversible.

Thanks for listening. I know you'd probably tell me something like *Keep moving forward*, or *Take it one day at a time*, and I'm going to keep trying to do that.

Love, Nat

I shut my Moleskine journal. I was almost out of pages in this one, and I made a mental note to pick up a new one next time I was at work. The late-spring sun was beginning to set, waking up all the frogs and cicadas, who sang their tunes into the dusky orange sky.

My letters to Dad weren't impeccable pieces of prose by any means, but they were what kept me writing, and what kept me grounded.

I started writing stories when I was young, when everyone my age started reading the *Harry Potter* series, and I was steadfastly Team Draco (I firmly believed he was misunderstood). Since that obviously wasn't who Hermione ended up with, I took it upon myself to write the story I thought should happen.

I'd stayed up late when Mom thought I'd gone to sleep, scribbling pages and pages of stories into little notebooks. The first few years after my dad had passed, I'd seen a children's grief counselor, and I'd shared with her some of my stories. She encouraged me to start writing my own stories about my own experiences and what I was feeling. At the time, I didn't really understand. When you're eight years old, you're old enough to know what's happened, but not old enough to understand the ramifications it's going to have on the rest of your life. What kind of story was I supposed to tell?

So instead, I started writing letters to Dad. They were simple at first, just telling him about my day at school or about a birthday party I'd gone to where we played princesses and dragons. Eventually they transitioned into homecoming parties, breakups, what TV shows everyone was watching, and what music we were listening to. I was telling him stories, even if they weren't fictional, and I looked forward to writing them. But these were mine—private conversations between me and my dad, as if we were still hiding in pillow forts and sharing secrets.

I thought back to *Harry Potter* and realized that part of the reason I enjoyed those stories so much was because there was an escapism factor to them, one I guess I'd needed. So I spent all of my college writing courses crafting short stories of magical realism. I got really into Stephen King and H. P. Lovecraft. I consumed all kinds of magic-based media. It was like finding my fictional escape velocity, and it worked for a while.

I had an interconnected anthology I'd written for one of my finals (very Lovecraftian in its format) and upon graduation, I sent the pitch for it to a few agents. Most of them gave me an obviously generic response they send to any submitting author when they couldn't be bothered to provide feedback.

Hi Natalie,

Thank you so much for your query. I read your pages with interest, but unfortunately your manuscript isn't the right fit for me. I'm going to pass, but do not be discouraged as every agent has their own tastes.

Stay well, and thank you again for sharing your work with me!

Best regards,

An agent who definitely had not read my pages

I was applying to entry-level jobs in publishing, too, in hopes that maybe I could finagle myself into the industry that way, and ironically enough got pretty much the same responses.

Hi Natalie,

Thank you for applying to our copy editor position. Unfortunately, we are moving forward with a different candidate for this role.

Best regards,

A company that wants six years of experience for an entry-level job

My only means of income right now was a part-time job at Stacks, a local bookstore downtown, where most of my time was spent reading, scribbling in my notebook, and shuffling through the jazz playlist that played throughout the cramped little store.

I knew I needed something fresh to pitch to agents in hopes of being published, but all I had so far was a half-completed beat sheet about a down-on-her-luck teenage girl who gets accidentally shrunken by a newly winged fairy experimenting with spells.

Maybe a change of scenery would help. So I moved from my desk to my bed. I changed positions about six times, switching from my stomach to my back to my stomach again. I played "Serotonin" by girl in red on repeat. I got distracted by my laundry. I folded and refolded my shirts (including the now coffee-free one).

Then I went downstairs to the kitchen and sat at the island and stared out the window at people walking by on the street, trying to differentiate the tourists from the locals and making up stories for them instead of working on my own.

Gracie found her way to my feet and let out a deep, far too burdened sigh for a dog who had a life full of naps and treats.

"Do you want to go for a walk?" I asked, optimistic that maybe a walk would help *me* too.

Even in her old age, the word *walk* perked her ears up. So I grabbed her leash, hanging from the ceramic fruit hooks by the back door, and took her out. She didn't really "walk" anymore, but rather ambled along casually, sniffing yellowing palm fronds that had fallen from the trees on the side of the road.

Of course, to the stranger walking by on the street, Gracie was still a big, scary horse-looking Borzoi, and sometimes they'd cross the street as they saw us coming, as if I was going to sic her on them.

"Don't worry, girl, I know you're the worst guard dog in the world," I cooed at her, reaching down to pat her big head.

Mom had found Gracie on Craigslist as a puppy about a year after Dad died, and thought maybe a dog would help me and Nikki cope. We had no idea how to train or handle a dog, but for some reason, Gracie didn't need much training. She was mellow and loving even as a puppy. Nikki always believed Gracie was sent to us for a reason, that she would help fill the void that Dad left, but I thought we just got lucky.

We did a short lap down to the beach and back, and as I approached our driveway, Mom was situating herself in front of a large canvas in our garage/her makeshift art studio, where she could get paint all over the walls and not feel bad about it. Fuzzy music from her Bluetooth speaker carried through the air as I walked up the driveway, and I followed the faint sound of Stevie Nicks's voice crooning out some soft love ballad into the garage.

Blues and greens in glossy paint splashed the corners, and she continued to paint the canvas with unwavering flow and elegance. She reached up and painted an aqua blue stroke at the top, then brought her arm down to the other corner and flicked her brush off the edge of the canvas. She was painting the waves, so she moved like one.

"What do you think?" She tilted her head to the side and studied the blank corner of the canvas with intensity. Blue paint dotted her cheeks like little freckles, and there were streaks of green in the flyaway bits of dirty-blond hair that had fallen out of her ponytail.

"It's pretty," I told her. "They're always pretty, Mom."

She frowned a bit and furiously mixed more blues and greens on a small plastic palette. Everything about my mom was soft and warm like a summer evening—that is, until she had a paintbrush in her hands.

"I feel so out of practice with acrylics now." She sighed, maybe more to herself than me. I took Gracie's leash off and let her meander over to the round plush bed in the corner of the garage, before walking over to Mom's side. "I spent the entire fall focused on watercolors, and now I'm having regrets."

"Spoken like a true artist." I chuckled dryly.

The whole reason we'd moved four hours east from Arcadia to Dahlia Point was for a job she'd taken as a featured artist at a local gallery. Mom was *from* Dahlia Point, but she'd never brought us here until we moved. I'd figured it was for a reason, but I never asked.

She was a painter by trade but had taught art classes at a private school for almost my whole life. Teaching provided her with a routine and stability when we were growing up, but now that we were adults, she could go back to her passion full-time.

"You seem even less enthused than usual," she said, not taking her eyes off the canvas. "What's bothering you?"

It wasn't *Is something bothering you*, because she didn't need to ask that. She knew, as she always did.

I groaned and lowered myself onto another stool beside her. "It's ridiculous. These companies want you to have experience, but how could I possibly have six years of experience for an entry-level job?"

Mom finally looked over at me, and sometimes when the light hit her the right way, I could see bits of myself in her, from the sheen in her hazel eyes to the mess of dirty-blond hair, knots and all.

"Have a little patience. You only graduated a few weeks ago," she replied. She dipped her brush in her mixture and continued with her elaborate stroking. "Have you worked on any writing at all?"

"No." I sighed. "I mean, I'm trying, but . . ." I let my voice trail off, watching her continue her brushstrokes.

"You'll find inspiration from where you least expect it. That's part of being a creator—making something out of what seems like nothing."

I smiled to myself. "When did you get so wise?"

"I've *always* been wise." She chuckled. "You were just too much of a stubborn teenager to realize that."

"Can't even argue with that."

I got up from the stool and gave her a side-armed hug, careful not to get paint on my T-shirt.

"Hey, wait," she called after me as I walked to the door leading into the house. I paused and spun on my heel with my hand still on the doorknob. "I have an idea that might jumpstart some inspiration for you."

She got up from her stool and dragged another large canvas to the wall by the open door of the garage, and I knew almost immediately what she was going to suggest.

"Paint balloons?" she asked.

"Oh boy." I shook my head with a faint grin. "Let me put a different shirt on. This is the last good white T-shirt I own."

Mom loved messes, and was a firm believer that she could produce art from them. We had done it a few times over the years, filling balloons with mixtures of paint, silicone, and water, and throwing them at canvases. The first one the three of us had done years ago still hung in our living room over the couch, its mismatch of colors perfect for our mismatched furniture.

We took turns filling balloons from a package she always had on hand and carefully placing them in a bucket. After putting a rain poncho on, I took one and chucked it underhand at the canvas, yelping as it exploded in a mess of green and blue and yellow. She did the same, and paint sprinkled down on us like rain.

"A friggin' masterpiece." Mom laughed. "Belongs in a museum, if you ask me."

We carried on for a little while, until the rays of the sun against the concrete floor turned to shadows and the sound of frogs and insects in the night echoed around the thin walls of the garage. I washed my hands in the slop sink in the corner as Mom moved our paint-balloon art to a corner to dry.

"Feel better?" she asked, trying to brush strands of hair out of her face without getting more paint on her.

"A lot, actually." I offered her a faint smile as I dried my hands with a rag. "I needed that."

"You know, Nat . . ." She heaved out a sigh as she sat back down on her stool in front of her canvas. "You're only twenty-two. You're so young, and I don't want you to live some of the best years of your life as a passenger, worried about the next stop you're getting off at."

I tried not to let the tension that settled in me show on my face, and I took a measured breath. "That's a pretty metaphor, but I'm okay. Really, I am."

She nodded, but seemed unconvinced. Silence settled between us, with nothing but the sound of Fleetwood Mac floating through the air, and even though I could have (maybe should have) ended the conversation, I still lingered. Sometimes I just needed my mom, but didn't know how to ask. Thankfully, she knew my looks as well as I knew hers.

"Your sister is going to be all right, you know."

"How do you know?"

"I'm your mother, I know everything."

A laugh escaped me, and I decided that for now, it was good enough. "Right, of course."

Mom called after me once more as I retreated to the door to the house. "Nat? Promise me you'll have fun this summer. Before you decide to go off and be a successful adult."

"I promise."

Three

I spent the rest of the weekend helping Mom finish painting the kitchen cabinets. Even though I was nowhere near as delicate with my brush handling as she was, I knew she was letting me help because otherwise I'd go insane cooped up in my room in front of a blank Google Doc.

Mom wanted me to "have fun" this summer, but a few weeks in I felt like all I was doing was *waiting*. Waiting to hear back from agents, waiting around until I could visit my sister, waiting for customers to visit the bookstore so I could point them to the sports-romance section, waiting for creative inspiration to strike me like lightning in an open field.

Waiting was *not* fun for someone like me—I wanted to be able to plan accordingly, so there were no more unexpected happenings that could unstick me from the solid ground I was comfortable on. My dad passing had filled my quota for unexpected happenings for the rest of my life.

So come the following Monday, I was bright-eyed and ready to *not* be waiting as I drove out to Otter House for visitation hours.

Even though nothing eventful usually happened during my visits, and Nikki and I would spend our time vegging, online shopping, and watching early 2000s rom-coms, I knew I needed to be there. I was her older sister, so there was nowhere else I *should* have been.

But when I parked in my usual spot and made my way up the cobblestoned path to Otter House's main entrance, the single most eventful thing that had happened to me since my summer had started was standing there underneath the shadow of the overhang, and he looked like he was *waiting*, coffees in hand.

He wore a Charleston RiverDogs T-shirt that was faded just enough to look intentionally vintage, and his hair was windswept just enough to look intentionally messy. When I got closer to him, I caught a whiff of fresh and clean cologne coming off his T-shirt.

"Hey," he greeted me with a similar smile as last time—unassuming but frustratingly enticing.

"Were you—" I turned around to make sure he was in fact talking to *me*. Wouldn't want to be embarrassed in back-to-back encounters. "Were you waiting for me?"

"I told you I owed you," he replied with a shrug. "I really did feel bad for knocking you over. I was in a rush to leave, and—" He paused and shook his head. "Anyway, I was hoping you'd come back around the same time."

He handed me an olive branch in the form of an iced coffee, sandy colored from maybe a bit too much milk or creamer, and when I took it, the brushing of my fingertips against his shot static up my arm.

"Well, thank you." I tapped my pink-painted fingernails on the plastic of the cup, hyperfixating on a chip on my pointer finger. I'd have to have Nikki fix that. "You didn't have to do that, but I will *never* turn down free coffee."

That got him to laugh, and the static moved into the pit of my stomach, buzzing and excited.

"I'm Brooklyn, by the way."

Obviously the latte assassin had a name, but now that I knew it, it humanized him and made him all too real.

"Like the city," I said with a soft smile.

"Like the bridge, actually."

It was my turn to laugh. "I'm Nat. Well, Natalie, but Nat to most people. Like the tiny flying bug, I guess?"

"Are you telling me you spell your name with a silent *g*?" He arched an eyebrow at me.

"What? No. You know what I mean," I said. "Guess I'm not nearly as funny as you."

"Guess not." His grin widened.

Not embarrassing myself in a second encounter had decidedly failed.

Guys didn't normally frazzle me, but the heat I felt spreading across my cheeks said otherwise, and I could have jumped off a cliff and into those gorgeous ocean-blue eyes of his to cool myself off. When I figured he was studying me in a similar way, that fuzzy static erupted through my whole body.

A breeze whistled through the trees, and it seemed to reground us both. He had a reason to be there too. We both moved to the front door at the same time, sharing a half awkward, half sincere chuckle.

"It's not really my business, but are you visiting someone?" he asked.

"I am." I nodded. "My sister."

"Got it." He paused and stopped in front of the door, pressing his hands together in front of his mouth. "I'm sorry, that was so—was that overstepping? I've been told I'm a yapper, and the foot-in-mouth stuff comes naturally to me. You don't have to tell me."

Whether I was put off by his blunt foot-in-mouth question

didn't matter, it got me to laugh all the same. I had never met someone who lent themselves to being so effortlessly endearing. It was nice, and *so* distracting. "It's fine, really. I don't mind. I mean, you're here, too, so."

He reached over me to open the door, motioning for me to walk in front of him.

"Are you visiting someone too?" We made it into the air-conditioned lobby, and I hadn't realized how warm I'd been out there. "Or are you just hanging around looking for your next latte assassin hit?"

I imperceptibly flinched, realizing there was no way he would have gotten the joke that only my internal monologue had heard. Instead, he seemed to take the joke in stride.

"Nah, you're my only mark." He paused, and the lines in his forehead faded as his expression softened. "So, the thing is—"

"You're late."

A red-haired nurse I didn't recognize stood beside Beck at the check-in desk, her hands on her hips and her gaze narrowed on Brooklyn.

Brooklyn made a dramatic showing of checking his smart watch. "By like three minutes."

"Punctuality matters, Brooklyn." Her voice was kind even as she scolded him. "You've got a week left. Let's try not to have any more setbacks before this is over, okay?"

Brooklyn heaved out a resigned sigh as he turned to me. "Guess I should go. I'll see you around?"

The realization of it all shocked me cold, like a bucket of ice water had been dumped on me. He wasn't there to visit someone. He was there because he had to be. I didn't have time to grapple with the revelation as he looked at me with those blue eyes, enticing me to jump off that cliff again.

"Sure." I nodded.

He gave me a comical salute before following the nurse down a separate hallway, and I watched him, tall and gently swaying like a big tree in the wind, until he was out of sight.

"Ready to go?" Beck recaptured my attention.

"What?" I whipped around to face her, looking up at me with a puzzled expression. "Oh, uh, yeah. Let's go."

I should have been less surprised. Otter House was big, and they treated a variety of different mental health illnesses and disorders. In the throes of my research, I'd learned that they also did partial hospitalizations as well as outpatient therapy. It just hadn't even occurred to me that *that* was why he was there.

As Beck took me back to Nikki's room like she had half a dozen times already, I couldn't stop the questions from swirling in my head. Why was he here? Was all that cool and charming bravado only a front? Was he going to get better?

When I walked through the door of Nikki's room, seeing her standing there braiding her hair, looking so goddamn *okay*, a feeling of gratefulness surged through me, and I flung my arms around her. The realization hit me all at once, and for the first time I truly believed that Nikki was going to be all right.

"Hello, hi, to you too." She hugged me back with a chuckle. "You okay?"

I pulled away, holding her face in my hands as I smiled at her. She and I shared the same hazel eyes as Mom, and for once in what felt like weeks, a brightness twinkled in hers. "Yeah. I'm all right."

I took a step back and cleared my throat. "Actually, I need you to fix a chip in my nail."

"How'd you chip it *already*?" She groaned. She turned her back to me to rummage through a drawer in her bedside table.

"All that hard work I put into making sure you have cute nails and you just *soil* it."

I held up my hands. "Mom and I were painting, and you know I type aggressively."

"You're lucky I like you," Nikki said as she sat down across from me on the bed.

I smirked back at her. "Yeah, I love you too."

>> <<

It didn't occur to me until later that week when Nikki and I were taking a walk around the courtyard that I had actually been *looking* for Brooklyn, but the way my heart careened into my throat when I finally saw him told me all the things I wouldn't readily admit. There he stood, big and tall but not nearly as imposing as you expected someone of his stature to be, having an animated conversation with another guy. The early afternoon sun hit him just right, and when he laughed at something the other guy said, I half expected a chorus of angels to come down in a beam of light singing "Hallelujah."

"Hello?" Nikki shook my arm.

"I'm sorry." I shook my head, trying to unstick my thoughts from whatever vapid daydream I was having. "What were you saying?"

"Are we continuing our Lindsay Lohan movie run or are we pivoting?" Nikki asked. "*You're* the movie connoisseur."

"Pivoting," I echoed. I subtly glanced over at him again, realizing I had already been lingering longer than I wanted to. I needed to casually pivot *us* without raising suspicion, before he noticed us and opened up the floodgates of Nikki.

"Yes, we're gonna pivot," I repeated as I took her arm in mine.

"*Herbie* is where I draw the line with Lindsay Lohan movies made before 2020."

I thought we were in the clear, but the moment I turned my back to him, he called out to me. So close, and yet so far.

"Hey! Wait!"

"I'm sorry, do you *know* that guy?" Nikki whispered, keeping her head down close to mine.

"Sort of, yeah. Wait a second." I sighed before resigning myself to the inevitable.

When I finally turned back around, there he was, backlit by those goddamn angels as he smiled down at us.

"Hey, Nat," he said breathily, and turned to Nikki. "And Nat's sister."

"Hey, yourself," I greeted him, unable to stop my lips from curling into a grin. Thankfully he seemed to have that effect on *everyone*, not just me.

"It's Nikki. Hi, I'm Nikki. Or Nik, or . . . whatever." My sister smiled up at him in a sickly sweet way, keeping her arm looped around mine.

"Hi, Nikki," he said, and turned to me. "I was actually hoping I'd run into you again, Nat."

"You were?"

He nodded, and a few stray locks of hair flopped onto his forehead. There was an almost intentional messiness to him, but instead of being off-putting, it added to his charm. All I wanted to do was steady his hands and fix him up. I could handle him better when he looked and acted more like other guys, instead of being so *him*.

"How tall are you?" Nikki blurted.

I inwardly groaned, but this was Nikki being her usual speak first–think second self, and I tried to let that thought outweigh the embarrassment. If she was feeling like her normal self, I'd take it, and if Brooklyn was at all deterred, he didn't show it as he grinned again.

"Six five."

"*So tall.*" Nikki sighed as she leaned into me.

"Yeah, tall enough to be the designated get-things-from-the-top-shelf person in my house." He chuckled. "Anyway, before we were so rudely interrupted the other day, I'd wanted to ask you something." He paused, rocking back and forth on the toes of his sneakers.

That sticky knot formed in my throat again, tangling up my words in it. There were a lot of uncertainties in my life, but one thing I was certain of was that a distraction like dating wasn't something I needed right now. My focus needed to be with my sister, my career (or lack thereof), and finding a shred of normalcy in my life here.

"Sorry, I have to get Nikki back inside," I blurted. "You know how strict they can be about unsupervised time." He flinched so subtly that I almost had to second-guess that it had happened at all, and guilt gnawed at my stomach. "But I'll see you around?"

And the effortless charm returned like it had never left. "You will."

He turned and walked away, thankfully before he could see me blush more intensely than I ever had in my life.

"Oh my *god.*" Nikki groaned when he was out of earshot. She led me through the courtyard by my arm like a puppy that had escaped its crate. "You have some major explaining to do. Who was that guy, and why, for the love of *Laguna Beach*, did you reject him before he even had a chance to ask you out?"

"Stop." I held my hand up to her. "This is exactly why I didn't say anything to you. He's just a boy."

"Um, no." Nikki stopped before the double glass doors leading back into her wing of the facility. "That wasn't a boy, that was a *man*. How do you even know him?"

"You remember how last week I came in with coffee all over me, and I said I tripped?"

She nodded eagerly, even though I was sure she knew exactly where this story was going.

"Well, *he* knocked me over in the parking lot and the coffee spilled everywhere. That's why I was covered in it. Then on Monday he actually waited outside in the parking lot for me and brought me coffee because he felt bad about knocking me over."

Nikki was ready to explode with excitement. "Oh my god that's *so* adorable. What else?"

I opened the door and gestured for Nikki to go inside before we were over our allotted walking/fresh air time. It wasn't my place to tell Nikki that he was a patient to some degree here too.

"Nothing else." I shrugged. "And now we're here."

"You're no fun," she grumbled.

We arrived back at Nikki's room, and as I watched her settle back in to her temporary room, guilt rolled through me. I didn't want her to feel like any of that was her fault. Maybe the other reason I didn't want to date was because of how invested she would get, and that I didn't want *her* to get disappointed if it didn't work out. Everything really did come back to her.

May 21
Hey Dad,

I've been thinking about this a bit lately, but today made me realize I need to come out and say it.

I feel like a bad sister sometimes.

All I want is for her to get better. Really, I do, but I can't help but feel resentful of her. It's only sometimes, and I actually recognize it even less. Usually I don't think twice about arranging my schedule around her, or keeping to myself because she needs my full attention.

It's only a flash of irritation, and then it's gone, and I hate this part of me. Because right after the resentment comes the guilt, and it feels so much worse. I think about how selfish it all sounds, and I can almost hear you saying I'm being too hard on myself. Maybe I am. But I don't have time to consider that part. At least not in those moments.

The truth is, I love her so much it physically hurts. That's what makes the resentment feel so shameful. I know I'm doing exactly what I should be doing, and I'm glad I get to be there for her.

Maybe that's how I justify rejecting people before they can disrupt that, even if part of me doesn't want to.

Anyway, I just needed to tell someone. You're the easiest person to tell, because you won't judge me. Or maybe you would, but I'll never know.

Love, Nat

Four

If there was one thing I'd learned since moving to Dahlia Point, it was that time didn't move unless you *made* it move.

The first few weeks after Nikki's admission were a blur of drives to Otter House, cleaning the kitchen until midnight, and pretending to "work" on my fledgling YA magical realism coming-of-age story about fairies when really I was just rearranging plot points in a scattered mess of an outline, like furniture that wasn't mine. Eventually Mom suggested I find something to do *just for the summer*, she'd said, in that way she'd say things to make it sound like a suggestion instead of an order.

That's how I ended up at Stacks, the local bookstore a long three blocks from my house. Maybe on a nice fall day I'd even walk there, but not in the throes of a humid Southern summer, when walking three blocks made you *look* like you'd run three marathons.

Stacks wasn't exactly a literary utopia. The air-conditioning rattled louder than the jazz playlist we had on rotation, and half the shelves leaned at odd angles, like they were as tired as the rest of us. But the smell—coffee, paper, dust, and something vaguely floral—was a kind of peace I hadn't realized I needed. I'd only been there a week and a half, but already I had a rhythm: unlock at ten, straighten displays, alphabetize the chaos left behind by some tourists, and lose myself in the steady quiet of other people's words.

It wasn't glamorous, but it was something. Something that wasn't *waiting*.

I was restocking a display of paperbacks—the kind that always had an impossible-to-remove sticker that screamed NOW A MAJOR MOTION PICTURE!—when the front bell jingled. I looked up just in time to see him.

Brooklyn.

He stood at the entrance like he wasn't sure if he was allowed to be here, wearing a faded tie-dyed T-shirt, a backward baseball cap, and that same careful grin that managed to be both apologetic and devastating.

He slid his sunglasses off, and if he was at all surprised to see me, he didn't show it.

"Hey," he said, like it was the most casual thing in the world.

"Hey," I echoed, painfully less casual. My stomach dropped and flipped at the same time, like it couldn't decide if this was excitement or panic. "What are you doing here?"

"Buying a book, presumably. Why, you appointment only?"

"What? No." Heat shocked my cheeks. I slowly strode around the display table, desperate for casualness as I straightened a stack of books that did not need to be straightened. "Surprised to see you here, that's all."

"*Surprised?*" He pressed a hand to his heart, feigning offense. "Ouch. I'll have you know I'm a big fan of books. They're like tiny movies for the brain."

He snapped his fingers beside his temples for maximum adorable effect.

"Wow," I deadpanned. "Poetic."

"Thanks," he said, still grinning. "Would it surprise you even more to know I'm *actually* looking for something specific?"

I tilted my head. "Depends. What is it?"

"*Gone to See the River Man* by Kristopher Triana."

It was significantly less surprising that he was into something obscure I'd never heard of, but I wouldn't dare endear him to that. "What genre is it?"

"Weird," he said immediately, which, for some reason, made me laugh.

"Okay, *so* not helpful."

"It's a short story." He sighed, as if he didn't want to relinquish the information.

"Unless it's in a collection or anthology, we don't carry individual short stories," I told him. "But you knew that, didn't you?"

He shrugged. "I'm open to recommendations."

"Fine." I sighed and turned on the heel of my sandal.

He followed me between aisles as I led him to fiction. He didn't hover and was just close enough that I could feel the air shift when he moved. It was disorienting how quickly I'd gotten used to his presence, like he'd already occupied a space I hadn't realized was empty.

"What about *House of Leaves*?" I asked, sliding a big paperback from one of the leaning shelves. "Weird, but beautiful, and a little bit haunting and unnerving."

He lifted the book out of my hands and flipped through the pages. "Jeez, this thing's like a thousand pages. I feel like you picked this one on purpose."

I shrugged, just like he had before. "This is my recommendation."

"Okay, fine." He snapped the book shut with a thud. "Why?"

"Because as nonsensical as it appears, the story does make

sense," I replied before I could stop myself. "Things aren't always the same on the inside as they are on the outside. That applies to people too."

"Then I'll take it."

>> <<

He came back three days later.

Same time in the afternoon, same casual stance leaning against the counter like he owned the place. I was midway through labeling a box of used paperbacks when his voice startled me.

"I finished it."

I jumped, nearly dropping the permanent marker. "Jesus Christ."

"Close, but not quite," he said, looking entirely too pleased with himself.

I pressed a hand to my chest. "You can't just appear like that."

"I knocked."

"On what?"

He grinned wider. "The innuendo is there, but I'll spare you."

"Oh, gee, thanks," I said. "So? Did you like it?"

"I did, although I don't think I ever want to move into a house, at the risk of it growing staircases and rooms." Brooklyn spun the marker cap on the counter. "I liked Johnny, though."

"Yeah, I thought you might," I said quietly.

Our eyes met unintentionally, as if simple magnetism was doing its job. This close up, he didn't look nearly as casually confident as he normally did.

Brooklyn cleared his throat, then pulled away and drummed his hands on the counter. "What's next? You seem like you have opinions."

I snickered. "I always have opinions."

"I noticed."

I smiled despite myself and walked around the counter to grab another book from the front table display. "Try this one. *Normal People*. It'll ruin your life in a slow, methodical way. Superfun."

"Perfect," he said, taking it from me. "And maybe you can tell me why over coffee."

I barked out a chuckle. Deflect, deflect, deflect. "You're asking me out to discuss literary trauma?"

"No." Brooklyn shook his head. "I'm asking you out for coffee. The trauma's just a bonus."

He said it lightly, but there was something under the surface—that nervous energy he tried to mask with charm. The same thing I recognized in myself.

"Tomorrow?" he added, and I realized I was already nodding.

"Tomorrow," I echoed, because in that moment, all alone with pretty books and pretty eyes, I couldn't think of a single reason to say no.

He smiled like a guy who was used to getting what he wanted but never stopped being satisfied by it. "Great. I guess I'll need that number of yours now. No sister to use as an excuse this time."

I blanched, but he kept grinning as he fished his phone out of his back pocket. We exchanged numbers, and just like that, he was gone again, leaving behind the faint smell of cologne and the promise of something that might have been good.

When the bell jingled as the door closed, I stood there for a moment, heart still racing, and wondered how something so normal could make the air feel so charged.

May 25
Hey Dad,

I might like someone.

Even writing that feels stupid. It's not like I planned it. I've spent my time here convincing myself that I'm better off keeping things simple and controlled. It benefits everyone that way. But then he showed up, completely unexpected, mind you, and it's like something in my brain short-circuited.

It's not even that he's charming. He is, and I knew that when I met him weeks ago, but it's different. He's quiet in this way that makes me want to fill the silence for him, to figure out what he's not saying. I think that's what's dangerous about it. I can feel myself trying to read him like a book—highlight the parts that make sense, skip the ones that hurt too much.

You'd probably say I'm projecting again. That I keep confusing empathy with intimacy. And maybe I am. I have a bad habit of seeing the cracks in people and wanting to patch them before they break. But this time I don't know if I'm drawn to him because he feels familiar or because he feels safe, and the difference scares me.

I keep telling myself it's nothing. That it's a distraction. But there's this flicker every time he looks at me like I'm not just background noise. It feels like recognition. And I don't know what to do with that.

I shouldn't be thinking about anyone right now. Not when Nikki still needs me, not when I'm supposed to be rebuilding myself into someone solid again. But then he smiles, and all my careful scaffolding starts to shake.

So, yeah, I might like someone.

But what I don't like is that I kind of want to see what happens if I stop fighting it.

Love, Nat

Five

I got up early to run the next morning, hoping I could steady myself with as much normalcy as I could before Brooklyn picked me up for coffee. I gave a friendly nod to the older man with the golden retriever, looped around at the Whale, and tried to keep my thoughts focused on the rhythmic pounding of my sneakers as they hit the wet sand. That was the whole point of exercise, right? To shut your mind off and focus on your body.

But traitorous thoughts trickled through in the silent split seconds between songs switching on my running playlist. What was I supposed to wear? What if he chewed with his mouth open or listened to crappy music like EDM or dubstep? Was this an actual *date*?

I gasped for breath as I abruptly stopped, linking my hands together on top of my head to stop my body from feeling like it was going to spontaneously combust. I'd done this run almost every day since I moved back, but I'd never felt my heart so eager to explode out of my chest. Even after I'd walked the rest of the way back home, I couldn't rein it in. It was like a wild animal that had gotten loose.

While I was out, Mom had texted me that she was going out to run a few errands (which to her probably meant Starbucks and HomeGoods), leaving me an empty house to tear through like a hurricane as I tried to get ready for something that didn't seem as simple as getting coffee with a guy. After inhaling half a peanut butter and banana sandwich, I dashed upstairs to shower and fired off a quick text to Mom.

NAT: sorry about the dishes in the sink. In a rush to leave

MOM: leave where?

NAT: coffee with a friend :)

Much in the same way Nikki didn't need to be privy, neither did Mom. For all any of us knew, this could be the first and only time I hung out with him, so there was no point in setting any of us up for disappointment. I'd even kept certain details from Dad, which I never did. Even writing it down felt blasphemous somehow.

After I showered, I turned my closet inside out before forcing myself to settle on a flowy long-sleeved white babydoll blouse and loose jeans. This whole outfit debacle really brought how alone I was to the forefront, because I had nobody to even consult on the five outfit changes I made.

At school, I had classmates and acquaintances, but I'd always been so focused on my writing and my work that actual *friends* seemed like a time constraint. But now, with all the waiting and all the time I seemed to have, an empty space had opened up in me, begging to be felt like a wound.

"Not too plain, and not too formal," I said as I surveyed myself in the mirror behind my door. I tied my still-wet hair into a braid, and when I checked my phone for the time, a text from him popped up in my notifications.

BROOKLYN KELLER (like the bridge): *be there in 10*

"Okay." I spun around to face Gracie. "This will be good. Right?"

Her ears perked up slightly, and drool trickled out of her mouth and pooled under her chin on my comforter. She eased her eyes closed, and I gave her a soft pat on her head before grabbing my bag and going downstairs where I could wait with more diligence.

Sitting on the stairs, I situated myself low enough that I could peer out the front window but high enough that he couldn't see me and my peering when he arrived.

My heart lifted in my chest when a bright-red Wrangler with the top off pulled up to the curb in front of the house. I watched with fascination as Brooklyn slugged back a can of Red Bull and checked his reflection in the rearview mirror, raking his hands through his mess of hair. Devastatingly, hopelessly endearing.

"He's just a boy," I told myself before hoisting myself up and walking to the front door.

When I opened it, there he was, halfway up the steps to the porch.

"Hey, I was about to call you." He grinned and pocketed his phone. "Were you waiting for me?"

"What? No?" It came out more like a question, and I felt myself stiffen. "I just happened to be coming down the stairs and saw you in the window."

Which wasn't technically a full-fledged lie. He seemed to buy it—for now, at least.

He grinned. "What can I say? I have impeccable timing."

I could tell myself over and over again that he was just a boy until I was blue in the face, but the way my cheeks flushed and my stomach churned in his presence told me it was more than that. He wasn't just a boy. He was a boy who looked like he was ready to disrupt my whole universe. With his haphazard mess of hair, his unintentionally cool faded T-shirt, and a crooked, white-toothed grin that was ready-made for making girls like me melt into a puddle, I realized how horribly unprepared I was for him, and I couldn't let it show.

"Besides, who comes to the door nowadays? That's what text messages are for." I brushed by him as I walked down the porch steps, catching a whiff of that fresh and clean cologne of his.

"Uh, people with manners." He chuckled.

"And you're one of those people?" I played coy.

"I am. In fact, watch." He strode ahead of me with those long legs of his and opened the passenger door of his Wrangler, and with a dramatic sweeping gesture motioned for me to get in.

"Cute." I smirked at him as I climbed into the passenger seat.

"I know."

>> <<

Cota Coffee was on the other side of the island, tucked away a block from the beach under a massive oak tree. It even looked like a little treehouse, and faint jazz music fluttered from a hidden speaker. But even in the shade, the late May heat was stagnant and thick, and I breathed a sigh of relief as Brooklyn came back out to our table with our lattes, the cups already dripping with perspiration.

"So, I should have told you this earlier, but I didn't wanna freak you out," Brooklyn said as he sat down across from me. "Cota is a locals-only secret spot. If you tell anyone about this place, you'll be cursed for eternity."

"I'll take my chances." I smiled, stirring my latte with the straw. "How long does one have to live here to be considered a local?"

"Well, how long have *you* lived here?"

"Technically since this past January," I told him. "But I was finishing school, so I've only lived here full-time for almost three weeks."

"Where'd you go?"

"Sky Valley." I sat back in the wrought-iron chair and folded my arms over my chest. "When do I get to ask *you* a question?"

"Whenever you want." Brooklyn mirrored my movements, sitting back in his chair and crossing his arms, and I wished I hadn't noticed how his biceps flexed against the thin cotton of his T-shirt. "Ask me anything."

"Anything?" I echoed.

"Yeah, anything."

I sipped my latte, contemplating my question carefully. Of course I wanted to know why he was at Otter House, but I wanted to know so much more than that. I figured starting with the basics was the best way to ease into it without sounding overeager.

"Fine." I nodded. "Where did *you* go to school?"

"Clayton University."

I chuckled and shook my head. "Oh my god, that makes so much sense."

Clayton University was the big, exciting D1 counterpart to the tiny liberal arts school of Sky Valley. They were a half hour drive apart, and the distance was about the closest thing about them.

Brooklyn, arms still folded and biceps still flexing, arched a challenging eyebrow at me. "You mean as much sense as you going to Sky Valley?"

"Oh, of course," I said. "What sport did you play?"

"Why do you assume I played a sport?"

"Because nobody goes to Clayton unless they play a sport."

Clayton was good at almost *every* sport, but football was the big one, and they were deeply steeped in tradition, like ringing the giant bell in the clocktower that loomed above the football stadium at the beginning of every game while "For Whom the Bell Tolls" by Metallica blasted from every speaker in the building.

I, of course, had only learned all of this against my will by being in such close proximity to it practically my whole life. Football in the South was a whole thing—it just wasn't really *my* thing. Hence my enrollment at Sky Valley, the school *without* a football team.

Brooklyn snickered. "Sounds like something someone who went to Sky Valley would say."

"You still haven't actually answered my question."

Brooklyn paused, and thank god he was wearing sunglasses because I was sure I would have melted like chocolate in the sun under the heat of his gaze. "Baseball. Full scholarship. Satisfied?"

"I just like knowing things, that's all."

"What else do you wanna know?"

I steadied myself and let out a sigh, trying to focus on the rivers of condensation on the side of his coffee cup instead of my uneasy reflection in the lenses of his sunglasses. "Why do you go to Otter House?"

"I knew that was coming." He snickered and held his hands up. "You sure you want to know?"

I sat up rigid, realizing I might have flung myself over a line that was not meant to be crossed. "I'm sorry. You don't have to tell me if you're not comfortable, or—"

"It's okay, I really do want to tell you." He heaved out a breath and ran his hand down the side of his face. "But first you need to understand, I have this really serious allergy. It's really only developed the last few years, but it's fucked with me pretty bad."

"To what?" I leaned forward in my chair, as if I could catch the words I was so eager to hear.

"Every time I do oxy, I break out in handcuffs."

It took me a moment to digest what he actually said, and when I looked up at him, I was met with a toothy grin that spread wide across his sun-stained cheeks. His brilliant laugh filled the little patio again, and I swore I could feel other peoples' eyes on us.

I scoffed. "You really think you're *so* funny, don't you?"

"What? It's not a joke," he insisted, still laughing between words.

"God, Brooklyn, are you always like this?" I asked him.

Brooklyn took a sip of his latte and then waved it around in his hand. "You mean charming, funny, and an absolute fucking pleasure to be around?"

Despite the fact that he was clearly joking, he was, to the detriment of my own willpower, exactly those things, but wasn't sure he actually knew that.

"Joking aside, that's what it is, then?" I asked. "You were doing OxyContin?"

Brooklyn nodded. "Started with Vicodin. Graduated up to oxy. I did my stint in rehab three months ago, and as of next week I am done with outpatient at Otter House."

There was a pause, and Brooklyn dropped his gaze into his lap. "If that's weird for you, or you don't wanna hang out again, I get it."

Without thinking, I reached across the table and put my hand on top of his. The way my body reacted to him without warning was infuriating, and my head couldn't keep denying what my physical being already knew. There was *something* going on here.

"If I've learned anything from what's going on with my sister, it's that you never really know what people are going through, and so it's kind of messed up to judge them for it," I said.

When he smiled at me, I smiled back. His energy was infectious. When I realized my hand was still on his, I recoiled as if he'd shocked me. He dropped his gaze again, but I was able to catch a faint blush spreading across his cheeks.

"Is she doing okay?" he asked. "Your sister."

"She is." I nodded, and I actually believed it when I said it. "And by the way, thanks for telling me the truth."

"Well, I've learned lying doesn't really get me anywhere, and I learned that the hard way."

"It seems like you're getting the hang of it."

"I'm trying." He shrugged. "That's more than a lot of people can say."

The softness of his voice took me by surprise. "Can I ask you something else?"

"Nope, any more questions and I've gotta start charging you by the hour."

He smirked and bumped my knee under the table with his, and I let out a giggle. I *never* giggled. He was back to effortlessly endearing, and it made me feel more at ease than I had with another person in a long time.

"What happened? *How* did it happen?" I didn't know how many lines I was crossing with him, but I'd never been so compelled to simply *know* someone the way I wanted to know him.

"It was pretty straightforward, honestly," he continued. "I was a center fielder, and all the hard throwing caused a lot of wear and tear on my elbow. I tore my UCL in the middle of my junior season, and I had to get Tommy John surgery. I got pumped with painkillers because I didn't wanna be sidelined my whole senior season, so I tried to rush my recovery, and sure, I wasn't *in pain*, but it got to a point where I couldn't function without them, even when I was technically *better*. That's really it."

It didn't really seem like *that was it*, but I didn't press him further. Like with Nikki, I wanted him to come to me on his own terms.

"I'm glad you're okay."

And that was enough for now.

We took the rest of our coffees to go and wandered up to the beach, watching teenagers on skateboards whiz by a pack of yoga moms pushing around their babies in strollers. The thick, salty scent of low tide filled my nose, and I could practically taste the fresh air as a forgiving breeze blew through us. A busy flower shop was situated on the corner across from the beach walkway, and next to it was the art gallery Mom had mentioned a few times. It wasn't until then that I realized I'd barely explored my new home, despite living here for a few weeks already.

"Okay, my turn for a question," he said, gently nudging me in the side.

"What?"

"You can't just ask me questions like that and then not expect me to ask one back. That's not how this game works."

"A game?" I echoed.

"Yes, a game." He smirked. "What can I say, I'm overly competitive and I like winning."

"Cute, but I'm no sore loser either."

"That's the second time you've called me cute today." He gently nudged me again. "Maybe you've got a little crush on me."

My whole body burned, and I forced myself to chalk it up to the early afternoon heat. "Stop deflecting and ask your question already."

He looked down at his coffee, but when he looked back up at me, another smirk pulled at his lips. "So, you've been given an elephant. You can't give it away or sell it. What would you do with your elephant?"

I looked at him with wide eyes, until I realized he was being serious. "Okay. Easy. Join the circus."

My heart lurched as he ran his tongue along his bottom lip. "Clever girl."

I laughed in response. "Please tell me you did not just quote *Jurassic Park*."

"And?" he scoffed. "What if I did? For your information, I quote *Jurassic Park* all the time."

"Okay, *now* I'm judging you a little."

My cheeks were starting to hurt from smiling and laughing so much. Part of me wished I was having a bad time and could go home with no attachment and no expectations. Despite his slightly self-deprecating humor, Brooklyn really *was* charming and funny, and gave me attention I didn't even realize I wanted. Or needed.

"Fine, then." He sighed. "What's your most quoted movie? And don't say *Mean Girls*."

He grinned wickedly, as if he *knew* he could see right through me.

I groaned. "But what if it actually *is Mean Girls*?"

"Then humor me and pick a different answer."

"Fine." My coffee was mostly empty now, and I rattled what was left of the ice cubes at the bottom of the cup. "Then it's a tie between *Clueless* and *Star Wars*."

"Ah, yes." Brooklyn nodded. "Because those two movies are practically interchangeable. I get them mixed up all the time."

"Well, I like movies." I shrugged. "A lot of movies, actually."

"I do too."

"Yeah?" This time I knew I sounded eager, and I didn't really care that I did.

Another soft breeze came in, lifting the loose locks of hair around Brooklyn's temple, and with grace and ease he brushed them out of his face. Never in my life had I ever used the word *cool* to describe anyone unless they were actually cold to the touch, but that was all I could think of when I saw Brooklyn. So candidly, unabashedly *cool*.

"There's a pretty sweet vintage movie spot around here." Brooklyn gestured with his coffee. "They've got a ton of old DVDs and lots of cool shit."

I squinted up at him. "To play old DVDs, you need a DVD player."

"I have an Xbox," he replied proudly. "Maybe we could rent a few, and watch them. Because it seems like you clearly need an education on quotable movies."

My heart was running away like it had before. I was a runner, but not a chaser, and I didn't want to be chasing my heart every time I hung out with him. And like with running, I needed to build my Brooklyn Keller stamina up.

"And *I* think you severely undervalue the early 2000s rom-com."

He draped his arm around my shoulder and lowered his head to mine. "So, is that a yes?"

Was it? There was no time for me to work out the pros and cons, not with how close he was and how that alone made my stomach go into a spin cycle.

I'd only ever had one real boyfriend before. Connor Halsey had sat in front of me in math class sophomore year, and on the first day he asked me for a pencil. On the fourteenth day, he asked me to go see a movie. He was nice, and he played trumpet in the marching band. We'd dated for five months but he never made me feel the way Brooklyn had in only one day of properly hanging out.

This feeling now—*whatever* it was—was a foreign object in my body, unsure of whether it should defend me or not.

Luckily Brooklyn's phone rang, providing a welcome distraction from the fact that I could have passed out from human contact. He frowned when he looked at the screen.

"Sorry, I gotta take this." He cleared his throat before answering. "Hey."

I tried to occupy myself with my surroundings—the group of teenagers kicking a soccer ball around and sending sand spraying up into the air, the two girls with longboards hoisted above their heads laughing as they made their way down to the water—but when he spoke, he drew my attention to him like a compass to magnetic north.

"I'm literally, like, five minutes away," he grumbled, keeping his voice low. "Sure, but—"

His scowl deepened as whoever was on the other end clearly didn't like his response.

"All right, all right." He groaned. Brooklyn's face twisted into an odd, almost hurt expression, and I felt a pang in my chest as his eyes darkened. It was gone as quickly as it had come as he hung up the phone and slid the sunglasses back over his eyes to no doubt hide the storm brewing in them, and I felt him tense up beside me before he spoke.

"I may have neglected to tell my mother I was leaving the house." He scratched the back of his head as he slowed to a stop. "Since her default assumption is I'm getting myself into trouble, I should probably go home."

"It's fine, really," I assured him. "It's no big deal."

"I promise we won't be long."

I let out a sharp exhale. "Wait, you want me to come with you?"

"Please." Brooklyn pouted and pressed his hands together in front of him. *So* goddamn endearing. "You're like living, breathing proof that I wasn't actually doing anything I wasn't supposed to be doing."

"Okay." I nodded. "Sure."

Going back to Brooklyn's house and meeting other people was not on my agenda, but I spun around to follow him back to his car anyway. The magnetic north also pulled me in whatever direction he went, and I would willingly go if that meant helping him out. Those cracks were starting to show, and here I was, pulling out the patches.

"You're the best," he said when we were both back in the Wrangler. He reached across the center console and put his hand on mine. "Seriously. I owe you . . . again."

Six

I found it increasingly difficult not to stare at Brooklyn as he drove us through the tiny center of town to the bridge that took us through the shallow marshes and toward his neighborhood.

His thumbs drummed against the steering wheel, in sync perfectly with every beat, and he knew every word to every song that came on, silently mouthing along. I found myself counting the freckles that trailed down the side of his cheek, creating made-up constellations on his face.

We rolled to a stop at a red light, and it felt like one of those movie moments in which everything slowed down, and he turned his head to look at me, already looking at him.

"What are you thinking about?" he asked with a grin.

My insides fluttered like I'd swallowed a thousand butterflies, and I had to force myself to look away from him.

"Taking in the town, you know? You grew up here, huh?" I leaned forward to fiddle with the air vents on the dashboard, trying to casually keep my attention elsewhere.

"Yep, born and raised and never left." Brooklyn nodded. "Most people don't leave. Everyone just grows up, marries someone else from town, and the cycle continues. It's like geographical inbreeding."

I laughed a little too aggressively, but it must have seemed endearing to him as he lit up with a smile once again.

"As weird as that sounds, I get it," I said. "I'm sure my mom would have stayed here and participated in geographical inbreeding if she hadn't met my dad, who whisked her away out west."

"What made your parents want to move back?"

I imperceptibly flinched, despite knowing how likely that follow-up question was. While it wasn't necessarily upsetting for me to share information about my parents, and especially my dad, it always sucked telling someone for the first time, and probably always would. But he'd been truthful with me all day, so I owed him the same.

"Honestly, my mom would have moved back sooner. I can see why she likes it here," I replied with surprising steadiness. "But my dad died in a car accident when I was eight. My mom chose the stability of her private school art teacher job while she was a single parent, but now that my sister and I are adults, she felt she could take a more art-focused opportunity out here and actually get back to what she's good at."

"Oh shit," Brooklyn said. "I'm sorry."

"It's all right." I waved him off. "It's been so long now that it being only me, my sister, and my mom feels so normal."

Brooklyn's features softened. "Your mom sounds like a good person."

"She's all right," I said playfully. "She did give me kind of a hard time last week about 'not wasting my summer.' She gave me a spiel about going out and having a good time, getting into trouble—but 'not too much trouble'—and whatever else not wasting a summer entails."

Not that my mother put any pressure on me (most of that came from myself), but she didn't want me to shoulder the burden of everything all by myself. I could put it down sometimes. It was just hard to remember that when it mattered.

"Yeah, I got read that riot act at home too." He nodded. "Maybe not in those exact words, but same sentiment. Guess we're in it together."

My face flushed. "I guess we are."

We pulled into a gravel driveway down a dead-end street shaded by tall, thick palm trees. Peaks of a house poked above the trees that were planted against the edge of the front lawn. Cars lined one side of the driveway leading up to a two-car garage attached to a perfectly picturesque house, as blue as the sky on a clear day. Trees and shrubs ornately dotted the side of the house, and a porch with white columns wrapped around the entire first floor.

"Is your mom having a party or something?" I asked, trying to count how many cars were parked. At least six.

"She hosts book club on Saturdays," Brooklyn replied, heaving out a tired sigh. "Really it's just an excuse for all the neighborhood moms to get together and gossip about stupid shit."

The subtext was loud. Whatever "stupid shit" they gossiped about involved him—at least partially.

He maneuvered his car in front of one of the two garage doors and killed the engine. He reached over for my hand like he had before, his touch soft and reassuring.

"Thanks for this, Nat," he said. "Seriously."

"Of course," I replied with a faint smile, pulling my hand away when I realized how clammy my palms were. When and how did *that* happen? There was nothing to be nervous about, but my body seemed to think otherwise.

He hopped out of the car and beckoned me to follow him to the front door. Light flooded the foyer as we entered, sending streaks of afternoon sun across the wooden floors. I wasn't sure why I expected a house that looked like it was staged for *Homes & Gardens*, but instead, it looked incredibly lived in.

There were shoes by the front door, along with purses and hats hanging from a coatrack topped with bronze sea creatures. As we walked past the stairs immediately to the right, I spotted several white bags from a store called Sandy Lane Boutique precariously perched on one of the steps.

As Brooklyn led me to the kitchen, we walked past a baby-blue credenza crowded with about a dozen framed photographs of Brooklyn and his family frozen in various stages of life. It was easy to single out some of the bigger pictures at the back, where what looked like a few of Brooklyn's high-school photos sat in shiny silver frames. He sported a wide, white-toothed grin like the one he'd been wearing all day.

"You can sit down if you want." Brooklyn gestured to one of the navy leather bar stools at the island when we made it into the kitchen. I perched myself at the edge of the stool and watched with more fascination than I'd admit as Brooklyn paced around the kitchen, yanking open random cabinets. He then walked over to the refrigerator on the other side of the island. It had a large black screen on the right-side door, and when he tapped it twice, its contents were illuminated.

"Wow." I gawked. "That's an impressive fridge."

"You want anything?"

I shook my head. "I'm good, thanks."

"It's a smart fridge," Brooklyn explained as he yanked the door open. "It's supposed to be some energy-saving thing. It's got a calendar, grocery lists, and a whole bunch of other unnecessary shit." He pulled a big bottle of SunnyD out and slammed the door closed with his elbow. "It's kind of ridiculous, but my dad is really into this stuff."

"Is he participating in book club too?" I asked as I pulled at the hair tie around my wrist.

"Nah. Right now he's somewhere in the Gulf of Mexico," Brooklyn replied. I must have made a puzzled face. "He's a drilling consultant on an offshore oil rig."

"That makes sense now. Is he gone long?"

"It depends." Brooklyn shrugged, then took a swig of SunnyD straight from the bottle and wiped his mouth with the back of his hand. "He usually does a month on and a month off, but he left about a week ago for a two-month tour, so he'll be gone mostly all summer."

For a fleeting moment there was a crack in Brooklyn's voice, and then it was gone as quickly as it came. But I couldn't miss it if I tried; I recognized the sound of missing my dad.

"You must be close," I said, choosing to pivot away from the negative side of it. I knew I'd want the same sentiment extended to me.

Brooklyn paused, and he spun the plastic cap of the SunnyD bottle on the counter, keeping his gaze hyperfixated on it when he spoke. "Our relationship is kind of weird right now. We had a bit of a disagreement right before he left, and, I don't know. I just wonder when he's going to stop being so hard on me."

He paused again and scrunched his face up. "I'm sorry, that was *way* too much. . . . Foot-in-mouth thing again."

"No, it's okay. I get it. The situation's not really the same, but I can be hard on Nikki too. I do it sometimes without realizing it, because if something happened to her—"

My throat tightened, and for the first time in a long time, talking about this was hard. No matter how kind and charming his smile was and how warm and comforting his presence made me feel, there were things that didn't need to be said. If I *didn't* shoulder it all the time, if I put it down even once and something were to happen to her, I'd live with it forever.

Even so, he waited and listened, decidedly not with his foot in his mouth.

"Maybe he's only hard on you because he cares, and he's afraid of something happening to you."

"Deep down, that's probably true." Brooklyn sighed as he leaned forward onto the island, lowering his head to meet me at eye level. "Thanks for getting it."

"Thanks for being so honest."

Goose bumps prickled down my arms despite the proximity of our faces making my body temperature climb by the second.

Brooklyn must have felt it, too, as he abruptly stood up straight and cleared his throat. "Whereas my mom isn't hard on me, she's just still getting used to me leaving the house by myself for extended periods of time. Hence you being here right now as my witness."

He tilted his head to the side as we heard a door slam, and a young woman sauntered into the kitchen from the back deck.

"And then there's my sister," Brooklyn mumbled, looking at me with wide eyes. "Who's just a bloodthirsty emotional cannibal."

"Rude." The girl smacked him on the arm. "Now please move. You're blocking me from very necessary alcohol."

She shooed him away from in front of the refrigerator, forcing him to slide around the kitchen island to stand beside me. As soon as the goose bumps had dissipated, they came right back with a vengeance.

"Excuse me, aren't you underage?" Brooklyn drawled at her while she fixed herself a mimosa.

"Only for another month," she quipped, spinning on her heel to put the SunnyD bottle back in the fridge. She slid her big movie-star sunglasses on top of her head, revealing the same bright-blue eyes Brooklyn had. "Besides, if you were forced to socialize with those little goblin women outside all morning, you'd be drinking yourself under the table."

The giggle escaped before I could stop it.

"Oh my god," she exclaimed, suddenly aware of my presence at the island. "I am so sorry. I'm Stella." She flipped her sleek ponytail over her shoulder and held out her hand to me. "You'll have to excuse my brother. I did say he was rude, didn't I?"

"Nat." I shook Stella's hand with a polite smile. "It's all right, mimosas are a pretty valid distraction."

"Do you want one?" she asked, and when she gestured back to the refrigerator, all the gold bracelets on her wrists clattered together. "You've been hanging out with him all day, you probably need one."

"*Now* who's rude." Brooklyn rolled his eyes.

He shifted beside me, and it dawned on me that if he was trying to stay clean, he probably didn't drink either. He'd made me so comfortable all day, I owed him the same.

"I'm okay, thanks." I gave her that polite smile again, and it seemed to satisfy her as she turned her attention back to her brother.

"Anyway, do us both a favor and *please* go talk to your mother," Stella said. "You have plenty of time to be annoyed later, but for now, at least show her you're alive and not . . ."

Brooklyn glanced down at me and mouthed *I'm sorry* before wandering toward the back door.

"Don't worry, us girls will hang out." Stella shooed Brooklyn away.

"I need her in one piece when I get back," Brooklyn called over his shoulder before shutting the back door behind him.

Stella leaned closer to me with her elbows pressed into the counter. She smelled like a vacation—all coconut and sunscreen and salt water—with the glowing sun-kissed skin to match.

"So . . ." She clicked her tongue. "You're a new face. Not that my brother brings any girls home to begin with, but regardless, I don't recognize you."

"We moved back a little while ago," I said. It wasn't hard to clock the interrogation, mostly because I would have done the exact same thing if Nikki brought home someone I'd never met before. "And Brooklyn and I are just friends."

She eyed me with a skeptical glance before sighing softly. "I'm sorry, I don't mean to be a bitch or anything. I'm trying to look out for him, that's all."

"I get it." I nodded. "I'm the same way with my younger sister."

"Do me a favor?" Her expression softened as she looked through the wide-open windows at Brooklyn, laughing and chatting with his mom's book club in that charming, endearing way of his. "Keep an eye on him, please."

"I will," I reassured her. "I like hanging out with him. As a friend, right?"

I inwardly groaned. If I could have kicked my own ass right now, I would have.

To my surprise, Stella offered me a soft smile. "My brother wouldn't readily admit this, but he really needs some good influences around him."

I held my hands up in surrender. "I can't promise his caffeine intake will be mitigated, but otherwise I'd like to think I'm a good influence."

Stella laughed, and it alleviated the tension that had crept into my shoulders.

"So how *did* you two meet?" she asked.

"Actually, he murdered my coffee in cold blood last week," I replied with emphatic casualness, and suddenly there was more laughter in the room that hadn't come from Stella. I'd be remiss to say I didn't already recognize his laugh.

"Murdered?" Brooklyn feigned offense as he reclaimed his position at the kitchen island beside me, clapping his hands to his chest. "*Murdered?* That's . . . that's cruel. Maybe we could downplay it to coffeeslaughter, couldn't we? You were half as guilty. Besides, Stella is gonna be a lawyer, so—"

"Excuse you," Stella scoffed and held up her hand. "Who said I'd be representing *you*? I'm on Nat's side."

"And together we can bring this latte assassin to justice," I continued.

"Unbelievable," Brooklyn grumbled. "I've never felt so betrayed, and *by my own family*."

Stella and I laughed, and I almost didn't hear the back door open again.

"What's so funny? You guys sound like a pack of hyenas."

A woman I assumed to be Brooklyn and Stella's mother joined us in the kitchen, standing beside Stella and taking a sip from the mimosa Stella had poured.

"Mom, this is Nat." Brooklyn gestured to me. "Nat, this is my mom."

"Annie, please. It's so lovely to meet you." She extended her hand to me. Her smile reminded me a lot of Brooklyn's, and it was easy to see where he got it from.

"Nice to meet you." I offered her a smile in return. We were doing *a lot* of smiling today, and I needed to schedule some scowl time before I lost feeling in my cheeks.

Brooklyn's mother was not what I was expecting, although to be fair I didn't know what to expect. She had sandy brunet hair like Brooklyn and Stella, but peppered faintly with gray, and done up cleanly in a claw clip. She was petite—perhaps a little too petite for her flowing floral sundress as it brushed against the wooden floors.

"Great, you've seen her," Brooklyn grumbled. "Now can we go? Nat has to get back home."

No, I didn't. But even though that seemed like a little white lie, it sounded great coming out of his mouth. Smooth and effortless and so true. I uncomfortably shifted on the stool as Brooklyn's mother turned back to me, still polite but a little more tense than before.

"Thanks for coming by," she said to me. "You're welcome anytime."

There was more subtext there, but I didn't have it in me to fully decipher it. I could tell from the way she looked at me, because her smile didn't quite reach her eyes this time.

>> <<

The drive back home seemed infinitely longer than our journey out to Brooklyn's neighborhood. Wind continued to breeze through all the openness of Brooklyn's topless Wrangler as we drove across the bridge and through the center of town, and I stuck my hand out, blissfully trying to catch air. We glided along in silence, with nothing but the grungy '90s rock Brooklyn played from his Spotify thrumming in the background. I watched him out of the corner of my eye, wondering why he seemed to captivate me so much.

"What?" He side-eyed me.

I could have said that I liked his eyes, and that I liked his smile, and that most of all, I liked the way he looked at me. I just didn't know I wanted to be looked at like that until he did, because I'd never gone searching for it myself.

"Nothing," I said instead, shaking my head. "Your mom and your sister seem nice."

By the time we had reached my house the sky had turned a milky lavender color, and streaks of pink and orange blended with the clouds as the sun slowly dipped below the ocean. Brooklyn pulled up to the curb and lowered the music so all that could be heard was the steady hum of the engine.

"Thanks for today," he mumbled. He looked up at me, his blue eyes gleaming in the dusky light.

"I should be thanking you," I replied with a faint smile. "For getting me out of the house, I mean. I actually had a really good time."

"Yeah, me too. Plus, I'm sure my mom and my sister are thankful I'm getting out of the house too." That identifiable sting had come back, spidering through his words like a crack in glass. "Look, I get it, it's weird. My mom treats me like I'm made of glass, and Stella's taken on this role as my protector, claws out and all."

"They just care," I reassured him.

"I know, I know." He sighed. "Thanks for reminding me, though."

"You're welcome. I know I need to be reminded sometimes too."

"I'll remind you, don't worry." The space between us began to close in what felt like slow motion, and his voice lowered to almost a whisper. "Just say the word."

Our elbows grazed on the center console, and I felt completely beholden to the will of my body, unable to rein myself in. Hot air filled my chest as the space between us continued to shrink, and for a moment I swore his eyes flickered down to my mouth. He paused, his lips inches away from mine.

Abruptly, he pulled back, taking all his warmth with him. "Look, I need to tell you something else."

A combination of words you never really wanted to hear. I tucked the loose strands of hair that had come out of my braid behind my ears and inhaled, bracing myself for impact. "Okay, shoot."

He rested a hand on the steering wheel and pivoted his body forward so that he didn't have to look at me so head-on. "They tell you when you're in recovery and stuff that you really shouldn't date people. At least not at first. So . . ."

A red-hot blush burst onto my face, and he must have noticed as he fumbled to continue.

"Not that I assumed that's what this was or anything." He cleared his throat. "It's fine if it wasn't, or even if it was, it's just that you're more prone to relapses in the first year, and all kinds of other stuff they talk about in group. I don't want you to think that I *don't* want to see you again, because I do. But—"

"We're friends," I interjected, trying to slow the thought train derailment. "Which is perfectly fine."

The tension rolled off his shoulders as he let out a deep, relieved sigh. "Yeah, it is."

Maybe this was what I had needed to cease my internal tug-of-war. I had a responsibility to be there for Nikki, and he had a responsibility to himself. We both had things we couldn't put down.

"I guess we'll talk later," I said as I fumbled to unbuckle the seat belt. I slid out of the buttery leather seats of his Jeep, desperate to escape the choking hot air around us.

"Hey, Nat," Brooklyn called as I was about to walk up the front steps. "I, um, meant what I said before. About hanging out again. If you want to. As friends."

"Yeah," I replied with a smile. "I'd like that."

Butterflies fluttered furiously inside of me as I watched him grin at me one last time before pulling away from my house, his grungy rock music carrying into the air of the night until it faded away.

A sudden gust of wind dried the sweat on the back of my neck, and for the first time all day, I felt cold.

Hey Dad,

I met with him again today and I might as well tell you his name now. It's Brooklyn.

We got coffee and talked for a while, and it wasn't awkward. It was easy. Too easy. He's funny in this sideways, wry kind of way. He asks about me like I'm interesting and listens like he's collecting every word. I like that about him. Most people only wait for their turn to speak.

He told me about his addiction and his recovery process so far. I already knew the basics, but hearing him dish out the details to me felt like being trusted with something delicate. He said people in recovery aren't supposed to date right away, and I get it. I really do. And it's not like I couldn't use a friend or two who doesn't live in the same house as me.

I think what scares me most is how familiar it all feels. How much he reminds me of Nikki—the restlessness, the self-deprecating humor, the way he apologizes for existing before anyone even asks him to. I recognize where the cracks are, and suddenly I think that must mean something. Like it's my job or responsibility to patch them. Do the things I couldn't do with Nikki the first time around.

I agreed with him and said being friends was perfectly fine, and IT IS. But maybe the smallest part of me thinks it's not, and that makes me feel selfish. I shouldn't be expecting him to mess with his recovery process just because I might have a little crush. Those can be temporary.

Kind of like when I had a crush on TJ Maxwell in the first grade and I chased him around the playground to tell him, and I came home very upset that I was rejected. But by dinnertime I was coloring and it was all better. I'm sure you remember that.

Anyway, I think you'd like Brooklyn. As my friend.

Love, Nat

Seven

Dr. D'Antoni always kept a box of tissues on the coffee table in her office between the stack of *Psychology Today* magazines and a small plastic basket of stress balls and sensory trinkets. We typically weren't tissue people, but Nikki leaned forward in the cushy armchair she sat in and picked up one of the squishy sensory toys with little dots you could pop like bubble wrap.

It was clear Dr. D'Antoni made an effort to make her office a cozy space for her patients, but the couch Mom and I sat on felt too worn and too lived in, and I was almost afraid I wouldn't be able to get up when we were done.

"It's important that *you* talk about what happened this week," Dr. D'Antoni said to Nikki, who kept her head down as she flipped the little popping dots back and forth on the sensory toy. Her pink zip-up hoodie hung off her shoulder, bony and protruding through her T-shirt.

Mom and I had a vague understanding of the topic of conversation today since she had spoken with Dr. D'Antoni earlier, but that didn't change the way my stomach jumped into my throat in anticipation.

"Nothing's happened." Nikki shrugged. "I'm just living the dream here, what with the gourmet meals and the constant attention and tending to. It's like I'm at a five-star resort."

"It's okay to be frustrated, Nikki. But you can talk to us." Mom reached over and put her hand on top of Nikki's. "Who's going to understand better than me and your sister?"

Nikki finally brought her eyes to mine, and she squished her face up like she was trying to clog the pipeline of tears before it burst. "But you don't understand. If *you* skip a meal, that's okay, you're just not hungry. But if *I* skip a meal, it's nuclear fucking meltdown, and everyone's gonna die."

Drama had been and always would be a linchpin of Nikki's personality. She did theater all through middle school to high school, and everything in her life was a show. In fact, she was such a good actress that she'd fooled us into thinking she was okay for as long as she had. But this was not the Dolby Theatre, this was her psychiatrist's eucalyptus- and lavender-smelling office, and my sister's dramatics made me squirm uncomfortably in the deep cushions of the couch.

Dr. D'Antoni, being the professional she was, took notice.

"Natalie." She addressed me in a soothing, even tone. "When you hear Nikki talk about her treatment and recovery like that, how does that make you feel?"

It made me want to scream and shake Nikki until whatever chemical imbalance in her brain was knocked loose, reverting her back to the person she'd been before all of this.

Instead, I said, "I wished she took it more seriously, sometimes."

Here I was, telling her to take it more seriously, when I was clogging up my own feelings, too, not taking it seriously in my own way.

"All the sarcasm and deflecting is because she's still not really accepting of what's happened and why," I continued. "So then how can she even begin to get better if she's still in denial?"

Nikki lurched forward in the armchair beside me. "That's rude. I learned sarcasm and deflecting from *you*."

While that wasn't directly true, Nikki certainly hadn't been the sarcastic sister of us two—not until she was really in the depths of her disease and it was her way of answering questions about her long trips to the bathroom and her change in appetite.

Mom gently touched my forearm as I was winding up a response, and it was just enough time for Dr. D'Antoni to step in to extinguish the fuming tension.

"Okay." Dr. D'Antoni gave us both a calm nod. "I hear both of you. Natalie, I'm hearing that you're frustrated because you want to see Nikki engaging more seriously with her recovery. And Nikki, I'm hearing that you think the way you are currently handling things isn't being validated, which feels unfair."

Nikki leaned back into the armchair with a sigh. "Life isn't fair, is it?"

"Okay, that's not—" I paused when I realized I was about to say *fair* and give credence to exactly what she was saying. In any other scene in my life, it would have almost been funny. "It's not that you don't have a right to go about your recovery in your own way, but—"

"But I'm not doing things *your* way," she muttered, and her words were like sandbags on my chest.

I exhaled slowly, trying to recenter myself. "Nikki, I understand this is hard for you. Really, I do. But maybe if you start taking it a little more seriously, you might find that everything else starts to come easier."

"Your sister makes a great point," Mom added. "All we want is for you to feel better."

A stagnant pause filled the air. Dr. D'Antoni was only a guide in these family therapy sessions—Emotional Focused Family

Therapy, she called it—and she'd only speak when she felt it was truly necessary, meaning she intentionally wanted us to marinate in the silence. Silence forced you to hear your thoughts.

"I'm not in denial, you know." Nikki's fingers tensed around the little sensory toy, then flicked one of the dots back and forth with a faint popping sound. She sighed again and pulled her knees up into her chest, curling inward like a turtle would for warmth and protection. "But sometimes, no matter what I say or do, it feels wrong."

I exhaled again, feeling the weight on my chest ease up slightly. "Well, that's not true, Nikki. I—" I forced myself to pause and to sit in the uncomfortable silence like I was sure Dr. D'Antoni wanted instead of rushing to give an explanation. "I don't know how to help because sometimes it feels like you don't want me to."

Dr. D'Antoni nodded and turned back to Nikki. "What do you think of what Natalie said?"

Nikki pulled at a loose thread on the sleeve of her hoodie. "She's disappointed in me."

I shook my head. "No. Not at all. Sometimes I get frustrated, but I'm not mad or disappointed." My throat tightened, but the confession squeezed past the tense desire to keep it together because I thought that would fix everything. "I don't want to lose you."

Finally her fingers stilled. She pressed her lips together into a faint frown, and signs of the emotion she had been trying to tamp down flickered over her face. She looked away, staring hard at the painting of an oyster shell on the wall on the other side of the room, like if she focused on something else long enough, the moment would pass and we'd move on.

Mom let out a quiet breath, her voice gentle. "Nikki, honey, we're here with you."

Nikki kept quiet, her response coming in the form of a slow nod. She swallowed, still staring at that distant spot on the wall.

Dr. D'Antoni let the silence hang in the air again for a few moments before speaking up, her tone unwaveringly calm. "There's a lot to process here, but this is good, Nikki. This *is* hard, and the instinct is to joke or deflect because it makes dealing with the situation easier. But I also want you to notice what happens when you don't." She paused and gestured to me and Mom. "See what happens when you allow yourself to hear that the people who love you are here for you."

Nikki exhaled slowly. "I'm trying."

It was the first time she'd said that word in these sessions. *Trying.* Trying was a start. Trying was good. I'd take trying.

>> <<

Mom made millionaire spaghetti that night, and it wasn't lost on me that it was a meal Nikki used to love and beg for when we were growing up. I sat at the kitchen island, where most of the painter's tape and tarp were now gone, and all that was left was soft baby-blue paint drying on all the cabinets.

"Well, that went about as well as it could have," she said as she scooped a chunk of spaghetti and sauce onto my plate. "Given the circumstances."

"Dr. D'Antoni said it was a *minor* regression," I added, stabbing the pasta with my fork. "But regression is regression, isn't it?"

Mom leaned against the island, electing to stand while she ate. "According to her, minor regressions like skipping a meal here and there are normal. It's almost impossible for people with mental health conditions like that to shut it off. They're habits, and we have to be understanding of that."

"Even though that makes sense, it doesn't make it feel any less shitty."

Mom looked up at me with a soft smile. "You're being too hard on yourself, Nat. You've been a fixer your whole life, so it's in your nature to want to fix what's going on with her, but it's not that simple. You have to let her try and fix herself, and you can only be there to support her."

Gracie sat at my feet and huffed out a weary sigh. Sleeping all day must have been *so* hard for her. Normally I would have given her some spaghetti, but Mom was taking her to the vet tomorrow for a checkup, and spaghetti was not an ideal part of a dog's diet, no matter how old and needy they were.

"I know that." The words escaped in a soft breath.

Mom stood upright and shrugged. "That's all you can do for now."

After we ate and moved to the couch to watch *Bake Off*, my mind wandered to Brooklyn. Did he have the kind of setbacks Nikki had? Did his sister worry like I did?

As if the universe was broadcasting my thoughts, my phone lit up with a text from him.

BROOKLYN KELLER (like the bridge): you working tomorrow?

I smiled to myself as I typed up a response.

NAT: depends, are you planning on playing Jenga with my new paperback releases again?

BROOKLYN KELLER (like the bridge): that was going great until you breathed on it

BROOKLYN KELLER (like the bridge): maybe I just need you to do your job and recommend another sick book

"Who are you texting?"

I snapped my gaze up to see Mom trying—and failing—to be discreet about leaning over and trying to peek at my phone screen while she balanced precariously on our squishy couch cushions and pile of blankets.

"Nobody." I shot her a sideways glance as I scooted away from her.

For a moment I thought she'd let it go, but as Netflix transitioned to the next episode, she casually chirped, "Could it maybe be the *friend* you met for coffee last weekend?"

The word *friend* flicked off her tongue tauntingly, and she knew it, too, as her lips lifted into a coy little smirk.

"Okay, maybe." I shrugged, settling back farther into the couch. "You know, you should be happy I'm making friends."

"I am, I am." She held up her hands in defense. "So, what's his name?"

"Who said it's a *he*?"

"Your face," she teased with another smirk.

And as if my face could give me away any more, I was sure it was now flushed and red.

I couldn't let her know about Brooklyn without running the gambit on who he was and how we met, and lying—especially to Mom—was never my strong suit.

"Regardless of gender, he's only a friend," I explained, and at the very least, that wasn't an outright lie.

"I *am* glad you're making friends."

But as soon as she finally diverted her attention back to the

Bake Off episode we were watching, I pulled out my phone (more discreetly this time) to respond to his texts.

NAT: I barter good recommendations for iced coffee

I was kind of joking, but his response came lightning fast.

BROOKLYN KELLER (like the bridge): you got a deal

Eight

Running had been a part of me for as long as I could pick out my own pair of sneakers at Sports Authority. Mom would have me run back and forth on the little makeshift track in the shoe section to make sure I liked how they fit. She signed me up for soccer to get me socialized over the summer, and while I was crappy at kicking a ball around, I was a good runner. I liked running. I believed in runner's high.

However, I wasn't sure even runner's high could calm the buzzing energy coursing through me. Sure, I could keep my cool on the outside, but on the inside, my nerves were all frayed live wires.

Last weekend Brooklyn and I had both agreed that we were friends. That was all well and fine, but as much as my brain agreed, my body insisted on rebelling. Friend or not, I'd never been so frazzled by a boy before. Boys were boys, but Brooklyn was, well, Brooklyn.

He was everything I'd read about in romance novels about the perfect "book boyfriend"—kind, attentive, funny, and honest almost to a fault. The thing about *reading* about those kinds of boys was that when you closed the book you were reminded of what they were: fictional. As in, not real, didn't exist, fantasy. Except now, here he was. And maybe for the first time in *forever*, maybe I wanted him to be that, a boyfriend.

I repeated that to myself (and Gracie) about fifty times while deep in contemplation about what I was wearing to work (*Is a summer dress too fancy?* I asked Gracie, to which she replied, *You can never be overdressed*), and continued to do so until the clock forced me to leave. I didn't exactly enjoy the fact that the knowledge of Brooklyn's presence had me changing up my whole work routine, but I wasn't sure what I could do about it by this point except grin and bear it.

By the afternoon the shop was quiet, the late-day sunlight slanting in dusty stripes through the front windows, the hum of the old ceiling fan wobbling just enough to sound like a sigh. I was perched behind the counter, nursing a cold brew that had melted into watery ice, trying to decide if I had the will to open my laptop and write something—*anything*—before my shift ended.

You'd think working in a bookstore would fill me with inspiration, but somehow, it made me feel worse.

The idea of publishing felt half myth, half miracle. I'd gotten a few "promising" rejections lately, which was the literary equivalent of being told you're almost pretty. I still checked my inbox too often, still imagined an email with *We'd love to discuss your work further* blinking in bold at the top, even though all I ever saw were *Unfortunately* and *Not a fit for our list at this time.*

Sometimes I thought about how Dad would've handled that kind of failure; if he would've told me to keep sending things out or to stop trying so hard altogether. I hadn't decided which advice would hurt less.

I was lost in that thought when the bell over the door jingled and Brooklyn appeared with a bag of chips in one hand and a bottle of soda in the other.

"You know," I said as I watched him shake the bag open,

"every time you bring snacks in here, I should remind you food's technically not allowed."

He shrugged and popped a chip into his mouth. "Technically, rules are meant to be broken."

"Yeah, that's what they say right before they spill salsa on a display copy of Harlan Coben novels."

He looked scandalized. "This is dry snacking. I've matured."

"Big step for you," I teased, leaning on the counter.

He gave me a mock glare before his mouth curved into a grin. "So, I've been meaning to ask you something, Nat. What do you *do*? Besides waiting around for me to show up and brighten your day?"

"What do you mean? That's literally all I do."

He pointed at me. "See, that right there? Deflection."

I snorted. "No. Observation."

"Deflection," he repeated in more of a singsong voice, smirking.

I reached across the counter for the bag of chips and grabbed one. "No, I'm snacking."

Brooklyn's laugh filled the empty store—loud, unrestrained, warm enough to echo off the shelves. I couldn't help smiling. The sound made the quiet feel less heavy.

"Well, if it makes you feel better, I *do* wait around to hang out with you, or my friend Alec. But he's always busy, and I'm pretty sure I'm starting to annoy him. He's put up with me since middle school, so . . . your turn."

"To put up with you or tell you what I do?" I sat back in the stool behind the counter and arched an eyebrow at him.

"Both."

I hesitated, suddenly aware of the way the sunlight hit the counter between us. "Well, I write."

He leaned forward, forearms braced on the counter like I'd confessed something top secret that he had no business knowing. "No shit, you're a writer? I guess the bookstore job makes even more sense now."

"No, I said I *write*," I corrected him. "Writer implies success. I'm not there yet."

"Success is subjective," he said, serious now.

I shrugged. "Tell that to my inbox full of rejections."

His lips quirked. "Maybe the world just hasn't caught up to you yet. I bet you're way better than you think you are."

I wasn't quite sure what to say to that, so I looked away and pretended to straighten a stack of bookmarks beside the checkout screen. But Brooklyn's curiosity was disarming; it made me feel seen in a way that was both thrilling and terrifying. While considering my next words would normally be the smart move, here it gave me too much time to study the way Brooklyn slid a silver pendant back and forth on a thin chain hanging around his neck, and the way the MCKINNLEY'S SEAFOOD logo on his gray T-shirt looked faded enough to either be vintage or just worn too often.

Finally, I surrendered with a sigh. "I've been trying to get a couple of short stories published in like an anthology sort of thing, but that's not really working. So I'm trying to write something different in hopes that maybe that works out better. I guess I'm distracted lately."

"I know how that part feels."

"Okay, then," I said. "Your turn. What do *you* do, besides being distracting and loitering around small businesses?"

"Absolutely nothing."

"Oh, I see." I nodded. "Very convincing."

He heaved out a sigh. "My mom owns a boutique downtown, and with my semilegit community college accounting degree, I help her do her payroll and books and stuff. Very serious business."

I scrunched my face up. "I thought you went to Clayton, Mr. Hot Shot Baseball Player."

"I *did.* I just didn't graduate from there." His face flushed, and he sat back on the bench. "That whole painkiller thing might have gotten me kicked off the team and out of school. But it's fine. I mean, I'm fine."

I heard my sister in him—the constant need to reassure people how badly you *didn't* need help because god forbid you asked for it, as if it was a crime to do so. Brooklyn handled it with admittedly a bit more humor and pluck, but the sound was still familiar enough. I offered him a faint smile, and swore I could see the tension leave his shoulders.

"I'm sure you are," I said, softer than I meant to. "But it's okay not to be fine too."

He tilted his head, studying me. "Spoken like someone who's been to family therapy."

I smiled faintly. "Yeah. I guess you would know, wouldn't you?"

"My family therapy sessions were *great*, okay?" Brooklyn scoffed. "My therapist, John, looked and sounded exactly like the guy from *Jurassic Park* who tries to steal the egg embryo things and gets attacked by the Dilophosaurus. You know, *Get the stick, stupid*?"

"The fact that you know exactly what dinosaur that is is astounding." I shook my head. "What is your obsession with *Jurassic Park*, anyway?"

"I was one of those toddlers who really loved dinosaurs, and I guess I never grew out of it."

That earned another laugh from me. "You're an endless source of unnecessary knowledge."

We fell into a companionable quiet then—the hum of the

fan above us, the soft shuffle of paper as the breeze through the cracked window flipped a page on an open book near the register.

Finally, I spoke up in a way I wished I had months ago. "You can tell me, you know. If you ever need to. I won't judge you."

After a moment that felt more like an eternity, he heaved out a sigh. "All right."

He *really* looked at me now, his eyes dark like the ocean in a storm, so sharply serious with the faintest glint of fear in them. "Fall semester of my senior year, I was at a party. I was in full-blown addiction by this point, although I either didn't realize it or was in denial at the time. I was drinking almost every day, and I was eating Adderall like candy so I could keep up with my schoolwork. So at this party, I was buying oxy from some guy I found through connections. I don't even know. Anyway, the cops busted the party, and I got caught with enough on me to get pinned with intent to sell controlled substances. The school and the team caught wind of it and bye-bye scholarship."

I was listening intently, but that silence we're told we should sit in must have unnerved him, and he squirmed on the other side of the counter.

"But, listen, Nat, I swear I was never selling drugs," he pleaded. "I would have been the worst drug dealer ever. I probably would have just done all the drugs."

It felt wrong for laughing at that, but I did, and when he laughed, too, it felt right.

"I'm sorry, I'm sorry." I put my hand over my mouth. "Continue, please."

"Well, that's really it." He shrugged. "My dad knew a lawyer, he got possession pled down because it was my first offence, and I went to court mandated rehab for ninety days. Got out, somehow finished my last semester at community college, and I'd been doing outpatient until about last week, which you know. So, yeah, I *am* fine now."

"I believe you."

Something eased in his expression then; his shoulders lowered, the tension draining from his jaw. It was the same look Nikki used to have after therapy, that quiet exhaustion of someone who'd spoken a truth they hadn't expected to share.

He tried to joke again. "Thank god. For a second, I thought you were going to whip out a polygraph test next."

I smiled, even though it ached a little. "No polygraphs here. Only curiosity. I like to know things. It makes life feel safer."

"So you can stop bad things before they happen," he said, not unkindly.

I met his gaze, startled by how close to home his words hit. "Exactly."

I sucked in a breath, suddenly hyperaware of how see-through I must have been to him, like I was made of frosted glass and all my wiggling organs were on display. But the thing was, I didn't mind. "My sister is supposed to come home next week, and I'm mortified about feeling like I'm going to have to micromanage her. For my own sake, not hers."

He nodded. "How about this: I'll mitigate you if you mitigate me."

"That's not even remotely how that word works," I said, laughing despite feeling like someone was hanging me upside down.

"Still sounds like a deal."

He held out his hand across the counter, and I took it. His palm was warm and a little calloused. His fingers curled around mine like he didn't want to let go too fast.

Just like that, the whole bookstore seemed to go still, because it wasn't hard to feel how perfectly our hands fit together.

June 2

Hey Dad,

I feel like I should tell you more about Brooklyn—or rather, what I'm starting to feel when he's around.

It's like he's actually paying attention. Not the way people do when they're waiting for their turn to talk, but like he's listening to what I'm not saying. It's strange how comforting that can be. For the first time in a while, I don't feel like I have to edit myself when I speak, to not have to appear so together and stable.

He told me things today that I don't think he tells most people. Heavy things. Messy things. I don't know why he trusted me with them, but he did. Afterward, he looked lighter. That should feel good, right? To help someone carry their load for a little while?

But here's what I keep wondering: Am I helping him by listening and being present or do I just need him to need me?

It's a bad thought, but it comes to me in little flashes the same way most crappy thoughts of mine do. I like feeling useful—not just because it makes me feel good, but also because it makes me feel safe. Mom tells me I was like that even when I was young. You probably remember. But I don't know where the line is between kindness and dependency, or if there even is one.

Even so, I don't want to have the same missteps I had with Nikki. I want to get it right the first time.

Love, Nat

Nine

There was millionaire spaghetti on the kitchen island again, but this time, Nikki was across from it, standing with her hands folded in front of her as Mom began to serve it.

"Actually, I can do it." Nikki perked up.

"Sure thing." Mom nodded and handed Nikki the serving tongs. When Nikki put a small serving on her plate, Mom and I shared a fleeting, uneasy glance, but kept silent. We moved to the table after we'd all served ourselves, and I realized it was the first time we'd actually eaten at the kitchen table since I'd been home from school.

Dr. D'Antoni outlined a few dos and don'ts for Mom and me when we were getting ready for Nikki to leave Otter House. Objectively, she was doing well—well enough to go home, obviously—but then we were cautioned that recovery was a long-term process that went well beyond her time at Otter House.

Dos: Express approval and affection (but not in a patronizing way, because Nikki would hate that), even when it comes to non-food-related things; make your communication meaningful; allow them to safely repair their relationship with food on their own terms.

Don'ts: Shame your loved one into eating; shield them from the natural consequences of their eating disorder; blame or guilt yourself.

While all that stuff made sense, it wasn't exactly easy to remember them in the moment where she was pulling the guts out of her piece of bread to lower the carb intake. I swirled around my spaghetti as I watched her, but when she ate the bread, relief settled in.

"I made an appointment at the salon tomorrow," Nikki said as she cut up her spaghetti. "If I have to go one more day with these grown-out roots, I might resort to shaving my head."

"I can take you," I responded, keeping my tone casual as I twirled around more spaghetti.

Nikki shot me a wary glance across the table. "I'm gonna be there for, like, four hours."

"That's okay." I shrugged. "I'm not working tomorrow, and I've got no plans."

Which wasn't even a lie. I'd queried a few more agents in the last few days but wasn't expecting to hear back from anyone so quickly. It was just going to be me, my struggling manuscript, and Gracie.

"Fine, then." Nikki offered me the same shrug and squirmed a little in her chair. "If you say so."

There had always been an agreement in our house that those who did not cook, cleaned—which was really Mom's way of getting us to help clean up when we were kids, and because the skillful cooking gene was obviously not passed to Nikki or me. We kept up the agreement even as we grew up, and now, I relished the normalcy of it.

"Do you wanna catch up on *Love Is Blind*?" Nikki asked me as she handed me a dish to dry.

"Sure." I nodded, running a dishrag over the bright floral-patterned ceramic dishes Mom loved so much even though they were older than I was. There was a chip on the edge of the dish

I was drying, and I remembered dropping it once as a kid. I was so distraught about it, thinking I'd done something so horribly wrong, but Mom consoled me and insisted that now the dish had "character." I must have been seven years old, but that memory had stuck with me.

Nikki and I settled into the couch to watch *Love Is Blind* with Gracie, who seemed happy that Nikki was back as she steamrolled herself all over her. Nikki laughed as she riled Gracie up (as much as a senior dog could be riled up), and I felt that wave of relief wash over me again.

My phone buzzed in my sweatshirt pocket, and I tried to angle myself into the couch so Nikki didn't curiously try to get a glimpse.

BROOKLYN KELLER (like the bridge): hey I know your sister's coming home today. everything is gonna be fine. I'm here if you need me

My heart swelled in my chest, and as I was typing a reply, a pillow smacked me in the face.

"Hello? Take a trip to la-la land?" Nikki waved at me.

"Sorry, what?" I put my phone down in my lap.

"I said I'm going to the bathroom."

I looked back up at the TV, which was now paused on Nick Lachey giving the spiel to the season six contestants.

"Sure." I nodded, swallowing the knot that began forming in my throat. "I'll be right here."

Nikki sighed as she sprang out of the couch cushions and walked to the bathroom in the front hallway. I scooted forward and held my breath, as if that could help me hear better. I wasn't even sure *what* exactly I was listening for, but I was just going to trust my instincts—for better or for worse.

Only when Nikki came out looking exactly the same as the way she'd gone in was I able to exhale and lean back into the couch.

"You good?" she asked, dropping back onto the couch and sending a few throw pillows to the floor. Gracie sighed a very labored sigh before rolling herself back into Nikki.

"What?" My words got stuck in my throat, like I'd swallowed a wad of peanut butter. "Yeah. I'm fine."

That seemed to be enough for Nikki as she pressed Play on the show, but even after an entire episode had gone by, the tightness in my chest had yet to disperse. I took a steady breath, and then another, but it was still there. I studied the way she absentmindedly twirled her hair.

She gave me a quick side-eye after she realized I'd been watching her and not the show, and I quickly dropped my gaze to my phone. There was my text from Brooklyn, still open and unanswered. I locked my phone and left it unanswered.

For now, I needed to be present for her. No distractions, and no guilt.

>> <<

Prior to going to Otter House, Nikki had a well-kept, high-maintenance blond routine. She'd found a hairstylist she liked at a trendy salon downtown called Tempest, complete with trendy plants (real? fake? who was to say) on every shelf and trendy, modern furniture. She went every three weeks, making sure to send me pictures every time she sat in the chair with foils in her hair, looking stunningly extraterrestrial.

Lula, her hairstylist, didn't ask questions as to why Nikki's roots were so grown out and why she hadn't come by in over a month. I'd prepared for it, ready to jump in with a well-practiced lie about how we'd been visiting a cousin's cousin in Florida and stayed longer than we intended to, but it never came up.

I couldn't pretend I understood the embarrassment aspect of it, but to watch Nikki squirm with the shame of it all hurt me in a different way. Almost secondhand, like putting your hand a little too close to the fire but not quite getting burned.

Instead, the two of them carried on yapping about who knows what while I sat in the empty salon chair beside them, refreshing and refreshing and refreshing my email.

Since he was clearly undeterred from my radio silence yesterday, a text from Brooklyn popped up on my screen.

BROOKLYN KELLER (like the bridge): we should do movie night friday or something

BROOKLYN KELLER (like the bridge): if you're up for it

BROOKLYN KELLER (like the bridge): need to start your reeducation of decent films and all

I smiled—the kind of smile that comes a little *too* naturally and *too* easily—and it was noticeable.

"*Who* are you texting?"

Nikki had spun around in the salon chair, the foils in her hair crinkling as she tried to move her head toward me.

"No one." I pulled my phone into my chest.

She gawked as she sat back in her chair. "You're a terrible liar. It's that guy from Otter House isn't it?"

"What makes you think that?"

"Because the face you're making is the same face you made when he came up to us that day."

She smirked a conniving smirk at me, and if I wasn't so taken aback, I would have almost been impressed.

"You've clearly learned your keen perception skills from me."

Her expression softened, and she nodded, more to herself than me. "You don't have to keep this kind of stuff from me, you know."

"I'm not," I answered a little too quickly.

She scoffed and shot me an unamused look, despite how hard it was to take her seriously looking like half a girl and a half a radio transmitter.

"Don't give me that look," I warned.

"Okay but *seriously*." Nikki slapped her palms down on the thighs of her jeans. Last summer, she and Mom had spray-painted bright-yellow smiley faces on the knees. "If you're talking to a guy, I want to know, mostly for my own selfish reasons so I can live vicariously through you. Since I am, obviously, not talking to anyone."

The subtle sting of that last sentence was what got me to surrender.

"Fine." I groaned. "We've hung out a few times. As *friends*."

"Uh-huh." Nikki nodded and rolled her eyes. "Friends."

"Yes, friends." I leaned forward in my chair, as if we were sharing secrets like we were little kids again. "And he asked me to hang out again this weekend, *as friends*."

"Okay, then." She shrugged, but hints of that conniving smirk remained. She was unconvinced, but so what? It was the truth. She could handle it. "Friends are nice, I guess."

"*You're* still my best friend, don't worry." I finally smirked back, and Nikki stuck her leg out from under the nylon cape to gently kick me in the shin.

"Well, *duh*. I'm irreplaceable."

That warm secondhand burning sensation spread through my chest, and even though *I* knew it was her standard dry humor, I wasn't sure *she* knew how true that was to me. There were days I genuinely contemplated that, but being here now, reveling in what felt like normalcy, made that hollow feeling seem further and further away.

Lula came back to the chair and pulled apart a few of the foils from the top of Nikki's head.

"We gotta let you cook under there now," Lula said to Nikki. "I'll be back to check on you in fifteen."

"Cook?" I chuckled.

"Yeah." Nikki nodded eagerly. "The color has to activate with heat from my head, or something like that. It sounds right, anyway."

I snickered. "I see. Maybe you should go to cosmetology school with all that insider knowledge."

"You know what? I've actually thought about that. I might."

We shared a true, genuine laugh, the way we used to before everything seemed to change, and it made me realize that maybe change was okay. Things weren't going to go back to the way they were before, but they could change into something else. Something good.

I opened my text messages and typed a response.

NAT: I'm in

Ten

I ran hard that morning. Gray clouds rolled through the sky, ready to unleash rain at any time, and even though rain was just rain, I ran like I could outrun it.

I came back from my shower in lounge clothes and with a towel wrapped around my head to find Nikki sprawled on my bed, and she jumped up like she'd been static shocked when she saw me stopped in the doorway.

"What are you doing?" she asked, scrunching her face up at me.

"Me?" I scoffed. "What are *you* doing in my room and on my bed?"

"Oh, well . . ." Nikki smiled that conniving smile as she scooted off the bed and gestured to a few articles of clothing (some of which might have been hers) laid out on the comforter. "I picked out a few outfit options for your date tonight. Which *you* are going to be late for since you took your sweet ass time out there."

I sighed as I leaned against the door frame, holding up a finger. "One, I need to run, it's part of my routine, and since I sweat when I run, I therefore need to shower afterward, and two"—I stuck another finger up—"it's not a date."

"Whatever." She flicked her wrist at me. "Please make a decision and I'll be out of your hair."

As I walked over to my bed to survey my options, rain started to patter against the window.

"Is this necessary?" I sighed, picking up a bright-yellow-and-pink-striped off-the-shoulder sweater.

"Absolutely." Nikki shifted her weight on her fuzzy-socked feet as she folded her arms over her chest. "I've carefully curated these outfits for maximum effect. I should be a personal stylist."

"After you go to cosmetology school, of course." I chuckled as I pulled on a pair of jean shorts. The oncoming rain would undoubtedly cool the air off, but it was still June in South Carolina. It would be hot from now until October.

"Maybe at the same time." She shrugged. "Who knows?"

I spotted something out of my own closet—a red-and-white-striped button-down—and plucked it off the bed. "Okay, I've picked my outfit. Happy?"

"Not yet."

She pulled the towel off of my still-wet hair and motioned for me to spin around. I had to crouch so she could tie my hair up in a claw clip.

"Perfect." She held me at arm's length to survey her work. "You look fab, Nat."

"Thanks to my fashion-slash-hair stylist hybrid sister." I nodded with a smirk.

After I dabbed some concealer on in my mirror, I reassessed Nikki, who'd curled back up on my bed.

When she was little and still learning to read, she'd come into my room sometimes at night, complete with a flashlight and her blankie and a book, and have me read to her under the covers. Part of me wanted to put lounge clothes back on and do just that.

"What are you doing?" She finally looked up at me and gave me a faint smile. "Go have a good time."

Seeing her sitting there made me hesitate, and once again, she was more perceptive than I gave her credit for. Or maybe I was more see-through than I even realized.

"I don't want you to feel like you can't do anything," she continued. "Contrary to what any of you might think, I can take care of myself. I know how to make mac and cheese, I haven't maxed out my credit card, and I have a valid driver's license. All that should get me by for a few hours."

A smile tugged at my lips. "I know you can."

"But I may stay here. Your bed is comfier," she told me with a shrug.

"Okay." I nodded, my smile widening. "You do that."

At exactly two o'clock Brooklyn pulled up to my house in his red Wrangler, this time with the hard black rooftop on. Rain had started to collect in puddles on the pavement as I made a dash to his car.

"You look nice," he said as I hoisted myself into the passenger seat.

I fumbled with the seat belt. "Thanks," I replied with a faint smile, hoping he didn't see the blush creeping up my cheeks. I glanced over at him, my face still warm, and realized it was impossible for him to ever look bad, even with his glasses, messy hair, and wrinkled green Smashing Pumpkins T-shirt.

Brooklyn shuffled through a few songs on his dashboard, settling on an upbeat house-style song I'd never heard before, and I sat in a quiet contentment, watching the small town fly by like a messy watercolor painting. But now I could pick out familiar things, like the flower shop on the corner by that Cota Coffee place Brooklyn took me to the first time we hung out. It was starting to really feel like home, and I tried not to think about how much of that was because of him.

>> <<

Film Press was filled with old, rickety shelves of even older movies, but that wasn't all. Racks of vintage movie posters hung from the exposed brick walls, and glass cases of collectible items like figurines, props, and all sorts of other knickknacks lined the far side of the shop by the cash register. Brooklyn and I snaked our way around the aisles of old DVDs.

"What about horror movies?" Brooklyn asked as he thumbed through the "Random" selection.

"I like 'em old-school. The cheesier the blood splatter, the better."

"Damn, that's too bad." Brooklyn held a DVD in his hand, tapping it on his chin. "My master plan of scaring you so you'd have to grab me has been *sorely* ruined."

"You've got jokes, I'll give you that," I retorted. "Does that work on other girls?"

"What other girls?"

Fine, he won that round. I quickly went back to shuffling through more DVDs. I glanced at Brooklyn out of the corner of my eye to see him smirking at me. For people who insisted we were *just friends*, the casual flirting came almost too effortlessly for both of us.

My hand brushed over an interesting cover—a photo of a young boy's profile with disheveled, windswept hair. The photo was grainy and had a murky, yellow tinge. But it was the actual title of the movie that piqued my interest.

"What's that?" Brooklyn suddenly appeared over my shoulder. I felt his breath, warm on my ear, as he reached over me to take the DVD box from my hands.

"'*Gummo*,'" I read, turning the box over in my hands. "Have you heard of this one?"

Brooklyn slung his arm around my shoulders, leading us away from the DVD racks.

He read the back of the DVD box like a radio show host, describing a town of odd and nihilistic residents that gets hit by a tornado. "Oh, and it says that critics have called this film fascinating, intoxicating, life-changing, and enlightening."

I looked at him with wide eyes, and he grinned that fierce grin of his again. "I'm in the mood to be enlightened," he said. "What about you?"

"I'd like to think I'm very enlightened already." I mirrored his coy grin. "But I guess this is my pick."

"And this is mine." He held up another DVD box with a picture of an upside-down sneaker hanging from a bloody knife. *Sleepaway Camp* was written at the bottom in a similar cartoonlike bloody print. "I've never seen it, but I've heard about it. Apparently the acting is terrible but there's a twist at the end that makes up for it."

"I'll never say no to twists."

We walked to the front of the shop where the registers were. I studied the figurines in the glass display case: a nightmare-inducing combination of grotesque creatures and trolls.

Brooklyn handed the young, mousy girl behind the counter his credit card, and I noticed the girl get flustered when she touched Brooklyn's hand. I was relieved I wasn't the only one Brooklyn had that effect on.

"The . . ." the girl piped up. She twirled Brooklyn's card between her hands. "The card isn't working."

"What?" Brooklyn's face twisted into a puzzled expression.

"Yeah." The girl fidgeted and avoided eye contact with him. "I ran it a few times, it keeps declining."

I watched Brooklyn's throat ripple as he swallowed and gently lifted the card out of the girl's hand.

"Do you want me to—" I tried to offer to pay, but Brooklyn shook his head at me.

"No. I got it." He thumbed through a wad of cash in his wallet, pulled out a twenty-dollar bill, and handed it to the girl. "Sorry. You can, uh, keep the change."

We left the store and lingered under an overhang, the rain coming down harder now than it had been, and thunder rumbling in the distance.

"Stay here," he told me. "I'll go get the car."

"I'm not gonna melt, you know," I replied with a faint smirk, hoping to diffuse some of the tension I felt building in the air. "Are you all right?"

"Yeah, of course." He put his hands to my forearms and forced a faint smile. "I'll be right back. Promise."

The way he emphasized *promise* repeated itself in my head. It was almost as if he thought I wasn't going to believe him when he said he'd be right back. When he did pull up to the curb, I decided to leave the thought behind on the rain-soaked sidewalk.

By the time we got to Brooklyn's house, the rain had become torrential. A clap of thunder vibrated the whole house as he led me through the front halfway and back to the kitchen I'd sat in during our last brief visit. Everything seemed smaller in the dimness of the storm outside, without sunlight flooding the rooms through all the open windows.

I took my same stool at the kitchen island while Brooklyn pulled a few things out of the fridge and placed them on the island—a tub of butter and a stack of yellow Kraft cheese wrapped in crinkling plastic.

"You hungry?" he asked as he grabbed plates from a cabinet

next to the fridge. "I don't wanna brag, but I make a pretty mean grilled cheese."

"Can't say no to that." I smiled at him, which seemed to alleviate the lingering tension in his eyes. I'd seen him smile so much, it kind of sucked to see him so uneasy.

Suddenly the speaker at the far end of the counter blared to life, sending some upbeat, chirpy pop I wasn't familiar with to every corner of the kitchen.

"Do you know this song?" Brooklyn asked.

"No, should I?" I almost had to yell over the music.

Brooklyn held his hand out to me. "Allow me to educate you."

The moment my palm slipped into his, he yanked me off of the stool and twirled me around the kitchen as the song picked up.

"What is this?" I tried to catch my breath between words, although I wasn't sure if it was Brooklyn's wild dancing or how close our bodies were that made my lungs beg for fresh air.

"I really refuse to believe you've never heard KC and the Sunshine Band." Brooklyn shook his head. "It's a classic."

Before I knew it, he was singing out loud, trying not to laugh as he belted out the chorus. He wasn't even a particularly good singer, but the way he crooned out the lyrics so naturally made my heart swell.

We both danced like idiots across the kitchen floor, so tuned in on laughing and trying not to trip over each other's feet that we didn't hear the front door open.

"Why the hell does it smell like burnt cheese in here?" Stella scurried into the kitchen with two bags of Whole Foods groceries and carelessly dropped them onto the countertop. Brooklyn and I stumbled over each other as we stopped our lurid dancing and realized there was bread and cheese burning on the stove.

"Oh shit." Brooklyn dashed to the stove and managed to salvage one of the sandwiches.

"Brooklyn." The warning tone of voice came from his mother, who walked into the kitchen shortly after Stella with her own bags of groceries. "How many times have I told you if you use mayonnaise instead of butter, it won't burn."

"I know, I know, except there's one problem with that: mayonnaise is disgusting." Brooklyn scrunched his nose up.

"Right. Of course." She chuckled and leaned up on her toes to kiss his cheek.

"Nice to see you again, Natalie." She turned to me and gave me a white-toothed smile that shone against her naturally tan skin. I felt like I was looking at Stella thirty years into the future, with her high cheekbones and lightly freckled nose.

"You too," I replied as I slid back onto my same stool at the kitchen island.

"Anyway, I have to talk to you." Brooklyn dropped a plate with half a sandwich on it in front of me but kept his eyes on his mother.

"If this is about that trip with Alec to Japan again, I already told you it's not happening." Brooklyn's mother brushed him off as she continued putting fruit away in the fridge.

"What? No, he's not even going anymore." Brooklyn crossed his arms over his chest. "Earlier today, I tried to buy a stupid DVD at the movie store, and Dad apparently locked my damn credit card."

"You mean *his* credit card," she corrected him.

"That's not the point," Brooklyn continued. "Can you just tell him to lay off? I don't know what he thinks I'm getting myself into, especially considering he's not even *here* to see what I'm not getting myself into. It's like he's out to get me or something."

"He's not out to get you. He's only trying to prevent you from doing unnecessary things with your money. But you can tell him all that yourself when he calls later." Even her words seemed to tiptoe. While her voice was nothing short of soothing, it was almost as if she was afraid to say the obvious. Meanwhile, Brooklyn looked more uncharacteristically unsteady by the moment.

"Mom, drug dealers don't take credit cards." He groaned.

On the other side of the kitchen, a snort escaped Stella's lips before she clapped her hand over her mouth.

"Brooklyn, maybe we should go start the movies," I interjected. "Before it gets too late."

Thunder rumbled outside, and that seemed to be the end of this tense but clearly familiar conversation. Finally, Brooklyn let out a resigned sigh and nodded. "Yeah, let's go."

I briefly made eye contact with Stella before leaving the kitchen, and a flicker of relief flashed over her before she turned away and continued unpacking groceries.

I followed Brooklyn down the front hall to the staircase, where photos lined the walls leading up to the second floor. I brushed my hand over the silver frames of Brooklyn's and Stella's senior high-school photos, all airbrushed with their white-toothed smiles and sun-kissed summer skin.

"I had baseball pants on in that picture," Brooklyn told me with a gentle grin, as if the last five minutes hadn't happened at all.

"Really?"

"They scheduled all the pictures during fall practice, but we only needed to be dressed from the waist up. So I kept my baseball pants on, threw a suit jacket on, took the picture, and went back to practice."

His smile made me smile. It was that simple.

"Cute," I said.

"I know." His grin widened.

As we walked farther up the stairs, the photos became older and faded, and Brooklyn and Stella got younger and younger as I passed each one. One trip to Disney. Junior travel baseball and cheerleading. A few Christmas dinners. They were so painfully normal, they even had one of those awkwardly staged family photos in white turtlenecks and jeans. Looking at them all in one place made my chest tighten. I didn't know how much I'd missed not having these kinds of family photos—picturesque and so *complete*—until I saw someone else's. It was a weird, hollow feeling.

"Is that your dad?" I pointed at one of the photos at the top of the steps, where Brooklyn, who couldn't have been older than seven or eight, was sitting on the shoulder of a muscular man, tall and wide and built like a tree. Brooklyn clutched a shining trophy in one hand, and they were both sporting big smiles.

"Yep." Brooklyn nodded, admiring the photo. "He looks pretty much the same now, except he's mostly gray."

"Your dad looks kind of intimidating."

"He wrestled in college," Brooklyn offered with a shrug as I followed him down the upstairs hallway to a room at the end. "But actually soft spoken, and he's a smart guy. I obviously completely take after him."

We shared another laugh before Brooklyn led me to his room. The way a man kept his bedroom said a lot about him. I didn't know what I expected Brooklyn's to look like, but it definitely wasn't what I walked into.

A queen-sized bed with gray sheets was pushed against the right-side wall, and a black comforter was kicked to the edge of the bed. A few Nike shoeboxes were neatly stacked next to the door, and a small, four-drawer dresser sat against the wall next to the boxes, the paint chipping at the edges. A TV hung on the wall across from the bed with a few wires and cords hanging down from it, but any other wall space was empty. The air felt thin, like there was too much empty space for it to fill. Everything looked shrunken and tiny, and the big windows that overlooked the ocean only added to the openness of the space.

"You can sit on my bed," Brooklyn said as he kicked off his sneakers and placed them on top of one of the shoeboxes. "Sorry I don't have a chair for you or anything. I got rid of most of my stuff moving from Clayton back home."

I nodded and slipped my sandals off by the door, then padded across the carpet to his bed. It creaked when I sat on the edge, and the sheets smelled like him—fresh and clean, like the air when it rains.

"This thing is ancient," Brooklyn said, waving around an Xbox controller. "But it gets the job done."

"Which one are we starting with?" I asked, trying to get comfortable but not *too* comfortable on his bed.

"Ladies first." He grinned and shook the DVD box for *Gummo*.

He loaded the DVD on the console, then flopped onto the bed and put his hands behind his head, his T-shirt sleeves straining against his arms. How was I supposed to sit next to him, desperate to keep enough distance between us for fear of spontaneous combustion from the heat his body gave off?

The beginning of the movie was grainy, and the sound quality was shoddy at best. The town in the movie was ravaged by a tornado, and the child narrating the film seemed almost amused by it.

I glanced over at Brooklyn, who seemed engrossed in the bizarre imagery of the movie. His breathing had steadied, and every so often his eyes would droop shut, just for a moment, before snapping back open. Looking at him was like driving by a car crash—it was wrong to stare, but impossible not to.

I tried to turn my attention back to the movie. The boy in the movie held a dirty gray cat by the scruff of its neck, then put it in a trash can and aimed a shotgun at it.

"Oh my god, are they actually going to shoot that cat? I can't watch that." On instinct alone, I turned my body into Brooklyn's, burying my face in his chest. His body vibrated under me as he chuckled, and I felt him gently snake his arm around my shoulder, but he kept the weight of his arm suspended over me, like he still wasn't sure if that was where it belonged. The sound of the gun went off with a muffled bang.

"We can change it to the other movie if you want to," he said.

"No, it's okay. It's fine." I shook my head and lifted it off of his chest, smoothing my hair back. "I can handle *a lot* in movies, but animal cruelty is not high up on that list."

"That makes sense. I can watch someone get hacked up and not bat an eye, but I cry every single time Atreyu loses Artax in the first *Neverending Story*."

"Exactly." I threw my hands up. "You get it."

In fact, I was growing exceedingly aware of how much Brooklyn *got it*. He got a lot of it, and the speed with which this was all making sense was much faster than the logic of it not making sense.

I let out a sigh and slowly, more cautiously this time, leaned my head on Brooklyn's chest. His fingers grazed my arm gently, sending goose bumps prickling up my skin. His chest heaved as he exhaled, and he finally let his arm rest on my shoulders. I eased my eyes shut, listening to the slow, rhythmic pounding of his heartbeat. I felt safe in his arms, like the world could end and we would still be exactly where we were, untouched and unscathed. Our bodies fit together perfectly. Almost too perfectly.

>> <<

"Is she sleeping?" a voice whispered.

I slowly opened my eyes, my cheek still pressed against Brooklyn's soft T-shirt and my hair obscuring most of my face.

"I think so," I heard Brooklyn say. He shifted his body underneath me, and I squeezed my eyes shut as tight as I could.

"Dad's calling," the voice whispered again. I finally recognized it as Stella's, but more tense and uneasy. "Mom thinks you should talk to him."

"Why?" Brooklyn hissed. He shifted again under me, this time gently sliding me off of him and resting my head on a pillow. I felt the bed rattle as he got off and walked to the doorway. I inhaled deeply and held my breath, trying to focus on their hushed words.

"I haven't done anything wrong, but he acts like he knows even though he's a thousand miles away." Brooklyn continued, "I was trying to buy a $12.95 movie, do you have any idea how embarrassing that was? And in front of her?"

"Brooklyn, I don't know." Stella sounded tired now, like she'd had this exact conversation before. "In fact, all I *do* know is that you're both being stubborn."

"I don't care how bad it looks, he needs to get off my back." Brooklyn spoke again, his voice tight. "Maybe if he fucking trusted me, we wouldn't have this issue."

"You avoiding him doesn't help your cause." Stella sighed. "Go talk to him."

Brooklyn let out a groan before his footsteps faded away

down the hall. I opened my eyes to see Stella still standing in the doorway. The perfectly manicured facade she usually wore was gone, replaced by her hair up in a messy bun and tired eyes.

"I'm sorry," Stella mumbled. "We didn't mean to wake you."

"It's fine," I said as I sat up. "Is everything okay?"

"Yeah, everything's okay," Stella said hurriedly. "My brother and my dad, they just bump heads sometimes."

Stella twirled a lock of dark hair around her finger. I thought maybe I could hear the faint sound of Brooklyn's raised voice, but Stella sighed and walked over to me, sitting on the side of the bed. She rested her hands in her lap.

"Are *you* okay?" I asked her.

"I'm fine." She let out a hollow chuckle and shook her head. "I love my brother to death. Really, I do. But sometimes he can be really selfish."

I gave her a puzzled look, and Stella had just opened her mouth to say something else when Brooklyn appeared in the doorway. His cheeks were flushed.

"I should probably take you home now," he said.

"Okay. Sure. Yeah." I nodded tensely as I got up, leaving Stella still sitting on Brooklyn's bed. I glanced back at her as I left the room, and she mustered up a faint smile.

After we left, Brooklyn flipped through several heavy metal songs on his car stereo before letting out a frustrated groan and shutting the music off. The rain pounded hard on the windows, and I couldn't steady my bobbing knees. In my head, I toed the line between asking out of care and keeping my mouth shut so I didn't overstep the whole damn thing. After all, what did I know about any of this? I could read about it as much as I wanted, but like I'd been learning with Nikki, real life experience was the only way you could *really* learn.

When we pulled up to my house, Brooklyn kept his hands white-knuckle tight on the steering wheel.

"Thanks for today," I said. "I had a good time. Despite the weird movie choice. That was on me."

"You're welcome," he replied. "I'm sorry we didn't get a chance to watch the other one."

"Next time, then." I nodded.

"Right. Next time."

And that was the end of that. I fumbled with the seat belt as I readied myself to step into the downpour. Before I shut the door behind me, I turned back to him.

"Will you text me when you get home?" I asked.

He finally looked up at me, his blue eyes glazed over with an emptiness that made my heart clench. "Of course," he said softly.

I shut the car door and watched him pull away. Rain came down on my head in fat blobs, and despite getting soaked, all I wanted was a warm shower.

I did just that, and afterward, I lay in bed, wrapped tightly in my plush blanket. When I checked my phone, there were still no messages from him. After some internal tug-of-war, I decided to leave him be. If I was in his shoes, I'd want some space too. At least, that was what I told myself.

Eleven

I woke up late the next morning, still without a text or explanation from Brooklyn. Nikki meandered into my room around ten and sat cross-legged at the foot of my bed, furiously scrolling through her phone.

"I cannot believe he doesn't have one social media account." She groaned. "I can't even find a goddamn Instagram. Like, who doesn't have Instagram?"

"What? Who?" The words were groggy as they came out of my mouth, and I sat up in bed and tried to rub the sleep out of my eyes. It was still raining out, and through my open window, the dark sky cast a gray haze across my room. A small pile of clothes (mostly running attire) had collected at the foot of my bed, and suddenly all I could think about was how badly I needed to do my laundry.

"Brooklyn." The *duh* was implied.

I followed up with the next obvious question, even though I could have probably predicted Nikki's response. "Why?"

"Because I need the insider info on who my sister is dating," she replied, again with a *duh* implied. "I need to know where he went to preschool, who his best friends are, identify any potential competition that comments on his photos . . . you know, the standard stuff."

"Please." I groaned as I swung my legs over the side of the bed and got up. My knees popped and cracked as I stretched. "We're not dating."

I didn't even want to speak it into existence, because that made *whatever* was going on that skirted the line between friends and more than friends too real. Not just for my sake, but for his too. I kept what he'd said at the forefront of my mind: People in recovery shouldn't date. Period.

"Do you have clothes you need me to put in the wash?" I asked Nikki.

"What?" She shot me a confused look. "Can you focus, please?"

"I *am* focused—on things I have to get done today. Laundry. Quick Mart for Mom because she's teaching back-to-back classes at the community center. Library to return a few books. Feel free to join me for any of those."

Nikki, whose head had been back down in her phone during my quick tirade (and may or may not have been listening at all), suddenly snapped upright. "Oh. I found something."

"What did you find?" I sighed.

She scooted to the edge of the bed and handed me her phone. An old article from ESPNU illuminated the screen, and the headline in big, bold letters read STANDOUT CLAYTON UNIVERSITY BASEBALL STAR BROOKLYN KELLER DISMISSED FROM TEAM FOLLOWING DRUG ALLEGATIONS.

She'd actually gone ahead and searched him, and while I should have been frustrated that she kept poking and prodding when I'd asked her not to, it was frustrating for a different reason—that *that* was the first thing that came up when anybody searched him. It didn't seem fair.

The lack of surprise on my face when I handed Nikki her

phone back was enough to throw her for a loop, and she tossed her hands up. "You knew?"

"Yes, I knew," I replied steadily, gathering the clothes on my floor. "He told me."

"And you didn't think to tell *me*?" She clapped her hands to her sternum.

"I obviously did not." I shot her a stern look. "It's *his* business, and therefore not my place to share it."

Nikki scoffed and sat back on my bed, leaning against the wall. "That's why he was at Otter House, wasn't it? Damn, this whole time I thought he'd been visiting someone. You think you know a guy."

"Now you know." I groaned as I bent over to pick up a stray sock that had fallen out of the wad of clothes in my arms. "Now, *please*. Laundry. Wash. Things."

With a dramatic sigh, Nikki slid off the bed as if she were melting onto the floor. "In a minute. I need to lie here and reflect on my deteriorating snooping skills."

"You do that." I nodded before maneuvering myself out of my room, trying not to drop any more stray clothes.

I was hanging halfway into our washing machine to load it when through the walls and the splattering of the rain outside, Nikki called my name. As I lifted my head out of the drum of the machine, I realized she'd actually been screaming.

With my heart in my throat I ran out of the laundry room, nearly slipping on the wooden floor in my socks as I darted up the steps two at a time.

"Nikki?" I called into what felt like the void. The darkness of the upstairs hallway lit up in a flash of lightning.

"In here!" Her voice cracked as she called back from Mom's room. Nikki was on her knees on the bed, hovering over Gracie, who was sprawled across the thick white comforter.

"She's not moving," Nikki croaked. Her shoulders heaved up and down as strained breaths came from her tiny frame. I trod across the carpet carefully, avoiding imaginary landmines as if the wrong step would blow us all sky-high.

Gracie's breath came out in short, ragged spurts, and her eyes remained closed even when I eased myself onto the bed.

"Come on, girl," I whispered to her. "What's wrong?"

And even though her responses were always in my head, even there it was silent.

"Okay." I got off the bed and stood rigid, desperately trying to keep it together in front of Nikki. "Okay. Okay. Okay."

I repeated it until I believed it.

"We have to get her to the vet." I forced the words past the tangled knot of tears in my throat.

"How?" Nikki bawled. "She's, like, a hundred pounds. I can't—" She took a wheezing breath, wrapping her arms around her waifish, trembling body. "We can't move her."

I slipped my phone out of my pocket and tried Mom, but I knew she kept her phone on Do Not Disturb during classes. My thumb twitched as I hovered over my text message thread with Brooklyn—still radio silent since yesterday—before quickly hitting the Call button next to his contact. It rang only twice before he answered.

"Hi." He sounded a little breathless, and a little surprised. I'd never outright called him before.

"Hi." I tried to stay cordial and not let the panic seep through my voice. I could keep it together. I *had* to keep it together.

"Hi." This time I could hear him smile.

I took a measured breath before continuing. "Are you, uh, are you busy?"

"No, I'm not." There was a pause. "Everything all right?"

"Um, well, no." I breathed out. "It's my dog. She . . . she's breathing but she's not moving. She won't get up. We need to take her to the vet, but she's big. We can't carry her."

This time there was no hesitation. "I'm leaving now."

I don't know how long we sat huddled on the bed, flanking Gracie as if we weren't too late to protect her from whatever was happening, but I watched shadows of clouds dance across the floor as rain gently pattered against the window, and it was almost peaceful.

When the doorbell rang, I used whatever surge of adrenaline I had to keep myself together as I dashed down the stairs. Just before I opened the door, I rubbed at my face and blinked away any stray tears that had made their homes in the corners of my eyes. God forbid I looked as distraught as I felt.

I swung the door open to see Brooklyn standing in the rain wearing a thick, square-framed pair of glasses and a backward hat. He looked out of sorts, with stubble prickling across his chin and a tired heaviness to his features. But then he stepped through the threshold of the door and pulled me into a hug, and his sweet, boyish charm overtook it all.

"It's gonna be okay," he mumbled into the top of my head. His jacket was damp and made goose bumps prickle down my arms, but I hugged him back like he was the warm little center of my universe.

"I'm sorry." I shook my head as I pulled away from him. "I'm sorry."

"Don't apologize." He put his hands on my shoulders. "It's your dog. That's family."

I gulped my heart down and nodded before turning and leading him upstairs. Nikki didn't care about appearing to keep it together; her eyes were puffy and red as thick tears rolled down her cheeks. She had her arm around Gracie's torso, and as we approached her, she tensed.

"Be careful," she pleaded before she finally let Gracie go.

We slid Gracie to the edge of the bed so Brooklyn could get his arms under her and lift her up safely. We flanked him like a doggie secret service as he trekked down the stairs with a gentle precision.

"Nikki, get an umbrella," I told her as we made it to the base of the stairs.

"I can drive," Brooklyn offered. Even though he was already doing enough, I didn't have the energy to debate it. I nodded and opened the door for him as Nikki jogged back into the foyer with a big umbrella. They stepped outside, and she held it over Brooklyn (for Gracie, really), and I slipped on whoever's jacket was hanging by the door before following them out.

Nikki sat in the back seat with Gracie, cradling her head in her lap, and I watched in the rearview mirror as Nikki sniffled and rubbed Gracie's nose. Nikki barely knew life without Gracie. I might have been Nikki's big sister, but Nikki was Gracie's. I knew what that felt like—the instinctive, almost carnal need to protect your little sister.

"Thank you," I said to Brooklyn, and it came out softer and more distressed than I wished it did.

"No need." He shook his head. "You'd do the same for me. If I had a dog."

I choked out a quick laugh, and it dislodged a few tears that had been choking me up. They rolled freely down my cheeks, and I let them. His lips lifted into a gentle smile, and at the very least, he seemed back to his usual self. Maybe I was just emotionally vulnerable, but I had to believe that whatever had transpired last night seemed to be gone.

>> <<

Nikki refused to leave Gracie's side and went into an exam room with a nurse while they took Gracie's vitals. I managed to get a hold of Mom in between her classes, and in the fifteen or so minutes (ten if she ran red lights) it took her to get from there to here, Brooklyn refused to leave *my* side.

"You really don't have to stay," I told him as I leaned forward in the creaky plastic chair of the waiting room. I'd had no time to change out of my lounge shorts and unintentionally oversized Sky Valley T-shirt, and the backs of my thighs had suctioned themselves to the sticky seat. "You've done more than enough."

He reached over and put a warm, reassuring hand on my knee. "I want to."

One simple touch was enough to make me want to give in to the unrelenting truth. Brooklyn had made it a point to wedge himself, in all his goonish ways, into the most uncomfortable spots in my life, and I was learning to accept the fact that he wanted to be there. *I* wanted him to be there.

Before I had a chance to respond, Mom stormed into the waiting room, rain dripping from the disheveled locks of hair that had fallen out of her once-neat bun.

She yanked me out of the chair and pulled me into a tight hug. "Are you okay?" I could have come undone in her arms (and trust me, I *wanted* to), but I put whatever energy I had left into keeping it together.

"I'm fine." I nodded as I pulled away, keeping her at arm's length. "Nikki's a wreck, though. All they're doing right now is vitals, but Nikki insisted on going into an exam room with them."

Mom took a measured step back, and as she nodded

contemplatively, her eyes fell on Brooklyn, who'd also stood up at some point. Sometimes it was easy to forget how big he was until he stood next to someone small, like my mom, who barely came up to his biceps.

"Hi, I'm Brooklyn," he said as he reached out to shake her hand. "I'm sorry we're not meeting under better circumstances."

"My friend," I interjected as Mom glanced over at me with curiosity. I might have neglected to tell her the details of our mad dash to the vet—namely, how we got here.

Recognition flickered in her eyes, and she gave him a polite smile as she took his hand. "Thanks for your help. I'm Natalie's mother, Melanie. Mel is fine too."

Thankfully there wasn't much of an opportunity to marinate in the awkwardness as a vet tech in bright-purple scrubs came out to greet us. I felt Brooklyn brush his hand against mine, and despite all the logic in me ringing alarm bells, my natural instincts begged me to stay put, to relish in the fleeting feeling of his skin against mine.

"Gracie's going to be all right," she told us, and there was an audible, collective exhale. "She'd been prescribed Acepromazine last week. It can be great to treat nausea and anxiety in dogs, but sometimes can have dramatic side effects with certain breeds, such as *profound* sedation, which is what Gracie is currently experiencing. We're not sure why it affects some dogs and not others, but all her other vitals are fine. She just needs some time to come out of it."

"Her vet did mention that, but I figured since she'd been fine the last few days it was nothing to worry about," Mom said.

"It's okay." The nurse shook her head with a kind smile. "We'll put her on something different. It's times like these when we really wish dogs could communicate with us, huh?"

While I was sure Gracie would sound exactly like she did in my head if she *could* talk, I was also pretty convinced she wouldn't be able to keep a secret (like Lady Whistledown) and let everyone know how in distress I'd actually been over everything lately. Nobody needed to know that.

"I'm going to go see how Nikki's doing." Mom turned to me and gave my arm a reassuring squeeze. Her eyebrows lifted as her eyes darted between Brooklyn and me, and I could only hope that only I could see her curious suspicion because I knew her well.

I heaved out a sigh after she retreated down to the exam room. "Now you really don't need to stay."

He snorted. "Damn, you really want me gone, huh?"

"No," I blurted, feeling my face flush. "No, I—"

"I'm kidding."

I let out a wry chuckle and pulled at the worn-down bottom hem of my T-shirt. As all the adrenaline began wearing off, I noticed the cold dampness weighing down my body. But he radiated warmth, and without consciously trying to, I inched closer to him just to feel it.

"You were right, you know," I told him.

"I know." His smirk widened, and then faltered. "About what?"

"About everything being okay."

"Oh, well." He gave me a one-shoulder shrug, and dug his hands into the back pockets of his jeans. "No point in thinking otherwise."

"Thank you."

"Anything for you."

It only took him a split second to realize the gravity of his words, but thankfully he seemed too preoccupied with fumbling to redeem himself that he didn't notice my cheeks flush.

"I wanted to say, um." He gave me a sheepish smile as he rubbed the back of his neck. "You're a good friend."

That was the reality check I unfortunately needed. Because that was exactly what we were—good friends. And that was *fine*. That was how it should be. I didn't need to be worrying about what had happened the night before, or anything else he wasn't willing to share. Friends didn't try to fix each other.

I pinched my lips together and nodded. "So are you."

"Anyway." He took a very intentional step backward. "The state fair is next weekend. Me and my sister and our friends usually go every year, so, if you need something to do, or something. I mean, you and Nikki."

"That sounds fun." I offered him a smile. "As good friends, of course."

"Of course," he echoed. We shared a laugh, holding each other's gaze for what felt like a bit too long for *good friends*. A large family came bursting in pushing a cat in a wagon, shattering whatever moment we had.

"Excuse me! My cat's in labor!" one of the younger girls cried as they sped past us.

"I am actually gonna go now," Brooklyn said as he turned his attention back to me. "But I'll text you."

He took a few steps backward to leave, stumbling over a garbage can by the front desk.

"Shit," he hissed as he collected himself, his face flushing bright red. Endearing, as usual.

I chuckled and shook my head at him, watching him back out of the glass double doors and jog out to his Jeep, dodging puddles and raindrops with a gracefulness nobody of his size should have.

Sure we laughed, and sure it was funny for now, but I did need to remind myself of the reality of the situation, because the more I realized how much I liked being around him, the easier it was to forget that we should be just friends. Maybe in another life, we wouldn't be.

June 7

Hey Dad,

It rained all day today, and it was one of those king tides that makes everything on the coast flood more than usual.

Gracie scared us. For a while I thought we weren't going to bring her home from the vet. Nikki panicked and I froze, and for a few minutes I think we both forgot how to breathe. At some point enough sense of mine turned on to know we needed help (I know you've never met Gracie but she is over a hundred pounds). So I called him, and he came without hesitation, in the pouring rain. He didn't even ask for directions.

I don't know why that part keeps echoing in my head. He came. Maybe because I don't expect that from people. It's the thing I'd DO, but not necessarily receive, mostly because I don't want to.

When you died, people said Let us know if you need anything, but most people don't mean that—it's just the "right" thing to say. So I learned to do things myself. To fix, to carry, to soothe, to fill the spaces no one else wanted to touch. I thought that was strength. But when he showed up, I realized how unbelievably nice being taken care of was, even for only a moment.

He said it was no big deal, because that's what friends do. I wanted to believe him, but it didn't feel small. It felt enormous. It felt like air after holding my breath too long.

I might be confusing comfort with closeness. I keep asking myself whether I needed him there for Gracie or if I needed him there for me. I don't want to need him—or anybody, really.

Is it wrong to let someone hold you up when you're supposed to be the strong one? Or maybe that's what being strong actually is, letting someone else carry the weight for a while.

You'd know the difference. I wish you could tell me.

Love, Nat

Twelve

"But like, how much do you *really* know about him?"

"A lot, actually."

"Like what?"

I groaned and shot Nikki a stern look as I rolled to a stop at a red light. While Brooklyn and I had casually continued texting throughout the week, the state fair hadn't come up again, and I didn't want to be the one to bring it up in case he had changed his mind. I thought if I could pick my sister's much more boy-experienced brain about it, I'd come to a logical solution. Instead, she'd turned it into an interrogation after I'd picked her up from her weekly group therapy session.

"Is this you actually asking me for my own sake, or are you being nosy?"

"Both."

I heaved out a sigh and lowered the volume on a boygenius song that was playing on the stereo. "He went to Clayton University. He played baseball. He likes movies. He listens to mostly '90s grunge. He has a younger sister. Should I continue?"

The light turned green and I fixed my gaze back on the road. Out of the corner of my eye I saw her lips curl downward.

"I'm really not trying to be a bitch or anything. I've seen people like him in rehab. They have an illness, Nat. I just want you to know what you're getting yourself into."

"I'm not *getting into* anything," I insisted. "He was upfront and honest with me from the get-go, and I feel like that counts for something. He also didn't have to help us out with Gracie last week, and he did, so I think he's proven he's a pretty decent guy. Just because you interacted with someone who had a similar problem as him does not mean all people with that problem are the same."

I really didn't like it when I became aware of the sternness in my voice—as if I was scolding Nikki like she was my child and not my sister. "Look, if you really need more convincing, then come with us this weekend. Actually, you should come anyway because it'll be fun. I think we *both* deserve that."

"I don't wanna third wheel you guys," she grumbled.

"First of all, you can't third wheel something that's most definitely not a date," I scoffed. "And second of all, his sister and a few of their friends are going too. It's like a whole social hangout thing."

Nikki snickered. "When was the last time you had a *social hangout thing*?"

"Exactly my point." I hit the steering wheel with the heel of my palm. "That's why I need you there. To help with my *social hangout thing* skills."

"You don't actually need any help, you know." Nikki's voice had softened, and when I stole another glance at her, she was pulling at the frayed edges of her bright-pink hoodie. "I know you like being on your own and all, but anyone you meet immediately likes you. You don't even have to try. It's kind of annoying, actually."

She smirked at me, and I reached over the center console to hold her hand. "I must have learned that from you."

Nikki snickered again. "No way, I'm not nearly as annoying."

>> <<

As it turned out, Brooklyn had assumed that since I'd said yes to going to the state fair last week, there was absolutely no need to confirm that and instead had simply informed me Saturday afternoon that he'd be picking us up at six. I hated being unprepared, and suddenly that was exactly what I was.

As soon as I yelled across the hall for Nikki, she immediately went into outfit-scheming mode, and despite the situation, it was nice to see her really getting back to being herself.

"Okay, okay, okay." She paced the shaggy carpet of her room while I sat cross-legged in front of her. "This is definitely the kind of thing that people dress up for. You know, social media photo ops and all. So, it's nice out, but it's gonna get dark, and it's still that time of year where the temperature drops when the sun goes down, so we'll need layers but ones that look like they're part of the outfit."

Nikki walked to her closet and shuffled through things, and the sound of the hangers scraping across the tension rod gave me goose bumps.

"You run a lot colder than I do," I told her. "I don't need layers."

That wasn't entirely true, but if I was going to be standing around Brooklyn all night, I could spontaneously combust at any given moment.

Nikki poked her head out of the closet. "Does he have cute friends?"

"I believe he has *a* friend. No idea what he looks like."

Nikki threw a pair of navy-and-white-plaid, boxer-looking shorts at me. "These are cute. You should wear them with one of your dozen librarian button-down shirts."

I scoffed. "They're not *librarian* shirts, they're very practical and they go with everything."

"Exactly, including those." She nodded to the shorts I'd picked up to study.

"These look like old-school men's boxers."

"They're very trendy." Nikki waved me off. "And will look great with *your* stallion legs."

I knew what my sister knew better than I did—like trendy fashion choices. So I steamed a white button-down shirt from Gap, threw on a pair of Vans, and quickly tied my hair into a braid. When I went back to her room, Nikki had pulled on a pair of purple-and-pink-checkered pants and a baby tee with an eight ball printed on it. Her clothes were really beginning to fit her again, and I didn't realize how much something so seemingly simple would matter. I smiled at her, and when she noticed, she shot me a suspicious look.

"What?"

"Nothing." I shook my head. "I like your pants."

Nikki eagerly stuck one of her legs out for show. "Yeah? They're so old."

"And they look great, so please don't do the thing you do where you change fifteen times right when we're supposed to leave, because he's going to be here in five minutes."

"I won't, I won't." She held up her hands in surrender. "Same goes for you. I told you those shorts were cute."

"They still look like boxers." I pulled at the hem. "But I digress. I'm comfortable and *somewhat* fashionable."

"That's the spirit!"

We both said goodbye to Gracie—who was much more cognizant and aware now that she wasn't doped up on Acepromazine (which, we learned, was *not* something Borzois should be taking), and as we made it downstairs, Brooklyn pulled up in his topless, doorless Jeep. Stella sat in the back with a guy I didn't recognize, meaning they'd left the front seat open for me, a small gesture that I unfortunately could not stop myself from reading into. The front seat was a thing reserved for the significant other of whoever was driving.

"Confirmed, friend *is* cute," Nikki whispered through her teeth as we walked down the porch steps.

Cute friend, with floppy dark hair and a strong jawline that didn't seem to match his rather small stature, was introduced as Alec—Brooklyn's close (and seemingly only) friend he'd mentioned in passing a few times. When I lifted myself into the passenger seat, Brooklyn silently handed me the aux cord. It took a certain level of trust with someone to let them play *their* music in *your* car, and the thought that he had that trust in me made my insides feel all warm and staticky.

"Cute pants," Stella said to Nikki as she slid into the middle seat.

"Oh, thanks, I actually got them at Goodwill."

"Love a good thrift," Stella continued. "I got a vintage Miu Miu pashmina last year at Reinvented downtown."

"*No way.*"

"This conversation is officially in a foreign language," I leaned over and whispered to Brooklyn, and he snickered in response.

In the rearview mirror I saw the three of them squished together, their knees and shoulders rubbing against each other with every dip and turn Brooklyn took; far too close to be comfortable, and yet Nikki smiled the whole car ride.

The fair was already crowded even though dusk had started to creep into the sky. The setup took over the entire parking lot of the old convention center that bumped up against the harbor, with everything from a Ferris wheel and the Gravitron ride to cotton candy and popcorn machines spanning every free corner of the parking lot.

"You know, one time Brooklyn rode that thing upside down," Alec, who'd naively wedged himself between us, mentioned off-handedly as he pointed to the Gravitron.

"Yeah, and then I puked afterward," Brooklyn scoffed.

"So I take it you don't want to ride it, then?" I asked him, and he vehemently shook his head.

"No fucking way. I still don't understand how it even works."

"Centrifugal force," Alec chimed in, keeping the slight monotonousness I'd learned was his usual tone. "Although actually, the reason you're pushed back against the wall is the result of inertia. For every action, there's an equal and opposite reaction. So as the wall pushes on you as the rider, your body pushes back against the wall, which creates friction, thus making you feel like you're stuck to the wall."

"You'll have to excuse Alec." Brooklyn draped his arm over his friend's shoulders. Alec wasn't short, but he looked it next to Brooklyn. "He forgets that not everyone is as fluent in nerd as he is."

"Well, I thought that was a very eloquent explanation," I told Alec with a nod. "I'm with Brooklyn, though, that doesn't make me feel any better about going on it."

"Maybe you should brush up on your nerd, then." Alec directed his comment to Brooklyn, wiggling out from underneath his arm. Their personalities were oil and water, but at the same time, they exuded a similar type of energy, bouncing off one another with an ease that was expected of two people who had been friends as long as they had. Middle-school playground love never died.

Neon lights from the rides dotted the pavement as we walked along the side of the carnival where all the games were set up underneath faded white tents. Alec had fallen back in step with Nikki and Stella, strolling a few paces behind Brooklyn and me, and every so often I could hear hushed whispers and silly giggling.

"I'm sorry, y'all have something to say?" Brooklyn called over his shoulder.

"What? I'm just trying to get some funnel cake," Stella shot back, which got Nikki to laugh.

Brooklyn stopped abruptly and grabbed my arm, pointing at one of the baseball throwing games.

"I'm doing that," he said.

Stella scoffed. "You know there's other ways to stroke your ego, dear brother."

"I always need my ego stroked," Brooklyn replied, and before Stella could respond, he pulled me in the direction of the booth.

It seemed to be a typical baseball toss carnival game: six cans were stacked neatly on a wooden pedestal, and if you knocked all of them over in a certain number of throws, you'd win. To me, all carnival and boardwalk games were the same, designed to sucker people in by making it seem easy enough at first and giving you a false sense of confidence. You'd hit a few, but it was always impossible to knock them all down, so you'd throw more money down, telling yourself you were *just* close enough to try again. Eventually you'd walk away defeated, with no stuffed teddy bears and an empty wallet.

The kid running the booth couldn't have been older than seventeen. His shaggy blond hair flopped into his face, which was turned downward, engrossed in his phone. He looked up at us with a deadpan expression.

"If you can knock them all down in three throws, it's free," he said with a shrug.

Brooklyn elbowed me. "What do you want?" he asked, gesturing up at the array of large plushies that hung above the booth.

"You haven't even thrown a ball yet. Besides, didn't you have surgery on your arm?"

"Do you know how Tommy John surgery works?" he asked me. I shook my head, and he leaned down closer to me, as if he was letting me in on some big secret. "To repair the torn ligament, they use a grafted tendon from another part of your body, and it's usually your ass. Most guys come back stronger after the surgery because of it."

I scoffed. "You're joking."

"Nope." He popped his lips, casually flicking the baseball up in the air and catching it with the same hand. "I've got a scar and everything. I'll leave that to your imagination."

"Oh, thanks." I snickered.

"Well, *we're* going to get fried Oreos, because nobody else wants to watch you show off," Stella interjected, pulling away both Alec and my sister. When I made eye contact with Nikki, I half expected to see some semblance of panic, but there was none. In fact, she grinned a wide white-toothed grin at me before folding into the crowd. Normally the obvious conspiring against me would be annoying, but it was nice to see her starting to really trust herself again.

"You didn't answer my question." Brooklyn nudged me, forcing my attention back to him and the way he effortlessly rolled the ball between his hands. God, even the way the muscles and ligaments in *hands* flexed was attractive.

I tried to blink the thoughts away. "Sorry, what question?"

"What do you want?" He pointed back up at the comically large plushies.

"Okay, hotshot, I'll humor you. That one." I pointed at a big green plush of Reptar from *Rugrats*.

"Good choice." He smirked before taking a measured step back. In one fluid, effortless motion he drew his arm back and threw the ball with perfect precision, hitting the bottom left can and causing half of the stack to topple. He picked up the second ball and glanced back at me for what felt longer than only a moment, his lips lifting into a faint smirk. Then he threw the ball with such force it knocked the rest of the cans clean off the pedestal and hit the back of the booth with a booming thud. Because of course he had the skill and the wherewithal to outmatch a carnival game, and while I had anticipated that, I was still surprised at *how* skillful he was.

"You're not half bad," I offered coyly.

"Good thing I told you to pick your prize in advance." He nodded at the Reptar plush as the kid working the booth got it down with a long hook.

"Were you trying to impress me?" I asked him as I was handed the plush.

"That depends. Were you impressed?"

"Maybe a little bit." I allowed my smile to soften.

"Hey, I know you," the kid piped up. "You were that baseball prodigy from Montgomery Prep. I recognize you from the pictures in the trophy case outside the gym. You still hold like five state records."

Brooklyn grinned sheepishly. "That's me."

Based on my lukewarm knowledge of sports culture in the South, I half expected the kid to ask for Brooklyn's photo or something, but he abruptly frowned instead. "Didn't you get arrested and kicked off of the team at Clayton? My dad said you were in jail or something."

My body lurched forward ready to defend Brooklyn (for what, I wasn't even sure), but he gently put a hand to my forearm, holding me in place.

"Not yet," he said to the kid. "Thanks for the prize."

We walked through the carnival quietly and made our way to where the parking lot met the edge of the harbor pier, the faint sound of an Oasis song fluttering from an unseen speaker. I clutched Reptar tightly against my chest, and he wasn't nearly as soft as I expected him to be, but that's carnival prizes for you.

Brooklyn leaned with his back against the railing of the pier. He took a long, heaving breath, his eyes closed and his head tilted back into the dusky sky. I leaned next to him, my stomach pressed against the railing.

"Are you okay?" I asked.

Brooklyn dropped his head and shifted his weight from one foot to the other. "I'll be fine."

"Don't let what that stupid kid said bother you." I gently placed my hand on top of his, still gripping the railing of the pier. "You're not that guy anymore."

"It doesn't matter what I am now." He groaned and ran a hand through his hair. "People only care about what I was, and they're always going to enjoy picking at my scabs."

I looked down at the beach, where high tide had rushed in, filling pockets of sand with foaming salty water. It must have been a twenty-foot drop from the pier into the shallow tide below us.

"Then prove them wrong," I told him. "You absolutely can, because you've done it already."

Brooklyn blew out another heavy sigh and shook his head. "I don't even think you realize how good of a person you are."

My heart swelled. "You are too."

"Come on." He rolled his eyes. "Don't be like that. I mean it, you know."

"So do I."

I looked down at the ocean rushing in below us, and when I looked back up at Brooklyn, his eyes shone just as blue and just as deep as the water. When you stood at the edge of the cliff, sometimes there was this overwhelming desire to jump, despite knowing the danger. It was called *l'appel du vide*—the call of the void. Somewhere in the breeze, I must have heard it calling, and suddenly I was very aware of *how* close we were now, felt goose bumps prickle up my arms in anticipation.

The call of the void was also often brief, which typically prevented you from actually putting yourself in danger. Even if I wasn't in any actual danger, I was scared. Scared of what this could become. There were so many unknowns, and to me, there was nothing more frightening than that.

"We, um." I recoiled, feeling the adrenaline in my body kick in. "We should rescue Alec from Nikki and your sister."

Brooklyn exhaled a sharp breath. Something flickered behind his eyes (regret? guilt? or something else entirely?), but it was gone as quickly as it came.

"Yeah. Good idea."

We started walking again, slower this time, as if we were trying to preserve whatever this moment was. For someone who talked as much as he did, when he was silent, it said more than words ever could.

"Hey, will you do me a favor?" he asked, pulling me back to the surface.

"That depends."

"Come on the Ferris wheel with me." He pointed across the fair at the Ferris wheel, and my heart dropped into my stomach.

"Brooklyn, I hate heights." I groaned. "Besides, shouldn't we—"

"I told you, they're *fine*." He extended his hand to me. "Now, come on. I got you."

I glanced over his shoulder at the creaking metal monstrosity. I had to admit, it looked pretty with all the lights decorating it, just starting to give off a glow against the darkening sky.

So I took his hand, and he didn't let go.

The line moved quickly, and before I could catch my breath, we were loaded onto one of the cold metal seats, slowly swaying back and forth with our legs dangling over the side. I felt the weight of Brooklyn's arm gently draped over my shoulder, and let myself unwind a little. He was warm and comfortable and everything a person should be.

My stomach churned at every creaking lurch, forward and upward higher into the sky. When we reached the top, the wheel groaned to a stop again, the chair still gently swinging.

"Jeez." I sighed. I kept my eyes down, intently focused on a chip in the red paint of the metal chair.

"See? It's fine," Brooklyn said. "It's totally fine. Look around. It's actually really nice up here."

After a few deep breaths, I glanced up and out at the world in front of us. Night had taken over, and all the lights from below were nothing more than little specks of color against the dark. A salty breeze blew in from the ocean, and even though I knew it was right below us, it sounded far, far away. It was quiet. A peaceful, honest quiet that I didn't realize I needed until that moment. But after a few seconds, I realized we were still perched at the top, our chair slowly swaying back and forth.

"I told you nothing was going to happen."

I glanced over at Brooklyn.

"You went through all this trouble just to say I told you so?" I jabbed him in the side.

He sighed and rubbed his hand down the side of his face, his forehead glistening with sweat. "No. Not really, anyway."

He held my hand delicately, interlacing his fingers between mine. With the colorful lights of the fair dotting Brooklyn's face in blues and whites and reds, and all the noise from below so far away I could hear his heartbeat as it thumped against his chest, I think I finally accepted how much I actually liked him. And despite all the warnings and all the unspoken rules, I think he liked me too. I was not a rule breaker by nature, but for him, I might have been.

Even though I was afraid of being up so high, all I wanted to do was fly.

"Then what is it? Tell me," I whispered into the night.

I didn't realize how close we already were until he reached up and brushed a lock of hair that had fallen out of my braid away from my face. The accumulation of all the subtle touches and lingering glances of the past few weeks led to this moment, with the moon lighting up his eyes and our lips so close I could practically taste his vanilla ChapStick. He pressed his thumb against my chin and tilted my head up to look at him. His lips grazed against mine, so soft and subtle that I second-guessed if it even happened.

"I've thought about kissing you all night," he whispered, his breath hot against my skin. "Can I?"

My heart careened into my throat, and I knew words would be useless. Instead, I leaned in and answered him the only way I could. I answered the call of the void, and I kissed him.

His hand moved up my neck, leaving little trails of heat everywhere he touched. He found the side of my face and gingerly pulled at my chin, begging me to let him in, and I felt myself completely unravel.

My first kiss had been nothing like this. My first kiss was in a closet in the eighth grade, with Joey DelVecchio, who played soccer and always smelled like grass. It was awkward and tasted like soda and sour cream and onion chips. But this? If I could go back in time, I would give up every kiss I ever had with anyone just so this could be my first. He was the sweetest thing I'd ever tasted, and I knew I'd be craving him long afterward.

We finally pulled apart, and I gasped for air as my heart threatened to explode in my chest.

"Wow," he whispered softly.

"I hope that's a good wow," I whispered back, still trying to catch my breath.

"It's a good wow. A very good wow."

Suddenly the Ferris wheel lurched forward with a loud creak and began moving again. I had answered the call of the void, and I'd jumped—but he was there to catch me.

June 15

Hey Dad,

I did something reckless tonight.

We went to the state fair—Brooklyn, his sister, his friend, Alec, Nikki, me. I remember going with you once, when Nikki and I were really young, and the only reason I remember it so well is because you and I snuck off to get one of those giant buckets of half-baked cookies and ate almost the entire thing ourselves, and I got sick on the car ride home. Mom was so pissed.

It's actually a pretty good memory.

This night should, in theory, be a good memory too. Brooklyn won me a ridiculous Reptar plush after knocking down all the cans in one of those baseball toss games that we're all so sure are rigged, and for a minute it felt easy to forget that some kid at the booth recognized him for the worst chapter of his life. I watched his face after, how quickly pride curdled into shame, and it hurt me too.

Later, he asked me to ride the Ferris wheel even though he knows I hate heights. "I got you," he said, and I believed him. Maybe that's what the reckless part is—believing. Up there, with the lights spread out like spilled confetti and the ocean pretending to be quiet, he took my hand. I liked that.

He asked if he could kiss me. I said yes, and I liked that too.

Here's the part I'm afraid to say out loud: I think he needs me, and I'm more okay with that than I probably should be. Is that having feelings for someone, or something else? Am I helping him heal, or am I using him to prove I can keep someone from falling this time?

I've told myself that I don't need to wrap myself up in some of the stuff going on with Brooklyn, because friends don't need to fix each other, that's not what friends do. There's part of me that thinks we'll keep pretending the rules make us safer—no dating in early recovery, no rushing, no naming the thing when it's still tender. And yet I'm already rearranging my days around the space he leaves. It's an unfamiliar feeling.

Love, Nat

Thirteen

I recounted the saga at the carnival to Nikki as I made us popcorn for our *Love Is Blind* catch-up binge. It wasn't that I was so willing and eager to do so, but Nikki had a sixth sense about this kind of stuff, and there was no point in hiding it.

"Oh that is bold," Nikki said as she hopped onto the couch with Gracie and the bowl of popcorn. "He *loves* you."

"Don't be ridiculous." I flopped back onto the couch and pulled one of our vintage crocheted blankets up to my chest. "It's really nothing. People kiss all the time and nothing comes of it, so stop being so dramatic about it, *please*."

Admittedly, reality had set in the next morning despite the fact that his touch and his scent had lingered on me. We'd had an agreement that neither of us should be dating, but we had kissed anyway, and now things were about to be awkward, which was probably one of the reasons we had that kind of agreement in the first place.

"Besides, you spent the *entire* night with Alec," I continued. "And you've been mum on all those details."

"Who says *mum* anymore?" Nikki popped another piece of popcorn into her mouth.

"People who deflect."

"Fine, fine, fine." Nikki shifted in the couch cushions so she could sit up, and Gracie let out a heavy, inconvenienced sigh as her own position was compromised. *How dare you?* I could imagine her saying to Nikki.

"He's a nerd," Nikki said flatly. "He builds robots or something. At some point he might have actually been speaking a different language. His hair is too floppy, and he wears Axe body spray for crying out loud. We're so *not* compatible."

Nikki's phone chimed under the blankets, and she dove for it immediately.

"Really? That's a shame." I smirked at her while her head was down into her phone, her thumbs furiously swiping across the keypad. "What are you doing?"

"I'm texting him."

"Of course you are."

The one detail I had left out was that Brooklyn and I hadn't actually texted much since the carnival. I hadn't gone out of my way to reach out to him, but neither had he, and it wasn't far-fetched to think the same thoughts were floating around in his head too. The same stinging uncertainty.

"Apparently they're doing '90s night tomorrow at this roller rink downtown, and Alec invited us." Nikki kept her head down as she talked, still texting. Her lips lifted into the faintest smile. When she finally looked up and realized I'd been watching her, she scowled. "Do you want to go or not?"

I tried not to let the fact that Brooklyn hadn't invited me himself get under my skin, and instead focused on what a walking contradiction I'd become by simultaneously being annoyed he hadn't texted me, while not wanting to text him myself.

"Do *you* want to go with Mr. Not Compatible?" I asked her, trying to distract myself from my own traitorous thoughts.

Nikki shrugged. "That doesn't mean he's not nice to look at."

"Uh-huh. Sure."

"What about *you*?" She shot me a conspiratorial glance.

"I might pass." I gave her a casual half shrug. "I need to send out a few more agent queries and whatnot."

That wasn't entirely a lie—the sudden and unexpected development of my social life had meant the time spent in front of my computer had dwindled. As much as Mom's words echoed in the back of my mind about *having fun this summer*, there were moments when I thought I should have been doing more; more emails to agents, more time spent developing a new manuscript, more focus on my future.

"What about Brooklyn?"

"What about him?" I quipped a little too quickly.

"Don't you want to see him?"

I sighed, and the admission came out with it. "He didn't exactly invite me himself."

Nikki didn't miss a beat. "Probably because he's nervous to talk to you since you went all radio silent on him after kissing him."

"How do you know—"

"Because I know you."

She knew me better than anyone else did, and recently, I'd spent so much time and effort worrying about her it was easy to forget that she did the same for me.

Nikki hopped across the couch cushions to squish herself beside me. "You should come anyway because it'll be *fun*."

She wiggled her eyebrows at me, satisfied with throwing my own words back at me when I'd convinced her to come to the fair. It worked; begrudgingly so.

"All right fine." I held my hands up. "I *suppose* I can take advantage of an opportunity to channel Cher Horowitz."

And that was exactly what we did. I wore a yellow plaid skirt I'd thrifted a few years ago in college (for this exact moment, perhaps?) and paired it with a white baby tee and knee-high white socks. My sister—whose maximalist style belonged more in the '80s—sported a variation of Britney Spears's live "Baby One More Time" outfit in a cropped neon-pink tube top and white flare pants.

Of course, nothing measured up to how effortlessly cool Brooklyn looked in his faded jeans and his Deftones T-shirt, like he was *made* for the '90s. Despite it being close to dusk, he wore a pair of Ray-Bans as he and Alec lingered outside the roller rink, waiting for us.

"Hey." He greeted me effortlessly, as if nothing at all had transpired last weekend.

What's the right move when you greet someone whose tongue has been down your throat, but whom you aren't dating, or are in any way, shape, or form romantically involved with? Do you hug them? Do you kiss them on the cheek? Or do you do nothing, for fear that touching them would cause some type of nuclear meltdown?

"Hey, yourself." I tried to echo his casualness, and his lips lifted into an easygoing smile.

"This place is sick." Nikki beamed as we followed the boys inside. She fell into step ahead of Brooklyn and me with Alec, who looked like he'd borrowed the flannel shirt limply hanging off his shoulder from Brooklyn as it hung off his shoulder.

We were blasted by the sound of the Beastie Boys as soon as we walked into the lobby. There were pinball machines and vintage *Pac-Man* games in the corner next to the bar, and then the entire room opened up into the actual roller rink. A disco ball hung over it, throwing a confetti of lights onto the slick rink surface.

"Where's your sister?" I asked Brooklyn.

"Oh, she . . ." He rocked on the toes of his Converse as we waited in line to get our skates. "She had to bail last-minute. Some kind of junior league emergency. Who knows."

Nikki glanced back at me over her shoulder, and gave me a wicked, conniving look. I blinked, and she turned her attention back to Alec, throwing her head back and laughing at something he said. *Not compatible* my ass.

When it was our turn to get our skates, Brooklyn paid before I even had a chance to grab my wallet from my purse. For someone who hadn't even reached out to invite me, he was certainly acting like he wanted me there. He lit up when he turned to hand me the skates, and his smile melted away the weird sense of unease building inside of me. He had that effect on me without even trying.

"You okay?" he asked as I sat on a bench in front of the rink, wrangling the skates.

It took only a moment standing upright for me to realize that this was *not* for me. I gingerly inched over to the cut-out section of the wall that separated the rink from the floor, and gripped the sides of the gate with white knuckles. "Yeah, but I'm not sure I'm entirely coordinated enough for this."

"Come on." He held his hand out to me. "You can do it, just don't think too much."

After another few moments of hesitation, I slipped my hand into his, suddenly hyperaware of how clammy my palms must have been. He slowly rolled backward, pulling me onto the rink, but didn't let go of my hand.

"See?" he said. "You're fine. Now push yourself forward slowly. Bend your knees a little and relax your body, you're too stiff."

I tried to breathe normally as I grasped the sleeve of his shirt. "How ridiculous do I look?"

"No." He shook his head. "You look great."

After a few timid laps, I started to feel less like Bambi on ice, but he kept a reassuring hand on the small of my back, and his touch damn near set me on fire.

We took a break and leaned against the wall, observing Nikki and Alec from the other side of the rink. My heart lifted as I watched Nikki laugh and act so goddamn normal, but then that weird sense of unease constricted my heart again.

"Your sister is fine. Alec's gonna take care of her."

I scoffed. "I didn't say—"

"You didn't have to," Brooklyn interjected. "I know you."

I winced as he echoed the same sentiment my sister had earlier. It was one thing for me to be so transparent with Nikki, but to him? I was so see-through he could see everything inside me—aching heart included.

There was no point in denying it, so I collected myself and pushed off of the wall, rolling forward slowly on my skates. "Still, no offense to Alec, but he doesn't *know* her."

"Maybe that's a good thing." He shrugged. "Did you ever consider that maybe your sister wants to be treated like a normal person instead of someone who had a bad lapse in judgment because of mental health problems and now feels like it follows her everywhere?"

"Wait, are we still talking about Nikki?"

Brooklyn shrugged again even though the silence was enough of an answer, opening a door for me to walk—or skate—right through. I pinched the sleeve of his T-shirt as we skated forward, slower than we had been before. I looked up at him, and as the lights reflected in his eyes the way the moon reflected on the ocean on a clear night, I recognized that flicker of guilt from that night at the fair.

"Is that why we're avoiding what happened last weekend?"

Brooklyn let out a wry chuckle. "That obvious, huh?"

"No, I'm just extremely perceptive."

This time his laughter was more genuine, and that sense of unease loosened its grip.

"I'm guilty too," I admitted. "I didn't exactly go out of my way to reach out to you."

"Honestly, I'm not sure what I would have said even if you had."

"Well, we kissed," I stated. "And if that was a one-time thing, getting something out of our systems, that's fine. I get it."

Even though I *did* get it, the sight of him was starting to sting. *Getting it* and being accepting of it were two different things, apparently.

"Yeah, I guess so." He rubbed the side of his face. "I'm sorry."

"Don't be."

"No Scrubs" by TLC started playing from the speakers, and even though we'd been casually skating along through a sea of people, they all seemed to come to life and started singing along. Including Brooklyn, who shot me a sideways glare when I laughed. At the very least, he always managed to do that.

"Come on, you can't just hum along to 'No Scrubs,' even if you're as bad of a singer as me."

"Well, you're no scrub," I chided, and we both belted out the chorus as it came on.

Without warning, Brooklyn stopped on a dime, and when he went to pull me back to him, my feet got tangled up in each other. Before I had a chance to steady myself I toppled over, taking him with me as he fumbled to keep me upright. I landed hard on top of him, and his body shuddered underneath me.

"I'm sorry," I blurted. "Are you okay?"

"Fine. Totally fine," he replied through breathy laughter. "Are you?"

Suddenly, we were all alone. It was then that I truly realized the position I was in. My knees hugged one of his thighs, and from there up, every single inch of our bodies, every dip and every curve, aligned too perfectly, like a lock and its one and only key. I had my hands pressed into his torso, feeling the way his chest moved up and down with every breath he took. Under the fabric of his shirt, his heartbeat thundered against his ribs. Mine did, too, reminding me of how precarious this whole situation was and how gossamer thin the line was between wanting to avoid him altogether and kissing him again like we had on the Ferris wheel. So, no, maybe I was not at all fine.

"I need to tell you something."

"Okay." I nodded intently, swallowing a thick wad of tension that had lodged itself in my throat. "Tell me."

It didn't seem to matter to either of us that we were still lying on the floor of a roller rink, people skating past us with confused glances.

But of course, my sister had impeccable timing.

"Oh my god." Nikki cackled as she skated up to us. "You guys absolutely ate shit, it was great."

We scrambled to our feet, my whole body still reverberating from the impact.

"You sure you're all right?" Brooklyn asked me, and in a seemingly thoughtless motion he reached over and tucked a loose strand of hair behind my ear.

"I'm fine." I heaved out a breath. "It was my fault, I'm sorry. I got a little too confident, I guess."

Brooklyn rubbed the back of his neck, rolling his head around a few times. "Yeah, me too."

Nikki slid me the most antagonizing smirk before skating away again, pulling Alec along behind her, who watched her with equal parts fascination and confusion.

"Anyway." I felt that gross wad of tension ball up in my throat again, and I had to force my words past it. "What did you want to tell me?"

Brooklyn heaved out another sigh as he shook his head. "Are we good now?"

"Of course we are," I told him.

Even though I'd come to the conclusion I selfishly wanted us to be more than maybe just *good*. We'd unlocked our own Pandora's box, and there was no way to stuff all the things I'd been feeling back into it.

"Excellent. Good. Great."

His voice was soft, and all the colorful lights dotted his face as he gave me a weary smile. I didn't know where I was, but I was not on earth; instead I was lost in the stars of his galaxy like a wayward comet. I wasn't sure I'd ever get home. I wasn't sure I wanted to.

Fourteen

When Nikki was sixteen, I found a half-eaten granola bar wrapped in a paper towel at the bottom of the bathroom trash can. It wasn't the granola bar that bothered me; it was that it had been chewed and spit out.

Back then, I didn't recognize it for what it was. I'd convinced myself it was one of her weird teenage experiments, like when she tried to cut her own hair with kitchen scissors or decided she could "manifest" better skin by drinking celery juice for a week. But the truth had been right in front of me, and I hadn't wanted to see it.

"Stop hovering," she'd snapped one night when I followed her into the kitchen after dinner, pretending to look for a glass of water.

"I'm not hovering," I'd said, which is exactly what a person who is hovering says.

She'd turned from the sink, face pale under the fluorescent light. "There's nothing wrong, Nat. I don't know why you don't believe me."

The words landed like a bruise. She didn't sound angry, just tired. Tired of me watching. Tired of feeling whatever this was that she was feeling.

Sometimes that memory sneaks up on me when I least expect it, like tonight, when we're all at the dinner table and everything is objectively fine and we're talking about Nikki dyeing her hair.

"I want a change," she insisted, pressing her hands into the table. "Some people cut their hair when they go through a breakup. I am, in a way, breaking up with my ED, but I don't want to *cut* my hair, because that's too dramatic. So, I'm thinking red—but not *red* red, like an orange red."

"Sure." Mom nodded. "Why not like a chestnut brown or a black?"

"Black hair would make me look like Matilda," Nikki stated, as if she'd already foreseen it and decided against it.

I sniggered. "Better Matilda than Leeloo from *The Fifth Element*."

"Lee-*who*?" Nikki groaned.

"Not Leewho, Lee*loo*," Mom sputtered between laughs, and eventually the three of us were cackling like hyenas, holding our sides with tears in our eyes. Moments like these were coming more often, but there was still a part of me that wanted to bottle it up in a jar and store it away, as if I would need it in the future. For what, I wasn't sure, but there were times I found myself looking upward without even realizing it, waiting for the other shoe to drop. Those moments still lingered.

"Fine, maybe I'll just get a trim," Nikki scoffed.

"You're born to be a blond," I reassured her. "Like Elle Woods."

We finished dinner, and to my relief, no shoe had dropped.

"I have exciting news," Mom said as we were clearing the table. Nikki had her hands elbows deep in the sink washing the Corningware while I scraped leftover chicken into Gracie's bowl.

"Oh yeah?" I perked up. "Do tell."

"There was a last-minute withdrawal from the Furman Gallery

showing next Friday, so they want to replace it with my *On the Bay* series." She paused and finally let herself beam with excitement while the news set in to us. "Obviously it goes without saying that I'd love for you two to be at the showing with me."

"This means I get to buy a new dress!" Nikki squealed in delight.

"That's great, Mom." I returned her smile. "You deserve it."

"Oh, can we bring dates?" Nikki asked, dancing around in circles while Gracie tried to keep up.

"You mean Alec?" I chided Nikki.

"Who's Alec?" Mom raised an eyebrow at her.

"*No.*" Nikki groaned. "I'm not dating Alec. Besides, he won't even be here, he has to go back to Stanford for some smart-people convention. I *meant* you could bring Brooklyn, Nat."

"Pot calling the kettle black. We're not dating either. We're hanging out." I waved a dishrag around.

There was a pause, and I caught sight of Nikki out of the corner of my eye, still grinning.

"Maybe you two can *hang out* at the gallery, then," Mom stated plainly, but she and Nikki traded scheming glances. "He seemed nice."

"Oh yes, he's very *nice.*" Nikki jabbed me in the side again, her grin widening by the second.

"All right, all right." I held my hands up in defense. "If I ask him, will you two conniving creatures leave me alone?"

"Only after we go shopping," Nikki insisted. "I need a dress, you need a dress, we all need dresses."

"Okay, Oprah, calm down." I chuckled. "We'll get dresses."

>> <<

In literature, *pathetic fallacy* is the use of weather to reflect tone or mood. Typically it was applied in a negative way, such as a storm to imply something detrimental or foreboding. But sitting out on the beach on a Saturday at the end of June, with the sun warm and high and glinting like diamonds against the water's surface, I thought maybe for once pathetic fallacy could be good. Genuinely good.

Nikki and I had met Brooklyn, Alec, Stella, and a few of Stella's college friends out at the beach by Sixth Street mid-morning (after going out of our way to pick up Bad Beans). Alec had been constructing a massive sandcastle (half child, half engineer), and Nikki eagerly skipped over to him, leaving me to the conveniently open lounge chair beside Brooklyn. Third Eye Blind played from a speaker clipped to his backpack hanging between the two chairs, and I dropped into it with a sigh.

"Not a bad way to spend a Saturday," he remarked, sipping his iced latte.

"Unless you forgot your sunglasses," I responded as I rummaged through my beach bag past a few bags of chips and my notebook. "I'll have to go back and get them."

"Oh, wait." Brooklyn leaned over the side of his chair to dig through his bag, then produced a worn-out Clayton baseball cap in the school's black and teal colors. He slapped it onto my head with a grin. "All better."

"I feel traitorous." I chuckled, adjusting the brim to shield my eyes.

"No, *stylish*."

His grin widened as he sat back in his lounge chair. Sweat glistened on his bare chest, and the way his sternum rose and fell with each breath, so calm and steady, was entrancing. Before I realized I had been gawking at him, he gave me a knowing glance over the tops of his sunglasses.

"You like what you see?"

I stiffened a bit, but let the faintest smirk grace my face. "It's . . . you're getting burned."

"Oh. I'll live." He gave me a knowing smirk before settling back in his chair again. He had me under a goddamn spell, and maybe he knew it. Time slowed when we were together, and nothing more than his presence made me feel so safe and so secure. I didn't have to try so hard to prevent bad things from happening, and I could simply be me. Nobody had ever given me that feeling before. I wondered if it would ever go away.

I reached back into my bag for my notebook, hoping the weather and the vibes would inspire me somehow. I took in my surroundings—Stella and two of her friends lying on towels, with hats and shirts over their heads; Nikki trying to follow along as Alec built up more sections of his sandcastle; a teenage couple beside us on a towel, giggling as they ran their hands all over each other. I clicked and clacked my pen about a thousand times, scribbling little hearts in the margins of my notebook instead of actual words.

"What are you writing over there?" Brooklyn asked.

"Literally not a damn thing." I sighed and snapped my notebook shut. "The words aren't coming today. Or this month, for that matter. But I've learned you can't force it, otherwise you're probably going to hate what you write."

"Very wise." Brooklyn nodded, pursing his lips. "Not that I can really relate, since I was technically supposed to be a corporate accountant, right?"

"I cannot see you as an accountant, all stuffy suits and business meetings and asking your secretary to get your coffee five times a day. You're too—"

"Devil may care?" He slid his sunglasses down the bridge of

his nose. I shook my head, but he continued. "It's okay, you can say it. It's not like that's really what I wanted to do, but I was good at math, so it made sense."

I sat up straight in the lounge chair and put my finger beside a ladybug that had crawled up the side of the chair. "What would you have done, then? Like if you had an honest to god calling, what would it be?"

"I used to think it was baseball. I'm sure at some point someone somewhere told me I was good at it and I should stick with it, but I really *did* like it. I didn't feel obligated or pressured to do it, and I was good. Like, *really* good. Now, I have no idea."

Uncharacteristic sadness lingered in his voice, and it clenched my heart.

"You don't have to know," I said softly, watching the ladybug crawl onto my finger and then flutter away. "I wanted to be a marine biologist when I was younger. Then I realized I was totally afraid of the ocean, and that went out the window."

That got Brooklyn to laugh, and hearing it made a sense of ease wash over me like a wave. It was an ease that I had almost gotten used to. An ease I felt only when I was around him.

"But you know now." He gestured to the notebook still in my lap.

"I guess so." I pulled my knees into my chest. "I like telling stories, but actual success can feel so intangible. I've been reaching out to agents for weeks and not even had one person interested in more of my anthology. That's why I'm trying to write something new, but—" I waved my notebook around. "No words."

I paused when I felt his eyes still on me. My heart pounded against my chest like it wanted to escape and leap right into his hands.

"What?"

Brooklyn slumped back into his chair and ran his hands down his face. "I feel like I've wasted so much time already with all my bullshit."

"I understand that. Sometimes I get nervous that I'll blink and suddenly I'll be my mom's age but I've done nothing."

"We're so young. We're not even old enough for quarter-life crises." Brooklyn sighed. "But I definitely don't feel young."

The air was heavy with heat and humidity, but the silence that followed was heavier. I knew I had to ask him to come to the gallery showing, and I knew he'd say yes. That wasn't what made my stomach turn over. Despite agreeing how *fine* everything was between us, something lingered in the air every time we were together. We continuously circled each other like wayward asteroids, and I wondered if it was only a matter of time before we collided.

I took a long sip of my iced latte to cool myself off. "Speaking of, my mom actually has this art gallery thing next week. I don't know if the art gallery scene is really your thing, but if you want—"

"I'd love to come." Brooklyn cut me off, and a toothy grin stretched across his face. "I've got a really great judgy art face."

He dramatically stroked his chin with his fingers and scrunched his eyebrows before letting out a long sigh. "I find this piece to be very lacking in purpose."

"You're missing *There's too much white space* or some other pretentious comment like that." I laughed. "My mom isn't like that, though. She's different. All my life she's been the happiest, most positive person I know. But you can't be like that all the time, right? Like, all the negativity has to go somewhere, and when you see her paintings, you can really feel them. They're raw and vulnerable, and I guess that's better than the right amount of white space or color tone or anything else."

Brooklyn nudged me. "Now you really sound like an artist."

"Oh no!"

Ahead of us, Alec's sandcastle had collapsed, and he and Nikki scrambled to save whatever was left of the turrets and . . . was that a moat with a bridge?

"Guess we better go help them." Brooklyn stood up and offered me his hand, like he already had so many times before.

I smiled and didn't hesitate, but I let our palms linger for a moment when he pulled me up. Maybe we'd already collided, and we didn't even know it.

Fifteen

I wasn't sure what I thought "normalcy" would look like when I settled full-time in Dahlia Point. Back at Sky Valley, I had a strict routine. I ran in the morning, went to class, went to the library, volunteered as a student editing tutor, went home, wrote things, read things, watched things. Rise, rinse, repeat.

Here, there were too many uncertainties—my post-grad career (or lack thereof), Nikki's health, and everything slightly more inconsequential in between.

But getting ready together to go to an art gallery show in Nikki's room while blasting some bubblegum pop music made it feel normal in a new way.

"God, I wish I had your boobs," Nikki said as she glanced over at me, capping her pink lip gloss.

"It's not too much, is it?" I looked back in the mirror to assess the silky baby-blue cocktail dress I'd picked out at a boutique downtown, pulling the sweetheart neckline up slightly to cover more of my very exposed cleavage.

"No way," she insisted, reaching over and yanking it back down to where it was. "If you got it, flaunt it. Body positivity and all that jazz."

"So *that's* what you're learning in group therapy."

"Something like that." She waved me off, and for a moment

the low tone of her voice triggered an alarm in me, but then she glanced at me with a faint smirk, and everything settled. "You might give Brooklyn a heart attack, but surely someone knows CPR."

"Oh, stop it." I rolled my eyes, holding out my hand for her lip gloss. "I'm sure he's seen a pair of boobs once in his life."

"Maybe, but not *yours*."

Before I had a chance to snap back, Mom called up the stairs for us.

"Girls! Uber's here!"

When I'd offered to drive, I had been brutally rebuffed. Apparently we were *all* going to have a good time tonight; whatever that meant.

Downtown Dahlia Point seemed picturesque on a quiet Saturday night. It was still a small beach town, with one main road lined with aesthetic but old gas lamps and few pedestrians dotting the sidewalks, but passing through it finally felt comfortable—a place in which I felt at home. The sun was sinking behind the tops of the palm trees, bathing them in a warm, dusky glow. Our Uber slowed to a stop in front of a tiny white brick building: the Furman Gallery.

Mom had talked about wanting to be featured at the gallery when she was in art school here. It hadn't happened, and when she met my dad, she'd moved out to Sky Valley, where he lived and worked. I always wondered if she'd felt a little resentful about it, but I never wanted to ask her.

Despite being in the center of a small beach town, the Furman Gallery seemed so official and professional. Apparently people from all over the state would be trickling in throughout the night to catch glimpses of pieces of art they could buy for their swanky city offices or sprawling modern ranches.

We'd headed over a little early so Mom had some time to take in her pieces being displayed so proudly, and when she turned to assess the two of us, tears glistened in her eyes.

"I'm so happy I get to share this with you girls." She put a hand on each of our shoulders.

"Come on." Nikki groaned, dabbing the corners of her eyes. "We just did our makeup, and I didn't put waterproof mascara on."

We laughed through the emotion, and Mom gave us each a hug. When she squeezed me, she held on a little longer.

"I'm proud of you," she whispered in my ear.

"Me? For what?"

She let go, holding me at arm's length with a smile. "Allowing yourself to be a girl this summer. I haven't seen you have so much fun in a long time."

"Thanks, Mom. I'm trying." I smiled at her, thankful that I *had* chosen waterproof mascara (even if it was by happy accident) as tears stung the corners of my eyes. Good tears, though. "Love you."

"Love you too." She pulled me into another quick hug before collecting herself and smoothing the front of her navy dress down.

A few of the other artists had arrived, and eventually so did some patrons. The event wasn't terribly crowded, which wasn't all that surprising, being a smaller gallery in a small town, but it wasn't empty, either, and quite a few people took an interest in some of Mom's paintings. Couples meandered by, champagne in hand, making offhand remarks about the flow of this painting or the coloring on that painting. Dainty piano music floated through the air, though there was no sign of an actual piano.

Thirty minutes had gone by and there was no sign of Brooklyn either. I'd sequestered myself in an empty corner and checked my phone for what felt like the tenth time, and it was still radio silent.

"Not even a text?" Nikki appeared beside me, tapping her pink fingernails on her champagne glass.

I slipped my phone back into my purse. "Punctuality isn't exactly his strong suit. I'm sure it's fine."

I wasn't sure who I was trying to convince more—me or her.

"If you say so." Nikki shrugged, not bothering to hide her unease.

As if I'd manifested him, I looked up to see Brooklyn stroll through the entrance to the gallery. One of the hostesses who carried around a tray of champagne, a petite blond girl, scanned him with curious eyes as he walked by. I had never paid attention to how other women looked at him, mostly because I didn't care, although I realized I'd be foolish to think that I was the only person who thought he was attractive. He was a different kind of attractive—not striking and goonish, but rather refined and rough around the edges—but that was what really made him so appealing to look at.

"See, being late's not a crime," I told her. "*You're* usually late."

"Whatever." She rolled her eyes as she walked away. Instinctively I took a step to go after her, feeling a pang of guilt shoot through my chest. I didn't want Nikki to be upset, especially because of me, but suddenly he was in front of me, and all the air left my lungs.

I couldn't have created someone better in any made-up schoolgirl daydreams. He wore all black, with his suit jacket open and the first two buttons of his shirt undone. He was clean-shaven, giving a view to how angular and strong his jawline was, but his hair was as intentionally messy as it always was, making him look just a little more human.

"Wow," he said breathlessly, his eyes trailing up and down my body. "You look . . . wow."

Prickly heat spread across my chest. "You look pretty wow too."

Brooklyn scooted closer to me as another hostess walked behind him, having to weave through the small crowd of people with a full tray of champagne, and placed his hands at my waist to keep us both upright. He smelled so good it genuinely made me weak at the knees. When he realized how close we were, he took a step back.

"I'm really sorry I'm late," he blurted. "I originally had a white shirt on, then I spilled coffee on it, and I couldn't find another shirt so I had to look through my dad's closet. It was a mess."

"It's okay," I said. "You're here now."

"I am." He brought his hand back to my waist with a little more intention this time, snaking it around to rest on the small of my back. He dipped his head down so he could whisper in my ear. "You really do look beautiful."

My body reacted to his touch, and I put my hands to his chest. "You really do too. Handsome, I mean. You clean up nicely."

Having an intimate moment with someone really changed the way you looked at them—no matter how small and seemingly inconsequential that moment was. Sure we'd kissed, and sure we said it was a one-time thing, but it didn't change how you hyperfocused on their lips and tried to relive the moment in your head, from the way they tasted to the places their hands rested on your body. I searched his deep ocean-blue eyes, wondering if he was reliving it too. He poked his tongue out to swipe it along his bottom lip, and I had to swallow down my heart.

But my sister, as always, had impeccable timing. Brooklyn and I separated like we'd shocked each other.

"*Thank god* you're here." She feigned distress, as if she hadn't been standing by me in the same exact spot not five minutes ago.

"Hey, Nikki," Brooklyn greeted her.

"Hi," she replied, but she kept her focus on me. "You need to talk Mom out of locking herself in the bathroom for the rest of the night."

"What?" I said. "Is she all right?"

Nikki shook her head. "She's been doing that awkward *HI, I'm Melanie, have we met before?* to people passing by, like Dory from *Finding Nemo*."

"Oh boy."

"It's fine," Brooklyn chimed in. "I actually *should* go find the bathroom."

Nikki didn't waste another second and pulled me away. Mom stood on the far side of the gallery, between two large oil paintings of the ocean. I remembered seeing her work on one of them, and it had taken her days to get the colors right for the water.

The closer we got to her, the more out of place I realized she looked. Even though I had watched her pull her hair tight into a sleek ponytail when we were all getting ready, frizzy strands had begun to poke out at her hairline. As a man and a woman walked by to admire one of her paintings, she gave them an awkward grimace.

"Oh god, Nat." She groaned as I walked up to her. "I don't know what's wrong with me. I don't know what to do with my hands or my mouth, and this dress is so goddamn itchy."

I put my hands down on her shoulders. "Everything's all right, you need to loosen up a bit. These rich artsy people can smell fear."

That got her to chuckle and her shoulders to ease up under my hands.

"Take a few deep breaths," I told her. "I'll stay right here with you and entice people over with the cleavage Nikki insisted I have out."

She laughed again and heaved out a relieved sigh. "I'm fine. You should go enjoy yourself. Both of you."

"Well, I've enjoyed the champagne enough and now I need to pee." Nikki turned to me and handed me her glass. "I'll be right back."

"If you see Brooklyn, tell him where we are," I called after her. When another hostess walked by with a tray of champagne, I felt compelled to grab my own. Despite the fact that I knew champagne needed to settle and should be drunk slowly, I immediately took a long gulp.

"Looks like I'm not the only one who needs to relax." Mom raised her eyebrow at me.

"What?" I scoffed at her. "You said enjoy yourself. I'm enjoying free champagne."

A younger man (and truly only younger compared to the posh older people walking around) walked by the two of us, assessing Mom's oil paintings with a musing smile. He then glanced at her and offered her the same one before walking away.

I nudged Mom with a sly grin, but before I could instigate any further, Nikki came waltzing back to us, and without Brooklyn.

"Did you see Brooklyn at all?" I asked her.

"No," Nikki replied. "I thought he was back out here with you."

I stiffened, feeling Nikki's eyes on me. "Oh, then I'm sure he's just wandering around, admiring some of the art."

"Oh that's sweet," Mom chimed in, but she was bouncing on her toes and looking for the younger guy who had walked by us before.

Nikki gave me a sideways glance. "It's not that big of a gallery, Nat, and he's also, like, built like a tree."

She swept her arm outward, where almost every corner of the space was visible from where we stood.

There was absolutely *no* reason for everyone to be getting so worked up, and I was about to relish the feeling of being right. I handed Nikki my champagne glass. "I'll be right back."

As soon as I was out of her line of sight, I made a beeline to the back hallway that led to the bathrooms and curator offices, and for maybe one fraction of a second my mind wandered to more sinister thoughts. I wasn't even sure what a relapse for someone like him looked like, but that was where I forced the thoughts to stop. Sure enough, Brooklyn emerged from the dimness seemingly on cue, looking as calm, cool, and collected as ever.

"Everything all right?" I asked when he made his way over to me.

"Yeah, it was a whole adventure to find a glass of water, and my bladder is the size of a quarter." He gave me one of those endearing smiles, and it made the tension whoosh out of my shoulders.

"I'm sorry." I sighed, silently kicking myself for even suspecting there wasn't a reasonable explanation for his absence. "I should have realized with you being sober, this might be uncomfortable for you."

"I'm fine," Brooklyn said. "Never was a champagne guy. Gives me bubble guts, to be honest."

I giggled and shook my head. I wasn't sure exactly what bubble guts were, but it seemed like a reasonable description for whatever was going on in my stomach now. No more champagne for me, that was for sure.

He offered me his elbow. "Shall we?"

I slid my arm through the crook of his elbow, and he felt as sturdy as ever as he led me back into the heart of the gallery. We did a few laps, admiring some of the more abstract artwork and making pretentious sideways comments as if we knew exactly what we were talking about. We laughed, and maybe it *was* simply champagne guts, but everything inside me warmed, the way the sun warms the ocean in the mornings.

We made our way back over to Mom, where Brooklyn effortlessly slipped into conversation with her about her creative process (and god knows she *loved* that). He was so good with people, I was almost envious.

We were debating if a painting had actually been hung upside down when his phone rang in his jacket pocket, and annoyance flashed across his features.

"I'm sorry, I gotta take this." He gave me a quick nod before retreating to the back hallway by the bathrooms again.

Out of the corner of my eye, I noticed a smaller painting on the back wall of the gallery that we seemed to have missed in our laps, and I wandered over to it. It hadn't gathered much attention compared to some of the larger pieces, but I was drawn to it. It was an oil painting like my mom's, but much darker. Parts of the ocean and sky were nearly black, and the only pop of lightness was a hand sticking out of the water.

I didn't know why, but looking at it for too long gave me chills. It was like something I would have nightmares about as a teenager—drowning, suffocating, and reaching out for help that wouldn't come.

"Where's your man now?" Nikki jolted me from my grim thoughts.

I shrugged in response, not willing to humor her sideways comment. "He got a phone call he had to take. Probably his mom. She likes to check in."

"Don't you think it's weird?" She scrunched her nose up and gazed around the room, where Brooklyn was nowhere to be found again. "Like, first he's late, and now he's basically been MIA since he got here."

"I don't think it's weird," I responded. "I think it's weird that *you* think it's weird."

Nikki scoffed and gave me another dramatic eye roll. "I'm saying it's sketchy. For all you know, he could be like snorting cocaine in the bathroom or something."

That one hurt. Not just because it was coming from my sister, but because there was the smallest iota of a chance it might have been true. But I wouldn't let her know that.

"I don't understand, Nikki, where is all this coming from?"

"Nat, he's got drug problems," she said bitingly, her tone hushed but still sharper than knives. "And I'm getting a weird vibe from him tonight. Something's not right."

"You know what?" I folded my arms over my chest, not bothering to hide my irritation anymore. "You of all people should be more understanding."

She scowled. "That's exactly the point. I've *seen* people like him in rehab, Nat. They sneak around and hide and lie and they're *good* at it."

"Well, you obviously haven't seen enough," I snapped back, immediately regretting it as she recoiled with hurt in her eyes. Desperate to regain any sense of composure, I paused and rolled my shoulders back. "Brooklyn's different, Nikki."

"Says who?"

"Says me."

"And you know *everything*, don't you?"

I paused and gritted my teeth. I didn't need to justify it anymore. I spent the most time with Brooklyn, and I *knew* that he was fine. I would know if he wasn't.

"More than you think you do." I lowered my voice. "I'm not having any more of this conversation. Not here, and not now."

"Everything cool?" Brooklyn came up behind me and draped

his arm over my shoulder. "Sorry about that, it was my mom. You know how she gets."

I shot Nikki a hard glare. *I told you so, again.*

"Whatever," Nikki grumbled, dropping her gaze to her silver stilettos.

"Everything's good," I told Brooklyn. "Great, actually."

He beamed at me, oblivious to the emotional standoff my sister and I were having. He led me away back into the gallery crowd, and it took everything in me not to look back at her.

>> <<

Mom sold two paintings that night, one of which was to the younger guy she'd been making eyes with. Otherwise, the gallery had mostly cleared out.

"You go, Nikki and I have this handled." She winked at me before looking over my shoulder at Brooklyn, who lingered by the door, his suit jacket draped over his arm.

"Mom, I don't know where you think I'm going except to bed."

Mom chuckled and shook her head in response.

I glanced across the room at Nikki, who'd been talking to one of the curators, still clutching an empty champagne glass in her hand. When we made eye contact, she scowled.

"Seriously." Mom swept me into a quick hug. "Thanks for all your help. Be smart."

"Oh my god." I groaned before walking away. "Pretending I didn't hear the implications behind that."

I met Brooklyn by the door, who gave me one of those effortless smiles. "What's so funny?"

"Nothing." I returned his smile. "Take me home?"

"That's what I'm here for."

We drove home with the windows open, and I tried to let the stinging sense of unease from earlier fly out of them and into the night air. Everything had ended up being fine—great, even—and maybe I shouldn't be so expectant of the other shoe dropping out of the sky. Brooklyn slowed to a stop in front of my house, and some old, soft rock song I didn't recognize crooned faintly on the stereo in the background. It was quiet; not the kind we forced ourselves to sit in during family therapy, but the kind of quiet that only came when you were just so comfortable with someone, words couldn't express it. I'd never had a person who understood me like he did, and it felt so good and so right that I almost had to wonder if he was even real, or if he was someone I'd made up because I wanted something like that more than I'd realized. Until him.

"We had a good night," he said over the faint lulling of the music.

"We did, didn't we?"

Brooklyn dropped his eyes to the stereo. He hit the Next button, and I couldn't help but notice his shaking hands. He pressed his lips together and furrowed his brows, carefully mulling over his next words.

"Everything all right?" I asked him, absentmindedly running my hands back and forth over the silky material of my dress.

"I don't know, Nat." Every time he looked like he was about to say something else, he pressed his lips together again. My heart began sprinting.

"What, Brooklyn?" I reached over the center console and gave his arm a playful shove. "Please say it. You can tell me anything."

He looked over at me, and the glow from the moon above us turned his eyes into little pools of light. "I feel like you're the only person I *can* tell anything to."

This time, I reached across the console to gently put my hand on his. "And I'm glad you feel that way."

"We really haven't known each other that long, but it feels like we have. I feel like you really get me, and not just the deeper stuff, but the dumb stuff too. Who else am I going to talk to about obscure freaky indie movies and books about how wonderful and fucked-up your twenties can be?"

"And disrupt my very busy workday with these conversations." I grinned and squeezed his hand a little tighter.

As much as I think I can keep my cool and composure, these were things I simply didn't have experience with—boys, dates, confessions in a Jeep after a long night out. But the thought of the unknown didn't make me nervous. Instead, I felt that call of the void again. Ready to jump in.

"I know I'm not *supposed* to date." He threw the word *supposed* out like a curse. "But for the first time in what feels like forever, I feel really good, and you have something to do with it. I almost think fighting this—whatever this is—is worse than just letting it happen."

He was so close now; close enough that I could count the faded web of freckles under his eyes and smell the vanilla ChapStick on his lips. "Being around you, feeling the way I feel and not acting on it, it makes my whole body ache."

"I know." I sighed. "I ache too."

He pressed his thumb against my chin and tilted my head up to look up at him. His lips brushed against mine, so soft and so subtle I had to second-guess if it even happened.

"What should we do about this?" He was practically breathing his words into my mouth.

My chest was on fire, but I craved the burn. I craved him. "Don't go. Not yet."

His eyes darkened, and I felt a storm coming just by looking at him. "I wasn't planning on it."

After fumbling through my purse for my house keys, I led him onto the dark of the porch and through the front door. We said a quick hello to Gracie, who barely lifted her head off the couch, side-eyeing us like we had such audacity to disturb her sleep.

When we entered my room, my face blanched in horror. I had forgotten how much of a mess it was, with both my and Nikki's clothes in piles on my carpet. Books were stacked against the wall beside my bed, and my desk looked like a hurricane had come through and upended all of my makeup, nail polish, and picture frames. Moonlight danced through the open window, giving the room just enough light that we could see the shapes and shadows of the mess, so I kept the lights off.

Brooklyn wove across the carpet, slowly slipping off his suit jacket and placing it delicately over the back of my desk chair. He lowered himself onto the edge of the bed, and I couldn't help but grin, seeing his large frame so out of place on my tiny bed, surrounded by fuzzy purple pillows and a paisley-patterned comforter.

"I'm sorry it's such a mess," I said breathily, running my hand through my hair. "Getting ready this afternoon was a disaster, and I haven't had time—"

"Would you stop fussing?" He chuckled. He stretched his arms out to me. "Come here."

After kicking off my heels, I walked over to him slowly and stood between his knees. His hands grazed up my bare legs to the hem of my dress, leaving blistering heat on every inch that his skin touched mine. I gripped his shoulders to steady myself as my head filled with static.

"Hi," he whispered against my mouth.

"Hi, yourself."

He gently bit down on his lip. "Can I kiss you now?"

I felt him squeeze my hips, and my body clenched in anticipation.

"I thought you'd never ask."

He gently ran his hand up the crook of my neck, letting his thumb brush over my lips before kissing me. Every movement of his was soft and gentle, and he tasted like everything good and sweet in the world. It was even better than the first time, and I wondered if it would feel like this every time we kissed. His hands explored me eagerly, from my flushed cheeks, through my mess of hair, to my neck, and down to my waist. Heat radiated through me, to the very deepest and darkest parts of my body.

I broke away for a moment and went to tie my hair up, but he grabbed my wrist.

"Leave it," he said in a husky voice. "I like your hair down." There was a pause as I felt him smile against my mouth. "And I like you."

Tiny fireworks went off in my chest, and I couldn't breathe.

"I like you too," I said softly.

He kissed me again, and I felt like I didn't even have to come up for air. It was as if he had breathed life into me.

He reached around me and found the zipper of my dress with ease, pulling the tab agonizingly slowly, as if he wanted to feel each of the teeth separate one by one. When it was finally undone, he tugged it over my head gently, discarding it on the floor.

"Wow," he said breathlessly, reaching up to smooth my hair back.

"What?"

"You."

If this was what it felt like to be lost in a moment, I never wanted to be found.

I smiled and shook my head at him as I carefully undid the buttons on his shirt, pushing the delicate fabric off his broad shoulders and tossing it into the pile with my dress. He wrapped his arm around my torso, and in one swift motion flipped us both over so my back was pressed into the mattress with his knees straddling my waist. His mouth continued to explore my bare skin, trailing down my neck to my collarbone to my shoulder.

"Brooklyn." His name left my mouth in a wistful sigh, and I felt him smile against my skin as he continued to dot kisses down my bare stomach.

"Sounds good when *you* say it." He lifted his head and grinned at me.

I scoffed. "Oh shush. I like your name."

Lust rippled through me in waves as he ran his hands up my thighs, his fingers finding the waistband of my thong. He paused for a moment to pull away and look at me, his eyes glowing even in the dim light.

"You okay?" He sat up, his legs still straddling my hips, and gently brushed his fingers down my stomach. My whole body buzzed under his touch, like I'd swallowed a hornet's nest.

"Yeah, I'm okay." I nodded. "I haven't done this in a long time."

"Me either," he admitted softly.

"What a pair we are, huh?" I chuckled.

"Like we're made for each other or something." He leaned back down and swept me into a deep kiss. We clawed at the last of each other's clothes, kissing and kissing and kissing like we were truly made for each other.

Sixteen

A persistent buzzing woke me from the deepest sleep I'd had in a long time. A warm breeze washed over me as my eyes struggled to adjust to the sudden light. I glanced over at the other side of my room to see that my window had been left open all night, bringing blinding morning sunlight and salty air pouring into the room.

The buzzing continued, but I ignored it. The boy lying next to me kept me preoccupied. His chest slowly rose and fell with each gentle breath he took. Even though I was still in a haze, I felt a sense of peace watching him sleep. His mouth hung open slightly but his breath was calm and steady. My stomach clenched as the events of last night rushed back to me in a fury. I still tasted vanilla on my lips. Vanilla and him.

I fumbled around the sheets to find the source of the buzzing, which I realized was Brooklyn's phone, not mine. When I went to silence it, a text message from a random number popped up on the screen.

Unknown: still owe me for those two shirts. elliot is on my ass man

"What time is it?" Brooklyn mumbled, his voice still heavy with sleep. I dropped his phone onto the mattress and shifted myself underneath the covers. It felt weird going through someone else's phone, and even though it was an accident, a knot in my stomach told me I should not have seen that message. I feigned a yawn.

"It's early," I mumbled. "Your phone has been going off."

"Oh." Brooklyn furrowed his brows, suddenly very awake as he patted around the sheets for the device. I watched his fingers dart across the screen, and his wide, hazy eyes following along as he typed a response.

He rolled over to face me and reached out to gently run his fingers down my cheek. "I have to get going, okay?" His voice was so soft it rolled over me like a gentle breeze, barely registering until he shimmied out of bed and began collecting his clothes from last night.

"Everything all right?" I asked as I sat up. Brooklyn looked over at me and gave me a tired smile.

"Everything's fine," he said as he slipped his shirt on. "I'd rather not start shit with my mom this early. I didn't exactly tell her I was spending the night."

"Right, well, I guess we didn't really plan that, did we? I don't want you getting into any trouble."

Brooklyn's tired smile grew into that charming, boyish grin that he knew I adored. He leaned over and gently placed a kiss on my forehead.

"Last night was worth all the trouble in the world. I'll call you later."

I squeezed his hand as he stepped away, and part of me thought that might have been enough to get him to stay, but he didn't.

There wasn't really a point in trying to go back to sleep, but I lay in bed, replaying last night over and over again in my head as a familiar warmth rolled through me. For a fleeting moment

I wondered if it was real, but then I inhaled, and my pillow still smelled like him, all fresh and clean and very real.

Of course, as reality began to really set in, so did the bad thoughts buzzing around my head like pesky little gnats, reminding me I was still in an emotional standoff with my sister. Normally I was above saying I told you so, but she'd crossed a line last night that I couldn't ignore.

I figured now was as good a time as ever to go for a run and enjoy the early morning before it got bogged down by the late June heat. When I got dressed and made it downstairs, I nearly tripped over my feet seeing Mom standing at the kitchen island, still in her pink-striped PJs and making a cup of coffee.

"Oh shit," I hissed to myself, but it was loud enough for her to hear and lift her gaze to me. I really should have just stayed in bed.

"Good morning," she greeted me, lifting her coffee cup up to her mouth to take a sip.

"Morning," I replied, putting a hand to the stair banister so I could stretch my calves. Maybe if I kept it casual, so would she.

"Saw Brooklyn leaving."

Now why on earth would I have thought she'd say anything else? Bad judgment on my part. I winced, shaking my head to avoid direct eye contact with her.

"We fell asleep." I shrugged. "It was an accident."

"Did you two rehearse that? Because he said the same thing." She smirked behind her coffee mug. "The last time I saw a *guy* do a walk of shame was when I was in college."

I groaned. "I am going for a run and pretending this conversation did not happen."

While that was a great idea in theory, I could only avoid the inevitable for so long. The inevitable being my sister, who was awake by the time I got back, drinking what was left of the coffee Mom had made earlier. The two of them had been sitting at the kitchen island, and as soon as Nikki clocked me, she scraped the stool back with a screech against the kitchen floor, scowling at me as she walked past and back upstairs to her room.

"What was *that* about?" Mom asked.

"Don't worry about it," I told her, making a beeline for the empty coffeepot. I stared into it, as if in the swirl of leftover grinds was some kind of spiritual response, like tarot cards or tea leaves. I didn't even believe in that stuff, but maybe I should. "She's being moody."

I couldn't loop Mom in without exposing all of Brooklyn's lore, but I was beginning to tremble with how much I'd been keeping in, so I tiptoed around it the best I could.

I spun around to face her and leaned back against the counter. "Look, Brooklyn has a history. Who doesn't? But right now, Nikki isn't being very understanding of that. That's all. It'll blow over."

Mom nodded as she continued to sip her coffee. "I'm sure it will, because you're a fixer, not a fighter."

"Who said we're fighting?" I set the empty coffeepot down on the counter a little too aggressively.

"That poor coffeepot," she replied. "Look, Nat, just be careful about how much energy you put into fixing other people."

"I'm not—" I groaned and pulled at the sleeves of my running jacket. "Who are we even talking about here?"

"I'm only giving you a general word of caution. I've been in your shoes. You can put an exorbitant amount of effort into fixing someone who maybe doesn't want it or isn't ready for it, and you end up just damaging yourself in the process."

"I'm *okay*," I reassured her. "I'm being supportive. Is that so wrong?"

"No, it's not," she replied. "I'm sure your sister could use some support too."

"I'm *always* supportive of her." I heard the patience thinning in my voice. "That doesn't mean I have to agree with some of the things she said."

"I understand, and I don't need to tell you she feels the same way." Mom got up from the stool and began fixing the coffee maker for another round. "And that's more important than whatever you two disagreed about."

"Sometimes I hate being the bigger person," I grumbled.

"You hate fighting more."

"Yeah, yeah, yeah." I waved her off. "Guess I should go shower and try to no longer be in disagreement."

"Sounds good." She nodded. "Because your hair smells like low tide."

"Thanks." I chuckled.

When I made it upstairs, Nikki's bedroom door was cracked open slightly, and rays of light from the suncatcher in her window cut across the hallway floor. I knocked on the door softly, but when she didn't answer, I nudged it open farther to see her in her bed with her headphones on.

"Can we talk?" I asked her, motioning for her to take her headphones off. After a few moments of glowering and being stubborn, she realized I wasn't going to leave, so she pulled them down.

"What?"

"I don't like fighting." I surrendered with a sigh, leaning against the door frame of her room. "As I have so astutely been made aware by our mother."

Nikki groaned as she sat up. "Me either."

I walked over to the fuzzy pink beanbag chair in the corner of her room under the window and dropped into it. "I'm trying to understand what even happened. I thought you liked Brooklyn, but last night felt like emotional whiplash."

"I do, I do." Nikki pulled at the distressed sleeves of her butter-yellow crewneck. "I got a bad gut feeling, and I'm sorry if it came across as mean, I guess. I'm trying to look out for you."

"I understand." I sighed, wishing it all made less sense. Maybe that would make it all sting less. "And while I appreciate it, I promise things are fine."

"How can you promise that?"

I groaned and threw my head back. "Because I am an all-seeing oracle."

Nikki got up from her bed and threw herself on top of me, smothering me in forgiveness and the scent of her orange blossom perfume. When I hugged her, there were fewer harsh edges to her, and it didn't feel like she'd crack in my arms if I squeezed too tightly.

People *were* capable of fixing themselves, and I needed to remind myself of that more often.

"Now tell me *everything* about last night. I want dirty details."

"There are no details."

"That is such a lie." Nikki groaned, rolling off me and slinking to the floor. She sat up and leaned back against the chair. "You weren't drunk, so I *know* you remember what happened."

"It's not that I don't remember," I said. "Honestly, I'm still trying to process that it even happened. It's not exactly like we'd planned it or anything."

"That means that it either was limp fucking noodles or it was totally earth-shattering."

"It wasn't limp noodles," I muttered. "It didn't feel real. Like I was watching myself from a distance."

"Nat, it's only sex." Nikki rolled her eyes. "It's not like you had an out-of-body experience."

But that was exactly what it was. Not the sweaty, scratching, moaning, dizzying, gut-unraveling part. It was after. It was the way he'd held me, almost like he could shield me from acid rain and falling stars.

My long silence prompted a snicker from Nikki.

"Oh my god, except you totally did." She batted her eyelashes and put her hand to her chest. "That's love."

I scoffed. "Now who's the dramatic one?"

"Doesn't matter, I speak the truth," Nikki replied.

>> <<

"I really can't believe you've never seen *Time Bandits*." Brooklyn shook the DVD box at me before loading it into his Xbox. "It's a cult classic."

Rolling over onto my stomach on Brooklyn's bed, I placed our bowl of butter-drenched popcorn on the floor in front of me. It felt so much more familiar than the first time I had been here. I casually splayed out across his messy sheets, and I could honestly have fallen asleep here. "You say that about every movie you pick."

"That's because I happen to be a cult movie expert," he said as he flopped down next to me.

Since neither of us had anything better to do on a Wednesday evening, we'd picked up two more movies from Film Press and were very determined to get through both of them this time.

Despite still reckoning with the night we'd shared last weekend, (even saying we *had sex* seemed reductionist, because it was more than that) lying next to him on his bed now felt natural, like we'd been doing it for ages. I hadn't given much thought to the text message I'd accidentally seen the next morning, but I told myself I wasn't going to bring it up unless there was a seamless way to do so.

I also wouldn't put it past myself to just be reading way too much into it.

"I won't lie to you, I kind of hated that." I got up from Brooklyn's bed to stretch my legs after we finished *Time Bandits*—which had an unexpectedly bleak ending that ruined the movie for me. This was a perfect example of why I rewatched the same things I enjoyed over and over again; no surprisingly bad endings to ruin things.

"I guess it's not for everyone." Brooklyn shrugged, rolling over onto his stomach and hanging his long arms off of the foot of the bed. I flopped back down beside him, absentmindedly tracing the *N-I-K-E* letters on the back of his T-shirt.

He tilted his head to look up at me and squinted like he was staring up at the sun. "Hi."

"Hi." I smiled down at him.

He lifted his torso off of the bed to bring his lips to mine, and it felt like as soon as we touched, we were interrupted by a gentle knock at the door. Brooklyn's mother poked her head in.

"Brooklyn, can I borrow you for a minute?" Her voice was calm but the pinched smile she gave us didn't quite reach her eyes.

"I'll be right back. Don't start without me," he mumbled into my neck before bouncing off the bed and shutting his bedroom door behind him.

I loaded up *Wish Upon a Star* (my pick for the night), then went back to the bed, lying on my back and counting the dark little rivets in the wood-paneled ceiling. I got to fifty before I realized at least ten minutes had passed. I pulled out my phone to text him.

NAT: everything okay?

I dropped my phone onto the bed and rolled back onto my stomach, watching the little blue DVD icon bounce around the idle TV screen. I picked at a hangnail on my thumb until it stung. Another ten minutes. I checked my phone again, and he hadn't answered.

"What the hell," I muttered to myself. I found myself padding across the carpeted floor of Brooklyn's room and easing the door open to stick my head out.

The hallway was dark and there was a stale silence, as if nobody else was in the house. After a moment more of silence, I swallowed hard and went back to the bed.

>> <<

"You all right?"

I awoke with a jolt to the sound of Brooklyn's voice. He sat up on the bed beside me, the light of blues from the title screen of *Wish Upon a Star* dancing across his face. Outside, the sun had completely set and a foggy night had taken over, the moon barely visible.

"What happened?" I asked, rubbing the side of my face to get some feeling back into me.

"You fell asleep," he replied.

I sat up too fast and all the blood rushed to my head. "No, I mean you. You were gone for like forty-five minutes."

"Oh." He frowned. "Nothing happened. It's fine. We were talking, that's all."

"You can talk to me, too, Brooklyn. You know that."

Brooklyn slid himself back until he could lean against the

headboard of his bed, and eased his eyes closed. "Nat, I'm sorry, I don't mean to be so weird."

Without giving it a second thought, I felt compelled to reach over and give his hand a gentle squeeze. "I know you don't."

"I had a bad conversation with my dad, that's all," he continued.

I didn't want to say it, but I couldn't help it. It just came out like word vomit (and suddenly I knew exactly how Cady felt in *Mean Girls*). "Does this have anything to do with the text message you got the morning you left my house?"

He let out a heavy breath, finally willing himself to look at me. He didn't look at all angry; he looked upset, and that felt worse. "You saw that?"

"I didn't mean to," I insisted. "Your phone was going off, but I didn't know it was your phone, I thought it was mine, so I grabbed it and there it was."

He tensed up beside me, dragging his teeth along his lower lip.

"Brooklyn, if you're in some kind of trouble—"

"I'm not," he said bitingly, uncharacteristically venomous. When he saw me recoil slightly, he eased up. "Not anymore, anyway."

I slid up to lean against the headboard beside him. "What happened?"

When I saw the hurt in his eyes, my heart clenched.

"I owed some guys some money. From before, *way* before. But I got nervous because I'm not really making any money right now, so I told my mom, my mom told my dad, and it turned into a shit show. But it *is* handled."

I rolled my shoulders back as I processed Brooklyn's story. I only really wanted to know one thing. "Why didn't you tell me?"

Brooklyn ran a hand down his cheek. "Nat, I don't know if I've made it obvious enough yet, but I really like you. I don't want you to think I'm this fucked up."

"I don't think that at all," I insisted. "Brooklyn, I trust you, but you need to talk to me if you want this to work."

I still didn't even know what *this* was. We'd already passed the point of no return, but I'd been so caught up in the moment I hadn't considered what came after.

"You're right." Brooklyn nodded. "Listen, everything's fine now, okay?"

He finally smiled at me in that effortlessly endearing way. He really could have convinced me to do anything when he looked at me like that. He reached up and gently caressed the side of my cheek, and all of the tense, hard edges of our night fell away. It was like the rain had come to extinguish a fire.

"Okay." I felt myself melt into his touch. "Because I really like you too."

"God I hope so," he whispered, leaning over and softly brushing his lips over mine. "You know, what happened the other night, that's a big deal to me, and I don't want it to be something that happened and then we forget about it."

"Yeah, me too."

He smiled and brought his lips back to mine. Even though we'd kissed quite a few times by now, it was as if we were kissing each other for the very first time over and over again. I moved my hands to the nape of his neck, pulling him closer as he ran his tongue along the inside of my cheek. He tangled his hands in my hair, and without breaking our embrace, we lay back into the bed.

I felt him everywhere, and the sensory overload consumed me. His hands roamed my body, gentle but eager at the same time, finding my waist and flipping me so I was pinned underneath him. I reached down and grabbed the hem of his T-shirt, pulling it off of him and tossing it to the floor. He did the same, gingerly tugging my sweater over my head. He smelled like vanilla and suntan lotion, and I was starting to believe that if the perfect summer romance had a smell, that was it.

A sharp knock on the door made us both jump, and in a knee-jerk reaction, I pushed Brooklyn off of me, sending him over the side of the bed and to the floor with a thud. I ignored his groans and jolted upright, patting around on the bedspread for my sweater.

"Brooklyn, I'm coming in," Stella called from the other side of the door. She swung it open just as I was pulling my sweater back on.

"Hi, Nat." She gave me a quick smile, either completely oblivious or completely indifferent to what she'd interrupted.

"Hey," I greeted her with a weary smile.

"What do you want, Stella?" Brooklyn groaned as he stood up, tugging at his shirt, which was clearly inside out.

"You ass, I knew you had my phone charger." She marched over to the wall beside the bed and yanked a charger out of the outlet, shaking it at Brooklyn. "Mine has electrical tape on it, so I know you stole it."

"Well I, uh, lost mine, so . . ." He spoke through a grimace. "Thanks for letting me borrow it. Now leave, *please*."

Stella turned to leave, but spun back around in the doorway. "Oh, Nat, we're all going out for my birthday slash Fourth of July next weekend, so obviously would love for you to come. Your sister too. I like her, she's funny."

"Sounds great," I replied. "As long as you promise not to tell her she's funny to her face, it'll go to her head."

Stella grinned and nodded before twirling on her feet and walking out.

"Sorry about that." Brooklyn gave me an apologetic grin. He put his hand on top of mine. "You're still gonna make me watch this movie, huh?"

I smirked and elbowed him. "*Yes*, it's a cult classic."

June 30

Hey Dad,

I'm sorry we haven't caught up in a while. I didn't mean to go quiet on you, time's just been moving faster lately. I used to roll my eyes whenever people said "time flies when you're having fun," but I get it now. I am having fun. For the most part.

There's been a lot of small, good moments. Things that don't sound like much when I write them down—the way the ocean smells driving home from the bookstore, the way Nikki hums when she's in a good mood again, the way Brooklyn says my name like he's trying it out every time, to make sure he still likes the way it sounds.

But there's also this other part. This buzzing, uneasy current under everything. Weird little things I can't quite name. Sometimes he goes quiet mid-conversation, like his thoughts disappear somewhere I can't follow. Sometimes I feel like I'm still waiting for the other shoe to drop, but it's not mine, it's his.

My brain keeps trying to warn me something could be wrong. But the key word is could, and my instincts, they say stay. This time it's different. This time I'm doing it all right.

So, yeah. I'm doing okay. I'm happy, even. And I'm trying not to question it too much.

Love, Nat

Seventeen

Brooklyn had picked up Nikki and me, and we'd planned to meet Brooklyn's sister and her friends at a trendy bar at the far end of the city by the harbor. Fourth of July was yesterday, but people were still setting off booming fireworks around town that sparkled against the quickly darkening sky.

"You're gonna love this place, it's all artsy and shit," Brooklyn said, lowering the volume on the stereo as he maneuvered around the surrounding side streets for a spot.

"Care to elaborate on *artsy and shit*?" Nikki leaned between the two front seats and pressed her hands on the center console.

"Well, it used to be a church, like a hundred years ago," he explained. "This local family, the Tenneys, bought it back in the '90s. They kept a lot of the old framework and windows, so it has those high cathedral ceilings and whatnot, but now they're all written all over. There's paragraphs from *The Art of War*, *Ben-Hur*, and all kinds of other crazy stuff, plus some local modern art freehand painted on the walls. It's kind of a dive bar but slightly cooler."

Brooklyn swerved into a spot a few blocks away and put the Jeep in Park, then glanced over his shoulder to give Nikki a sly grin. "So, yeah, artsy and shit. But it's also kind of the only legitimate bar on the island that isn't attached to a restaurant or anything, so it's become sort of a rite of passage to go to when you turn twenty-one."

"Oh, did you also participate in this deeply steeped tradition?" I asked him as he opened the passenger door for me. I didn't think I'd ever get tired of that, no matter how seemingly simple it was.

"Obviously." He smirked. "I don't remember much after walking through the front door, though."

A warm breeze rolled in from the harbor, tickling all the exposed skin on my back from the silky green corset top Nikki insisted I wear. We walked along cobblestone side streets to the bar, and as I hobbled around in a pair of Nikki's wedges (also at her insistence), I felt Brooklyn place a gentle, supporting hand on the small of my back, his thumb finding exactly the right nerve on my spine to send blaring sensory alarms to every extension of my body—the kind that the longer he touched, the more likely I was to be overcome with the urge to pull his clothes off.

When we approached the small line outside the door of South Church, Brooklyn pulled me aside. He snaked an arm around my waist, bringing me in close so that our chests were pressed together.

"Have I mentioned how gorgeous you look?" he muttered as he brought his head down to mine.

He, of course, was a vision in dark jeans and a black short-sleeve button-down. Locks of his sandy-brown hair stuck out from the brim of his beige hat, which read DO NOT DISTURB in black script. It was something so simple, but he wore with enough charm and grace to probably get away with wearing it in a Michelin-star restaurant.

"You could mention it again," I murmured back, smiling as he swept me into a kiss.

"You're gorgeous," he whispered against my lips, his hands

finding that same spot on my back that would have made my knees buckle if he hadn't been holding me up.

For a moment it was easy to forget there was anybody else in the world—at least until someone loudly cleared their throat. We both whipped our heads around to see Nikki, arm flailing outward to prompt us to move forward in line.

Brooklyn wasn't kidding about the "artsy and shit" part, and when we walked into the bar, I was immediately sucked into all the words painted on the high cathedral ceilings. One block of text caught my eye, stark white in contrast to the black backdrop of the ceiling. ALL WARFARE IS BASED ON DECEPTION.

But he also wasn't kidding about the dive-bar part, and it felt like everyone in town between the ages of twenty and thirty was jammed between the long bar that ran along the left side of the room and all the high tops spread around the rest of it. On the far back wall was an open space in front of a small raised platform, where a DJ (or at least someone who controlled the music) was at his laptop, blasting "Stacy's Mom" from the two big black speakers on either side of him. Strings of Christmas lights hung from the rafters, bathing everyone in a colorful confetti of light.

We made our way to the back of the bar, where a small group of people congregated around Stella. She sat on a cracked leather bar stool at the end of the bar, but slid off and immediately strode over to us in high fuchsia-colored heels that matched her sequined barely there halter top.

"Happy birthday!" I greeted her as she pulled me into a tight hug.

"I'm so so so glad you came," she squealed. The scent of fruity liquor wafted off her breath. She turned to Nikki and did the same, as if they'd been best friends their whole lives, but that wasn't surprising. Nikki could make friends with a tree if given the opportunity. It was obviously the same for Stella, and I was slightly envious.

"I'm going to find the bathroom real quick." Brooklyn pressed a kiss to my temple before walking away, and I found myself warm under his lingering touch. It wasn't hard to figure out these were all people who knew Brooklyn (or knew of him) as he high-fived and greeted people he walked past, and yet he was comfortable enough with us together to show me affection in front of them.

"Drink?" Stella asked us. "We've already got a tab, and I have the bartender's full attention, if you know what I mean, so if you want something . . ."

Nikki snickered. "Oh I would *love* a Long Island, since I am *definitely* twenty-one."

"I'll have whatever you're having." I gestured to the fizzy pink drink in Stella's hand.

"Oh, it's my fav, although they can be *so* dangerous," she gushed. "I've had like, three already, and you can't taste the alcohol at all. They make their own blackberry lavender syrup that goes in it."

I didn't mind a little danger tonight, and I wasn't about to play protective big sister with Nikki here—the prospect of a good time tonight (a good time that we'd both earned) outweighed any of that.

After Stella had gotten our drinks, I took a spot at the bar a bit removed from the group of Stella's other friends, some of whom I recognized as her sorority sisters from Larocca University, and who'd been out at the beach with us last week. On the outer orbit of their circle, Brooklyn leaned against the bar and spoke to Alec. When I glanced over at Nikki, her eyes dropped to her Long Island.

"Everything okay?" I asked her.

"What?" She snapped her gaze back up at me. "Yeah, of course. I'm gonna go dance with the birthday girl before they start playing shitty music."

"You do that." I smirked at her as she slid off the bar stool and grabbed Stella's hand, dragging her away to the makeshift dance floor.

I continued to watch Brooklyn and Alec, who looked more like an old married couple arguing about furniture than best friends. I tried my best to lean closer inconspicuously, catching bits and pieces of their discussion, but someone wedged themselves up to the bar beside me.

"Hey," they said, dull and nearly muddled up in the music and other voices. I turned to face a tall stocky kid with a shock of dirty-blond hair. "You're one of Stella's friends, right?"

"Yeah, I am," I replied, giving him a polite smile as I tapped my fingers on my glass, wet with perspiration. I tried to crane my neck around him to get another glance at the other end of the bar, but his bulk and mass blocked my view entirely.

"I'm Dalton," he said, sticking out his hand. "I go to Larocca with Stella."

"Natalie."

His hand was warm when I took it, and with his red cherub cheeks, he had the disposition of a teddy bear. I probably could have been nicer, but I'd lost Brooklyn and Alec in my line of sight, and for some reason, I didn't like that.

"I see you've met Big D." A pair of hands brushed against my waist, and with them came a whiff of Brooklyn's all-too-identifiable fresh and clean cologne. I felt relief roll off my shoulders.

"What's up, dude?" Dalton greeted Brooklyn, and while they did the standard bro handshake, their eyes were not particularly friendly. "I was wondering if I was gonna see you tonight."

"Well, here I am."

"Big D?" I craned my neck to look up at Brooklyn, who still had his arms draped over my shoulders from behind. "That is *not* an endearing nickname."

"It was at the time." Dalton chuckled. "So, you two are . . ." His voice trailed off as he gestured between us.

"Yeah." Brooklyn rushed to answer, moving his hands up to my shoulders and giving them a gentle squeeze. "We are."

It wouldn't have been difficult to buy into the fact that whatever we were didn't *need* a name, except we hadn't explicitly talked about whether or not to give it one. Although I wouldn't have minded calling him my boyfriend. That would have felt right too.

"Got it." Dalton pinched his lips together and nodded. "Well, I'll be around all night, so—"

"Yep." Brooklyn cut him off again. "I'll see you."

"What was *that* about?" I asked Brooklyn the moment Dalton was out of earshot. I spun around to face him, his arms still wrapped around me, but less warm and more cagey, like he was trying to protect me from something.

"Nothing." Brooklyn shook his head. "He's kind of scummy, to be honest. I'm pretty sure he used to spike girls' drinks at parties."

"Ew, really?" I scrunched my nose up. "He seemed so nice too."

"They always do." Brooklyn sighed. "Anyway, forget about him. Dance with me?"

He slid his hands back to my waist, as if he knew exactly where to touch me to get me to do whatever he asked.

"I don't know." I played coy with him, reaching up to absent-mindedly mess with the top button of his shirt, undone and exposing a glint of silver from the chain I knew he always wore. "I'm not a good dancer."

"You don't have to be. I am."

Without another word, he took my hands in his and whisked me away.

The music had shifted from poppy and familiar '90s into something bassy and unidentifiable, shaking the floor underneath us to the beat. At first it was innocent fun. We danced and laughed like we were in our own little universe. Strobe light supernovas and music that exploded like stars. After a little while, everything started to muddle together. Colors. Hands. Sounds. Bodies. When Brooklyn spun me around, I fit a little too perfectly into him, like our bodies were two pieces at the edge of the puzzle, made only for each other. He put his hands on my hips, and I arched my back so that my head sat in the crook of his neck. We were holding each other's hands, breathing each other's air, swaying to a beat neither of us knew, and it was everything.

Then he spun me around again, looking down at me while the lights flashed in his deep-blue eyes like fireworks. I read once that when you looked at something you really loved, your pupils dilated, and that was how he looked at me, eyes wide and cheeks red, chest heaving to catch his breath. I brought my hands to his chest, where his heart pounded through the thin fabric of his shirt, as if it wanted to jump out of his chest and into my hands.

I grabbed his hand and pressed it to my sternum so he could feel my same runaway heartbeat, and no matter how in shape I thought I was, nothing could help my lungs from the sight of him.

This time when we moved, we really were the only two people in the room, pressed so intently together as we swayed to the beat that I wondered if our bodies were trying to become one.

"See, you can dance." He brought his head down to mumble

against my ear, and the feeling of his breath on my skin chilled every burning nerve in me.

"You're a good teacher," I told him, relishing the feeling of his hands so eager to touch me. "But I've filled my dancing quota tonight."

He held me at arm's length and clutched his chest. "Break my heart, why don't you?"

"All right, I confess." I surrendered. "It's because my feet hurt!"

He smirked. "That makes me feel better."

Brooklyn led me back to the bar, gesturing for me to sit at an open bar stool as he ordered a refill for me and a water for himself. The rest of the night went by with ease as we all talked and drank, and I fell into a good conversation with two of Stella's sorority sisters about the recent season of *The White Lotus*. Brooklyn had retreated to the far end of the bar with Alec, and was deep in conversation about who knew what. He seemed distressed at first as he spoke animatedly with his hands, but when he saw me looking over, he waved and gave me a smile so glowing that put the sun to shame.

"I have to use the bathroom." Nikki had to shout to get my attention.

"I'll come with you."

It was instinctive for me at this point, but thankfully she didn't fight me this time, nodding and sliding off the bar stool.

Nikki took my hand and we wove in and out between people to get to the back hallway where the bathrooms were, which were two individual unisex rooms. There was handwritten graffiti all over it like the rest of the bar, and the lights above the sink flickered and buzzed. I leaned forward against the sink to clean the smudge of lip gloss at the corners of my lips. On the wall beside the mirror, someone had written WHERE IS HER HEAD? in what looked like red lipstick.

"What's going on with you and Alec?" I asked Nikki as she came to the sink to wash her hands.

"What do you mean?" She kept her gaze down to furiously scrub at her hands.

"I don't know." I leaned back against the wall beside the sink. "You've been avoiding him all night. I thought you two were talking."

"We're not anymore. It's no big deal." She shut the sink off and brushed past me to dry her hands.

"You can talk to me, you know," I told her as we walked out of the bathroom.

She abruptly stopped and spun on her heel. "Can I?"

I took a cautious step closer to her, furrowing my brows at her. "Of course you can. Why do you think you can't?"

She scoffed, her mouth gaping open. "You've become, like, so obsessed with Brooklyn, you don't even realize this is something you could have asked me a week ago."

Obviously things were nowhere near as normal as I thought they were. I took a step back, suddenly very off-balance in shoes I wished I hadn't worn.

"That's not true" came out softer than I wanted it to.

"Okay." Nikki pressed her lips together and nodded. "If you say so."

As we got closer to our designated spot at the back of the bar, I wished I didn't recognize the raised voices. Sure enough, we came upon Brooklyn and Alec, inches away from literally being at each other's throats.

"Dude, what the hell is your problem tonight?" Alec groaned, raking his hair back off of his forehead.

"Right now, you're my fucking problem," Brooklyn spat back.

"Brooklyn, don't be like this," Stella, who approached him the way you'd approach a lion in a cage, pleaded.

"Stay out of it, Stella," Brooklyn snapped, and she recoiled with a scowl.

"What the hell is going on?" Nikki muttered in my ear.

"I feel like we should do something." My voice sounded so detached from the rest of me that I had to second-guess if I'd even spoken. But when I stepped forward, Nikki grabbed my arm.

"Don't." There was pleading in her voice, as if the conversation we'd had hadn't happened at all. "This doesn't involve us."

While it was loud enough that most of the bar outside of our group had carried on with their night without noticing, some of the direct outlying people started to key in to the scene.

"I'm getting tired of trying to understand you." Alec's voice became weary, and even though I hadn't known him that long, there was more affliction to him now than I'd ever heard.

"I'm not asking you to."

Alec paused and pursed his lips. "She really doesn't know, does she?"

"I mean it," Brooklyn hissed through clenched teeth. "Don't go there. Leave her out of it."

Nikki squeezed my arm again, now silently willing me to intervene, since it seemed it actually *did* involve me. I gulped down my heart before speaking.

"Alec, what are you talking about?" It took everything in me to keep my voice steady, since the rest of my body was rattling.

"Ask him." Alec jerked his head in Brooklyn's direction.

"Don't drag her into this," Brooklyn warned, putting his hand on Alec's chest and gripping his T-shirt.

Someone else stepped in beside me, pulling Alec away from Brooklyn and standing between them.

"Why are you doing this right now?" Stella hissed at her brother, squaring up to him as if he wasn't a whole foot taller than her. "It's my fucking birthday and you can't even keep it together for one night out."

I felt like someone had glued me to the spot I was standing in with tar. I glared hard at him, willing him to *feel* my eyes on him so he'd at least look at me, but he didn't. It was like I was watching from behind a two-way mirror; I could see them, but they couldn't see me.

"Forget it," he grumbled, shouldering himself away from our circle, not even so much as glancing in my direction.

My heart slammed against my chest, and through some force of sheer willpower or divine intervention, my body moved on its own, following him to the back.

"Brooklyn?" I called into the back hallway. A group of girls brushed past me, and two of them consoled a third one, who had streaks of tears and mascara running down her cheeks.

I stopped next to one of the bathroom doors, hearing the water run behind it.

I knocked on the door softly. "Brooklyn?"

A few moments went by before he answered. "What do you want?"

"To see if you're okay," I called through the door.

The water kept running, and another few moments passed without a response. I felt the hairs on the back of my neck stand on end, as if I was waiting for lightning to strike me in an open field. Or maybe a deep, recessed part of my body knew that something bad was on the other side of the door, like in a horror movie—the kind you have to go through to get out. So I turned the handle and pushed the door open.

I had never actually seen anyone in the act of doing drugs before. Even in college some of my more adventurous roommates who did cocaine occasionally would do it in the bathroom with the door closed. But here it was, like something out of one of those cautionary films they showed us in health class in middle school. There was a dusting of white powder like freshly fallen snow on an old water-stained copy of *Sports Illustrated.* I studied Brooklyn carefully, his throat rippling as he swallowed down all of his shame and anger.

Anything I could have thought to say was swallowed by the sick, greasy knot that balled up in my throat. I tasted pennies, like you do when you're about to vomit. I wanted to stick my face in the sink under the running water to shock my senses awake. Every time I blinked, I hoped that when I opened my eyes I would be dreaming, but I wasn't.

"I don't understand," I managed to croak.

"I'm not asking you to." He kept his head down when he spoke, echoing what he'd said to Alec before.

I slid into the bathroom and shut the door behind me. "What's that supposed to mean?"

He stood upright, his hands pressed into the sides of the sink. "Forget it."

I felt my heart cracking the way his voice did.

I reached for his arm but he jerked away. "Brooklyn, I would have helped you if you needed it."

"I'm not going to do that to you, Natalie," he said in a low voice, and the way he threw my full name at me hurt more than it should have.

I shook my head, desperate to keep the tears stinging the corners of my eyes at bay. "Brooklyn, please." I could hear myself begging. "Let me help you. Let any of us help you."

"You want to help me?" There was venom in his words now, and it stung as it seeped under my skin. "You can help me by leaving me the fuck alone."

"Brooklyn, it doesn't need to be like this," I pleaded. "I can help you."

"No, you can't." He sighed, and an all-too-eerie calmness came over his voice. "So just go . . . before you make this any worse."

I wasn't sure of the feeling coursing through me now, but it burned through me like my nerves were being set on fire.

"Fine," I hissed. "Maybe you're right. Maybe I can't help you."

I stumbled out of the bathroom and into the hallway, feeling my knees shake with every step I took as I went back to the bar. I gritted my teeth as I shouldered my way through the crowd of people, desperate to escape what suddenly felt like crushing. Music thumped through the air, vibrating my entire aching body, and strobe lights flashed too brightly. I had to keep going because if I stopped, I might have turned around and given in.

By the time I made it outside, I was gasping for air. Night had completely taken over and fireworks boomed in the distance in time with my throbbing heart. I hugged my torso with my arms and started walking, nearly busting my ankle on the uneven cobblestone street, but I willed myself forward, sniffling and swallowing down tears.

I trembled and shook, and my chest felt heavy, like I was being suffocated. After I'd made it a few blocks I slowed down to catch my breath. The initial shock passed over me like a cloud, and suddenly I could identify what was coursing through me. It was anger, but not at him—at myself, because I should have known better.

I thought I'd been doing everything right, and that was what hurt the most. Instead, I did myself wrong. I let what I was feeling for him consume me, and it made me forget the *one* thing I'd learned this summer—you cannot save people. But damned if I'd tried anyway.

Fireworks burst above me, staining the night sky in rivers of smoke and lights. I walked and I walked and I walked until somehow I made it home with aching feet, letting the hot summer air dry the tears that streaked my face.

Eighteen

The rain started early the next day, and it came down hard and didn't let up all weekend. Stacks was closed for the holiday, and I couldn't even run, which meant I had zero mental reprieve, giving me plenty of time to think and overthink every single thing leading up to what happened.

Since the entire town was half underwater for Fourth of July, Gracie and I spent the day buried under a mass of blankets and pillows rereading my favorite Stephen King novel (because obviously reading about other people's misfortunes with killer interdimensional clowns made us feel better about our current situations).

"Do you plan on sitting in here forever?" I heard my bedroom door open and Mom's voice, and felt the bed shift as she sat down on the edge of it.

"I'm not *sitting*. I am *very* busy," I replied, muffled through my comforter. I stuck my arm out and flailed around my thick copy of *It*.

There was a pause, and Mom pulled away some of the blankets until I was greeted with the dim light of my bedroom. Gracie sighed as her peace was disturbed.

Mom put her hand on my forearm and gave it a gentle rub. "Come on, I'm going to pick up sushi. You should come, just to get out of this room."

"I'm fine." I shrugged her off.

"Nat—"

"I said I'm fine!" I snapped. Gracie, who never liked it when people raised their voices, promptly got up and huffed at me as she left the room.

If that wasn't something that filled you with immediate regret, nothing would.

"I'm sorry," I mumbled, rubbing my face with my hands.

"You have nothing to be sorry for. I wish I had better advice." She took a pause and reached over to brush a few strands of staticky hair out of my face. "You've always been like this, even when you were young."

"Like what?"

"Nurturing and supportive. You get that from your dad."

I glanced over at my notebook on my bedside table. I hadn't even told Dad what had happened. I wouldn't know what to say to him. It wasn't like it was embarrassing to be wrong, but the whole thing made me sad.

"I remember when your sister first started playing soccer," Mom continued. "She must have been four or five with practically no hand-eye coordination. But you went to every game to cheer her on, and not because we asked you to, but because you wanted to."

"Also because I was seven and couldn't stay home alone," I reminded her.

Gracie poked her long snout back into the room, and when Mom called her over she hopped back onto the bed and rested her head in my lap. I absentmindedly stroked the swirling gray and white fur on the top of her head. She'd come back, even though I'd scared her off.

"You can't force people to get better, Nat." Although still soft,

Mom's tone had turned serious. "You know that, but you need to remind yourself more often."

I nodded. "I'll try."

"That's a good place to start."

I willed myself up and went with Mom to pick up sushi. By the time we returned home, the rain had become torrential. Little waterfalls tumbled off the house gutters, creating dirt-filled puddles in the flower beds my mom had been trying to fill. Despite the rain, one rose had popped out of a dying bush, desperate to live its life against the odds.

>> <<

I'd fallen asleep at some point Monday afternoon with *It* open on my lap, rain still gently pattering against the windows. I awoke with a startled jolt as Nikki shook me, half expecting Pennywise the clown to be standing over me.

"What? What's going on?" I groggily rubbed my eyes, trying to shift my body out of fight-or-flight mode.

"Get up. You've got a visitor."

"I do?"

I asked the question despite knowing the answer, as if somehow asking would change it. My body shook with anticipation, very much back in flight mode. I slid out of bed and padded downstairs as I pulled on a sweater, pressing myself against the window that peered into the porch.

My heart seized when I saw Brooklyn sitting on the wicker rocking chair on our porch, casual in a Clayton baseball hat and Nike shorts. I caught a glimpse of a small bundle of colorful flowers in his hands.

"I told him he had to wait outside," Nikki said tersely.

I scoffed. "Why would you do that? It's raining."

"Because he's up to something," Nikki snapped, pointing at the window. She sighed and put her hand to her forehead. "Whatever's going on with him, you need to sort it out before it gets out of control."

I thought about what Mom had told me the other day about not forcing people to get better. I shouldn't—*couldn't*—strive to control any of it, but how else would I prevent it from getting out of control to begin with? It made no sense. I had to drive it, because who else would?

"Hey," Brooklyn greeted me, his voice weary as he stood up from the rocking chair. It squeaked a few times as it continued rocking, banging slightly against the side of the house.

I felt a weird wave of déjà vu wash over me as I looked at him. So much had changed since the day he first showed up at my house, but the familiar sight of him standing there, smiling down at me, made all of the uncertainty evaporate. It almost tricked me into thinking we could go back to that first time.

"Hey," I replied. Brooklyn tensed when I walked closer. "Everything okay?"

"I'm not sure Nikki likes me," Brooklyn said, rubbing the back of his neck.

"She's being defensive. It's like her job," I responded as I twirled a lock of hair around my finger. I looked down at his hands, calm and steady holding a small bundle of mismatched flowers in an array of pinks and purples and oranges.

"Are those for me?" I asked.

"Oh, yeah." He handed them to me. "I'm sorry, they kind of suck."

I ran my hands across the soft petals of the flowers. There was one rose, an orchid, a few carnations, and an azalea, tied at the stems by a thin string. Like outcasts from a garden that didn't match their own kind but instead complemented each other's differences. Just like we did.

"No, these are beautiful, thank you," I said with a nod. "But what are they for?"

Brooklyn scowled, looking down at them as I cradled them in my hands. "For trying to help me the other night. I'm still kind of ashamed you had to see me like that. I'm sorry."

I looked back up at him, and he smiled at me the way he always did—calm and bright and so assured of himself. It reminded me why it was so hard to walk away; it was for that Brooklyn. That Brooklyn was worth it.

"I like flowers," I told him.

Brooklyn stepped closer to me and ran his hand up my arm. He gave me a weak smile and kept his hand on my shoulder. "Will you just hear me out, Nat?"

I swallowed the lump in my throat. "Fine. We can sit out here if you want."

He sat back in the rocking chair, looking out at the road as a car drove by slowly, sloshing through a puddle. "I like the rain."

"Me too," I told him, sitting in another chair across from him. "It's so calming when it's like this, and I love the smell. It has a name, you know."

"Does it?"

"*Petrichor*," I replied, running my fingers over the petals of some of the flowers. "It's from the plant oils and bacteria in the soil that build up when it's dry, and when it rains, the smell of it all is released."

"Wise girl."

"I try."

Brooklyn shifted in the chair, accidentally sending it back

against the house with a smack. He rubbed his palms on the thighs of his shorts.

"I want to start with I'm sorry, and I'm an idiot."

I nodded, and after a moment, he looked at me expectantly.

"I'm sorry, did you want me to tell you you're not?" I chuckled.

"Guess I deserved that one." He sat back in the chair with a faint smirk.

"All joking aside, the only thing I want right now is an explanation," I said to him. "God, I look back at some of the things that happened, and I wonder—"

I knew *what* I'd seen, but that didn't make reckoning with it any easier for either of us. As much as being lied to hurt, sometimes the truth hurt too; it just hurt in a different place.

"I feel like you see right through me and all my bullshit," he muttered.

I wanted to reach over and squeeze his hand, but I kept mine wrapped around the stems of flowers. "Let it out. Like ripping off a bandage."

"I want you to understand that I'm not like seeking any of this out, you know? I'm not going out looking for it, and I swear that's the only thing I've done since I've been clean." His voice splintered, and he paused, desperate to mitigate the damage. "I used to buy from Dalton. He and a couple of guys had a few grams of coke, and I couldn't help myself. I thought I could handle it."

All I could do was listen. It was about all I knew how to do at this point.

I could see his hand tremble as he rubbed the side of his face. "I wanted to fit in so badly. To prove I didn't have these kinds of problems and that I could be the Brooklyn people think I am. But I lost control, and the next thing I knew I was so loaded I couldn't see straight."

"Ironic, isn't it?" I said softly.

"Yeah, and I hate it," he grumbled. "Anyway, at that point I gave up. I knew I'd relapsed, and I felt like shit about it. I didn't want to push you away like that, but I couldn't even imagine that once you found out you'd want to be with someone like me anyway."

I finally gave in and reached for his hand, and he took it, his hand clammy and still shaky.

"I'm sorry. I'm so sorry." Brooklyn's breaths caught as he tried to hold back whatever storm was brewing inside of him. He rubbed at his eyes, glassy and on the verge of tears. "This was a slipup. That's all, I swear."

"It's going to be all right, Brooklyn," I said, trying to keep my voice steady. It was hard not to cry when watching someone else cry, but one of us had to keep it somewhat together. "You can't lie to me anymore. I want to help you, but there's no way I can if you keep pushing me away."

He nodded and brought his hand up to my face, wiping away a stray tear from my cheek with his thumb. "I promise. No more lying. No more pushing away. Just me and you."

"Me and you, huh?" I asked, giving him a tired smile.

Brooklyn replied with a chuckle. "I'm not good at this, Nat. Any of this. I haven't had a real girlfriend since high school, and that was a disaster. I don't bring girls flowers, get into fights over them, or—" He took a deep breath and his cheeks reddened. "Or beg them to forgive me when I know I don't deserve it. But you? You make me want to be good."

"You *are* good. You don't have to try," I reassured him. "But there are things you have to do. Not for me, for yourself. For one, you need to go back to group therapy. It helps my sister, and I can't imagine why it wouldn't help you. I'll even go with you, if you want."

"I get stuck thinking my problems aren't as serious as other people's. Like I'm better than it all or something."

"I admire your self-awareness." I chuckled. "But you're wrong."

Was I trying, like I told Mom I would? Maybe. But Brooklyn needed someone to prop him up right now, and if I didn't, who would?

Nineteen

Everything at Otter House always felt clean but not sterile like a hospital. Instead, it was more like when we expected company growing up and we cleaned the house more than we usually did for our weekend chores. Everything had a place, and it smelled like citrus disinfectant.

This room for group therapy was similar, but it seemed like it hadn't seen company in a while. There was a circle of mismatched chairs that might not have had a place anywhere else in the facility, and some of the colorful motivational posters stuck to the walls were peeling at the edges.

However, I'd come to find that the people were always the same, no matter what room you sat in. It was people who, despite looking like a similarly mismatched group, were trying to salvage something from the wreckage of their current situation. Like my sister, and like Brooklyn.

"Take a seat anywhere that's open," John, the group leader, said to us as we walked in, his round cheeks red and blotchy like he'd run a 5K. *Just John*, Brooklyn had told me he liked to be called, instead of Dr. Lachlan. Brooklyn was right, he really *did* look like the guy from *Jurassic Park*, albeit with a Southern twang in his voice.

Brooklyn looked like he might have been more comfortable

taking a seat on a cactus. He hadn't said much since we'd walked in, and when he took a seat beside me, he rested his elbows on his knees and wired his jaw shut tight. He kept his eyes on the people who walked in, trying to decode their state of being. Were they worse off than he was, or had they figured it all out already? He forced a half-hearted smile when he realized I'd been looking at him.

"All right, let's get started." Just John clapped his hands and rubbed them together. "So something I want to talk about today is self-forgiveness. I know this one isn't easy. A lot of people here feel like they've done things that can't be forgiven. Hurt people they love. Made choices they regret. But the truth is"—he paused and glanced around the room, making slightly prolonged eye contact with all of us, like I was sure he'd been taught to do in med school—"beating yourself up doesn't get you clean or keep you clean. Instead, it keeps you stuck."

There were a few murmurs of agreement. A heavily tattooed man who looked to be in his thirties let out a dry laugh. "Yeah, well, tell my ex-wife that."

A few more chuckles filled the room. The air didn't feel as heavy as it had when we got here.

Just John nodded. "Of course, it's easier said than done, but I still want y'all to think deeply on it. What's something you haven't forgiven yourself for, and why haven't you yet?"

We sat in silence again, and I wondered how many people were truly contemplating what Just John had asked versus waiting for someone else to speak so they didn't have to. Finally, a younger woman with tired eyes spoke up. "I stole from my little sister," she admitted, voice tight. "Cash, mostly. She was the only person who still trusted me, and I ruined that. *She's* forgiven me, but I still think about it almost every day."

Brooklyn flinched almost imperceptibly, trying to cover it by shifting back in his chair and crossing his legs.

Then one of the oldest men in the group cleared his throat. "I understand that. My daughter had a dance recital when she was about six. I was drunk, passed out at home, and missed the whole thing. She's a teenager now, and I'm not even sure she remembers it, but I do."

Just John, like the professional he was, let us all sit in the silence for a moment. "And what do you tell yourself because of that?"

The man stared at the floor, rubbing his beard, which was patchy with gray. "That I'm a shitty father."

Just John nodded. "Does saying that serve you at all?"

He let out a hollow laugh. "Not really."

For some reason, Just John's eyes found mine. He knew I was there for support, but he searched for something in my eyes in the same way I assumed he would a patient. Like he was waiting for a revelation to come over me, that I was the same as everyone else here in the sense that I was also deserving of self-forgiveness for the things I blamed myself for. I was not a shitty sister because Nikki's eating disorder had escalated to the point of hospitalization, and I was not a shitty sister for not seeing signs earlier.

In my head I knew all that, but the *feeling* was still there, and I had nowhere to put it all. I felt it when I looked at Brooklyn too.

"Self-forgiveness isn't saying what happened was okay," Just John addressed the group. "It's saying you're still worthy of moving on. That you're still here, trying. And that matters."

This time, I thought the silence that we all sat in was intentional, allowing us all to let what he'd said sink in. After a few more moments, Just John clapped his hands again. "All righty, let's take a five-minute break."

As people moved around and stretched, I sat back in my chair, waiting for Brooklyn to make the first move. But he stayed put, too, staring down at his hands, lost in thought.

I nudged him lightly. "You okay?"

His lips twitched into something that wasn't quite a smile. "Yeah. I—" He exhaled. "I don't know how to do that. How to forgive myself."

I reached for his hand and gave it a small squeeze. "Does my forgiveness help at all?"

This time, his smile was more obvious. "Yeah, it does."

"Then we start there, and we keep doing this together. I'm with you."

Brooklyn looked at me, something unreadable in his expression. But he kept his hand in mine. "And I'm with you."

For now, that was enough.

>> <<

I'd put my phone on do not disturb during the session, and when I finally checked it, I had about ten missed calls and a barrage of texts—mostly from my sister.

"Jeez," I muttered, thumbing through the texts as we walked to Brooklyn's Jeep. "So apparently my mom's in the hospital. She hurt her ankle."

"Do you need me to take you over there?" Brooklyn asked as he started the car.

I wasn't going to ask, but I wouldn't say no. I wondered if maybe he was still trying to make up for the night of Stella's birthday, struggling to find that self-forgiveness that Just John preached.

"Sure, thanks."

"Yeah, anything."

I blinked in confusion, wondering if I'd misheard him say *any time*. But it sank in, and I knew I'd heard him right. *Anything*—for me.

His mood seemed to have improved from all the forlorn dismay of group therapy, and he jammed out to Caroline Polachek on the way to the hospital, singing so badly that it might have been good.

"What's he doing here?" Nikki hissed through her teeth as we approached her in the emergency room lobby. No *Hi*, no *Everything's fine, Nat, don't worry*, just venom.

"How else did you expect me to get here?" I replied. "You took my car, and I was already with him."

Nikki scowled as she glanced over my shoulder at Brooklyn, who hung back with his gaze down and his hands in the pockets of his jeans.

A tense moment (that felt more like ten minutes) passed, and I kept myself very much in between them, like a barricade. Then Nikki took a step back, and suddenly nothing was wrong. "She's all right, they're getting her set up in a cast. She broke her ankle."

"How?" I asked, lowering myself into one of the thick-cushioned paisley chairs.

"Tripped going into the community center." She shrugged in reply. Then her eyes found Brooklyn again, who sat two chairs away from us. "So, you're really not needed here."

"Oh." He sat up in the chair, looking back and forth between us. "Yeah, I guess not."

"I'll walk you out," I offered. I didn't want him to leave, but I didn't want Nikki eviscerating him either—metaphorically, of course.

Brooklyn got up, and I followed him through the sliding

double doors of the emergency room. We lingered off to the side under the overhang of the building.

"I'm sorry," I blurted over the wail of a siren in the distance. "About my sister."

"Hey, listen." Brooklyn took my arms and pulled me closer, wrapping them around his torso. He reached down and gently caressed the side of my cheek before pulling me into a soft kiss. "It's all okay."

I nodded, feeling far too at home in his arms, and we kissed again, as if it was always the first time.

"How about you go on a date with me," he said softly as we separated, staying close enough that his lips still brushed against mine when he spoke.

"A date?" I echoed.

"Yeah." He finally pulled away, and his eyes twinkled in the sunlight. "Like an honest to god, hold my hand, I'll even wear a collared shirt kind of date. Seems like the logical next move. At least, that's what certain early 2000s rom-coms tell me."

"I knew you paid attention." I reached down to intertwine my fingers in his. "Well, I already like holding your hand and everything, but I won't lie, I like seeing you get all dressed up and stuff."

He chuckled. "Yeah, yeah, don't get used to that."

He kissed me one more time before backing away, smiling to himself until he eventually turned around and jogged to the parking lot. The moment I stepped back through the sliding double doors, I reeled on my sister.

"*What* is your problem?"

"Me?" Nikki squeaked as she clapped her hands to her chest. "What's *yours*?"

"I don't have one," I told her plainly.

"Really? Because I happen to know you do. He just walked out."

I sat back in the chair and pressed my hands against my thighs. "That's—" I sighed, shaking my head to see if I could rattle out better words. "That's kind of fucked-up."

Not at all better, but got the point across.

Nikki put her hands to her forehead. "You really don't see what a bad idea this is, do you?"

"No, but I can *feel* the whiplash you keep giving me with this," I drawled with an eye roll. "First you're all happy and excited for me, then you're not, then things are fine, then they're not. It's like, *please*, make up your mind already."

"I have." Nikki looked at me with a stony expression. "And I've decided I don't like it."

"Nikki, I don't know what you think you know that I don't."

She shifted in the chair and her gaze dropped to her pink Adidas sneakers. "Enough."

Suddenly it all slid into place, and the revelation drenched me like a bucket of ice water had been dumped on my head. "What has Alec told you?"

"Nothing," Nikki answered curtly. "I told you, we don't talk anymore."

"Really?" I asked. "Why is that?"

"Stop making this about me." Nikki groaned and smacked her hands on the thighs of her leggings.

"No, I want to understand," I insisted, folding my arms over my chest. "It's my turn to criticize your decisions."

"Because of you," Nikki blurted, jumping out of the chair and glowering down at me. The few people lingering in the emergency room lobby were suddenly very attuned to our conversation, lifting their gazes up at us and waiting to see what would happen next.

After glancing around, Nikki slowly lowered herself back into the chair and pinched her lips together. "I don't want to commit time to someone when I have you to worry about."

The worst part about all of this was that I knew *exactly* how she felt, and it made me feel small. I wondered how much I'd deny it if someone had told me that when it came to her.

"That's—" I exhaled. "That's ridiculous, and *so* not necessary."

"It *is*. You don't—" Nikki paused and sat forward in the chair, keeping her gaze on the sliding double doors that led back into the emergency room. "You understand way less than you think you do."

"Then enlighten me."

Nikki lowered her voice to a harsh whisper. "Do you get what it's like to be someone like him? How easy it is to fall back into their shit?"

I shifted in my chair to face her, tucking one leg underneath me. "You underestimate what I *do* know. He's been clean aside from that one incident. He's going to group therapy. And I know he's *trying*."

"Trying doesn't mean *you* won't get hurt."

"I can take care of myself."

"That's the problem." Nikki brought her hands down on the wooden armrests of the chair, wrapping her fingers around them tightly. "You always think you can handle things yourself. But what happens if this goes south? What if he relapses again and doesn't get better?"

"Then . . ." I paused and swallowed hard. "Then I'll deal with it."

And I believed what I said.

"That's what you're not getting. You shouldn't have to deal with it." Nikki groaned and pinched the bridge of her nose. "You shouldn't have to be the one picking up pieces of other people."

"I've been doing that my whole life, haven't I? I was eight years old with a grieving mother and suddenly had to learn how to parent you, then my freshman year at college I had to figure out why Mom's getting a call from the high-school nurse that you fainted in PE because you haven't been eating lunch all week. I skipped graduation when you were admitted to the hospital and spent every day I could with you until you came home. But you know what? I'd do it all again exactly the same. So I'm not going to wait around until it's that bad for Brooklyn. I'm just not. This is it, Nikki, and I can't just shut it off, no matter how hard you and Mom tell me I should."

I was on fire, burning down the entire room with us in it. Nikki sat back and nodded slowly, pinching her facial features together to hold in her emotions. I didn't realize that I'd become this person, constantly teetering on the edge of *something*, though I couldn't even figure out exactly what that something was.

"Nikki, I—" I reached for her but she shifted away from me in the chair, keeping her gaze fixed on those emergency room doors. They slid open, and it seemed Nikki recognized the nurse who walked through them, as she stiffened in the chair.

"All right, she is good to go," the nurse told Nikki. "I'm sorry for the wait, we had a mix-up with her paperwork."

"Great, thanks." Nikki forced a smile through tears that glistened in the corners of her eyes. She dabbed at her face with the sleeves of her sweatshirt as another nurse rolled Mom out in a wheelchair.

If there was one thing my sister and I were both good at, it was putting on a face, and if anyone had seen us in passing, they would have thought nothing was wrong.

"Remind me again, how did you manage to bust your ankle

up walking into the community center?" I gazed at Mom in the rearview mirror. She had to sit sideways in the back seat so her leg could be properly elevated.

>><<

We had to drive all the way across town to a specific pharmacy to fill the prescription for her pain medication, and it was almost dark by the time we made it home. Nikki and I didn't directly speak the entire time, instead trading uneasy glances that I wasn't entirely sure Mom caught onto, seeing as she was a little preoccupied with broken bones and all that.

"It's really not a big deal." Mom rubbed at her temples. "I'm clumsy sometimes, right? I wasn't watching where I was going and I tripped."

"Maybe now if you go and sell some paintings, people will feel bad for you and make pity purchases." Nikki snickered while she helped Mom inside the house, as if things had gone completely back to normal. But I knew better.

After we set Mom up comfortably on the couch, Nikki immediately dashed for her room, and I nearly tripped up the stairs trying to get to her before she shut the door.

"Nikki, wait." I reached for her wrist before she could cross the threshold of her bedroom.

"What?" She groaned, but lingered in the doorway, leaning against it as she looked at me with tired eyes.

"I want to apologize," I said. "I didn't mean what I said to come off as so cruel."

She arched her eyebrows at me, expecting more, but I wasn't sure what else I could say that didn't sound like I was making excuses.

"Sure." She turned to walk into her room, but I pressed my hand to the door to stop her from shutting it.

"That's it?" I asked.

"Yeah. All good."

This time I let her close the door on me, and I had to believe her, even though it was against my instincts to.

Twenty

"Your prince here to whisk you away in your carriage?"

Nikki leaned in the doorway of my bedroom, eyeing me as I sat at my desk, finishing applying my mascara.

I could tell Nikki was trying hard not to sound bitter. While we had "resolved" our argument from a few days ago, we tiptoed around each other and all the splintering cracks around us, like we were on thin ice that could give anywhere at any time.

"Princes are boring." I offered her a faint grin. "Knights are better. They're the ones with the swords and armor, and they do the fighting."

"I guess that makes you a knight too." Nikki shrugged. "Just don't get too hung up in trying to save each other from trolls and dragons, or whatever it is that knights fight."

The hint of comical smarm in her voice was her version of an olive branch. One time when we were in elementary school, she'd pushed me off the monkey bars because she wanted a turn, and at the time, skinning your elbows on concrete was pretty much the worst feeling in the world. I was beside myself for what felt like days. Instead of asking me for forgiveness, she drew me a picture of me with bandages on my arms and wrote (in very illegible five-year-old handwriting), SORY YOU ARE NO GOOD AT MONKE BARS. Everything was fine after that.

"So wise." I rolled my eyes. "Although I don't think there are any trolls or dragons around here anyway."

"True. Well, have a nice time."

Nikki gave me one last smile, faint and fleeting like she was saying goodbye for what felt like more than one night, before leaving me to my own devices. Despite everything Brooklyn and I had done and had been through already, this was technically our first date, and it was still a little nerve-racking in its own way. I still felt like I was on the edge, but when I walked outside to see Brooklyn leaning against the door of his Jeep, I realized maybe it was an edge meant to be jumped off of.

A blast of the dipping sun in the oncoming dusk nearly blinded me, and Brooklyn's bright-orange button-up shirt didn't help. I smiled to myself at the wrinkles at the bottom hem of the shirt, as if he'd gone back and forth several times on whether to tuck it in or not. I knew he cleaned up well, but there was something about this version of him I liked better. The slight unruliness gave him a more unrefined attractiveness, and it made him more human.

"Are we going to direct traffic?" I joked.

He gave me a coy smile as he opened the passenger door for me. "I'm not giving anything away. You know, maybe I just like the color orange."

"I'll keep that in mind," I replied.

He hopped into the driver's seat, and the engine roared as he sped away down my street. The wind whipped through the car, and I silently thanked past me for a hairstyle that wouldn't undo in the open air of the topless Jeep.

Brooklyn fiddled with the radio the way he always did, cranking the volume of his Deftones playlist to counteract the sound of the wind. It was moments like this when I wished I could stop time. We really *were* happy, laughing and holding hands with the sun bathing our world in a golden light.

We hit the parkway, driving farther away from Dahlia Point than I'd been since living here. After enough speed and enough wind and more distance than I had been prepared to handle, Brooklyn pulled off at an exit and into a small town with one quiet main road, where a few pedestrians seemed to pay no mind to the one car driving down the street. He slowed to a stop in front of a tiny old brick building. I could barely make out the dark script imprinted on the front window.

"Villalobos," Brooklyn told me. "It means Town of Wolves. My dad's friend from college owns the place. It's in the middle of nowhere—obviously—but they do killer business, and they have, in my unprofessional opinion, the best tacos on the East Coast."

"You're setting awfully high expectations here." I went to unbuckle my seat belt when Brooklyn stopped me.

"Oh, we're not eating here, I'm only picking up the food."

He winked at me before jumping out of the car. Through the large front window I watched Brooklyn chat with the petite redheaded hostess, her eyes wide and fixated on him as he chatted and laughed with her like they were best friends. I was never the jealous type, but then again, I had never been around someone like him. His sweet, easygoing charm was part of this pull that he had, almost like a planet ready to ensnare any wayward comets in his gravity. At this point I was definitely one of those comets, sucked right in and fated to exist in his atmosphere.

After he returned we drove away and pulled down a small offshoot, a quiet suburban street lined with one-story brick houses and large oak trees with branches that danced in the soft breeze. The street abruptly ended in a thicket of bushes and tall marram grass, but over the tops of them I could see the sky, clear and starting to turn an ombre of orange with the setting sun.

Brooklyn parked the car at the dead end and ran around the front of it to open my door. It was something so small and insignificant, but I'd never get tired of it. He grabbed a backpack from the back seat and led me to the bushes.

"Now would be a *great* time to tell me what's going on," I prodded.

He shook his head. "Follow me. You trust me, don't you?"

Whether the gravity to his words was unintentional or not, it gave me pause. Against the odds, against the past, against my sister's apprehension, I really *did* trust him.

I took his hand as he led me through the brush, thankful I had picked a good thick pair of jeans to wear. When we made it through to a clearing, it felt like someone had pumped so much air into my chest that it threatened to burst. In front of us was a strip of beach with white sand, probably no bigger than my living room, surrounded by the same brush and beach grass that we had walked through. A small dock stretched into the ocean, which was so calm it looked like glass as the sun began to dip below its surface.

"Wow" was all I could manage to breathe out.

"Is this a good spot for our tacos?" Brooklyn beckoned me to follow him along the dock. He pulled a tribal-printed blanket from his backpack and laid it at the edge, sitting down so that his feet dangled over the water. I sat down beside him, letting the warmth of the dusky sun wash over me.

"Brooklyn." I sighed wistfully. "This is amazing."

He stayed quiet, his eyes trained on the ocean. But he put his hand over mine, brushing his thumb over my knuckles and filling me with warmth.

We ate in a comfortable silence, watching the sun slowly set and turn the ocean into a messy watercolor painting of blues and purples and oranges. Every time I glanced over at him, he was already looking at me, his blue eyes deep and veiled with something I didn't recognize, but whatever it was, it brewed a storm inside of me. I looked down at my feet dangling over the ocean, but my skin prickled as I felt Brooklyn's eyes still on me.

"What?" I asked.

He gave me a faint smile but stayed silent.

"Why are you looking at me like that?" I continued. "Like—"

"Like I adore you?" Brooklyn's smile widened, and his eyes gleamed like they had stolen the stars right out of the sky. "Because I do. I fucking adore you."

I swore I heard a pop in my chest, like my heart had just exploded. "Brooklyn."

"Seriously. You're like the best thing that's ever happened to me."

I was a mess of thoughts and emotions, and any words I wanted to say knotted up in my throat. I knew the feeling that was starting to bubble up inside of me, and it scared the hell out of me.

"Me too," I finally said, leaning my head on his shoulder. "I mean it."

The rest of our dockside dinner passed by in a blur, but I danced on clouds the entire time. We talked about nothing at all, like the weather and our favorite sneakers and bad music, but somehow Brooklyn made it seem like something. I hinged on every word he said and felt my cheeks aching from smiling so much.

When Brooklyn dropped me off at my house, I took my time gathering myself, silently pleading for our night to not end. Brooklyn fiddled with the radio like he always did, and I could tell he was stalling too.

"So . . ." He clicked his tongue.

"So . . ." I echoed. The fuzzy static of the radio filled our silence.

"Do you have plans for Sunday?" he asked, cracking a small smile.

"Well." I tapped my finger on my chin. "I have a very important date scheduled with my copy of *The Road*."

Brooklyn chuckled, still smiling that same smile that made my stomach feel like I was on a rollercoaster. "Would you be willing to forgo your date with the nameless character Viggo Mortensen plays in the movie adaptation to have dinner at my house?"

"You mean like, order takeout and get a movie?"

"Not exactly." Brooklyn grimaced. "More like a family thing. My dad will be home this weekend, and . . . it would be nice to have you there."

He fiddled with the radio again. I tried to read the expression on his face, strained somewhere between unease and uncertainty. I delicately pulled his hand away from the knobs on the radio and laced my fingers between his.

"I'd love to," I told him. "Remember what you told me the other day?"

Relief washed over him. "I meant everything I said before. I *do* mean everything I say to you, always. I don't know what I'd do without you."

"You'd have nobody to yap with about obscure indie movies from 1992, obviously."

"Obviously." Brooklyn smiled at me again, and leaned over to kiss me the way he had so many times already, and the way I hoped he'd continue to do for a long time.

Twenty-one

Brooklyn's father, Charlie, was nothing like I anticipated. He was mild-mannered for a man of his size, and far softer around the edges than Brooklyn had made him out to be. When he found out I'd been writing (which Brooklyn had to proudly state), he recommended a few nonfiction books on creative philosophy.

It was also Charlie's family lasagna recipe that was made for dinner, and Stella eagerly played sous chef, yapping his ear off about junior league and some inconsequential drama in her friend group. But Charlie listened attentively.

"Don't let the tough-girl act fool you, she's a daddy's girl." Brooklyn nudged me and smirked.

"Does that make you a mama's boy?" I asked. We'd taken on the task of setting the dining room table after Brooklyn had so graciously volunteered.

"No way," Brooklyn replied. "At least, not in the negative connotation of the word. But god forbid men are nice to their mothers."

"Don't be so smarmy." Annie had appeared beside us to hand Brooklyn a stack of napkins. "You know you're my favorite son."

Brooklyn blinked. "I'm your only son."

"Exactly."

I snickered behind my hand, and Brooklyn playfully jabbed

me in the side, causing me to squeal and capture everyone's attention.

"Nothing to see here." Brooklyn came to my rescue. "Maybe a casual kidnapping."

We sat down for dinner, and they carried on as if Charlie had only been gone two days instead of almost two months.

"On the rig, sometimes it's hard to pass the time," Charlie was saying. "A bunch of us take turns doing the questionnaire from the *Colbert* show. Have you ever done it?"

"No, but I like personality quizzes."

Charlie nodded. "You'll like this, then. So the first question is what's the best sandwich."

Definitely *not* what I had expected, and I was sorely unprepared for an answer—which I guess was the whole point. "Wow, that's actually kind of hard, because I don't think I've ever thought about that in my life."

Brooklyn lurched forward in his chair. "Grilled cheese, obviously."

"For you maybe," Stella scoffed with a flick of her wrist. "You have the eating habits of an eight-year-old."

Stella's comment lit up places in my memory, and the answer surfaced. "Okay, I've got mine. When I was younger, my mom used to make me turkey and lettuce with mustard on really good sourdough that she'd get from the farmer's market in downtown Arcadia. I know that's not the *best*, but I ate that for lunch every day from fourth grade to seventh grade, and back then I thought it was pretty great. With some classic Lay's, of course."

"Best to *you*, though," Charlie said. "That's the point."

Brooklyn casually draped his arm over the back of my chair, and his father continued the questionnaire. Despite knowing there was some kind of tension between Brooklyn and his father, they kept it away from the dinner table, and we all laughed and ate lasagna and debated if apples or oranges were the better fruit.

When I thought about what family normalcy looked like, this was it. As well adjusted as Nikki, Mom, and I were with our situation, that didn't stop me from occasionally wondering about what our whole family would have looked like having dinner on a Sunday summer night. I wondered if my dad would have still been a history teacher, and if my mom would have kept collecting those little ceramic animals that had been all over our kitchen.

And suddenly, it sank in, deep into my bloodstream, as to Brooklyn's desperation to fit in and be normal. It was for them. People like Brooklyn (and by extension my sister) might have been victims of their illness, but their families were victims of everything else that came with it.

The realization of that stung—that meant *I* was a victim, instead of someone who was handling things because it's your family and you care and you want things to be okay. I didn't like to be thought of as a victim, because it didn't feel right to identify as something people who had serious trauma identified as, but maybe Nikki was right about something—I didn't know nearly as much as I thought I did.

I helped Stella load the dishwasher after dinner, and even in the comfortable silence I felt her gaze on me.

"What?" I asked.

"You really are good for my brother," Stella said with a casual shrug. "But I think you knew that already."

"We're good for each other," I replied, rinsing off a plate in the sink before handing it to her.

"Right. I do mean it, though."

I offered her a smile. She jerked her head in the direction of the back doors, where Brooklyn was outside on the deck. "Don't worry, I'll finish this."

"Thanks. For saying what you said too."

I made my way onto the back deck but stopped when I realized he hadn't heard me come out. He had his back to me, his silhouette faintly illuminated by the dim glow of the lights coming through the windows of the house.

It was the smallest of things. The way the wind whipped his hair in every direction. The way he'd crack his neck every so often. Every little move he made captivated me. I was beginning to accept how deep into this I was; so deep the light barely reached me.

"Hey, you," I said as I finally approached him.

Brooklyn turned around, and his eyes lit up.

"Hey, yourself."

Without a word, Brooklyn wrapped his arm around my shoulders and pulled me into his chest, resting his chin on the top of my head. My cheek brushed against the soft, threadbare material of the Clayton baseball sweatshirt he had thrown on, and I inhaled his usual fresh and clean scent that I had grown so used to. He really did smell like a rainstorm, in the best way, and I would have stayed there all night if I could.

"Thanks for coming tonight," he mumbled into my hair.

"Of course."

"Everything felt so okay, for once," he said. "*I* felt okay."

"You are okay," I replied, reaching down and grabbing his hand, feeling him melt under my touch, as if all the icy tension was turning to water. We stood outside for a while in silence, the gentle sounds of the ocean floating through the night air.

"It's getting kind of chilly, let's go inside," Brooklyn said, pulling at the sleeves of his hoodie. I nodded in response, and let him lead me through the back door and up the stairs. A warm feeling radiated through me as Brooklyn pulled me into his room, something I barely recognized as lust until he quietly shut the door behind us and studied me with dark, hungry eyes.

In a split second his lips were on mine, his touch like a spark that set off fireworks inside me. We slowly meandered across the floor of his room, refusing to separate as we stumbled to his bed. I had kissed him dozens of times, but the way his hands glided so effortlessly but still so sensually along my skin put me on another level—one that damn near separated my soul from my body.

"Nat," he whispered softly, still so close to me I felt his lips brush against my ear.

"Yeah?"

He exhaled heavily, his breath hot on my cheek. "I can't thank you enough for everything you've done for me this summer."

My heart nearly burst. I smiled at him, letting my fingers gently run down his cheeks. "Don't thank me. You've done so much for me too. Everything that's been going on, it would have been really easy for me to lock myself in my room all summer, but you made sure I didn't. Remember what you said to me when we first hung out?"

"Tell me again anyway."

"We're in it together."

I wanted to stop time entirely. He kissed me again, pressing his body into mine. I was in such a haze, his scent and his touch clouding all my senses, that I barely registered the voice calling from the hall. We jerked away from each other as someone pounded on his bedroom door.

"Brooklyn," his father called from the other side of the door. "Can you please come downstairs for a minute?"

Brooklyn let out a heavy sigh and shot me an apologetic look as he shimmied off of me and rolled off the bed. He pulled at the strings on his hoodie.

"I'm sorry," he said. "Guess I spoke too soon."

"Don't be sorry." I gave him a faint smile in response. "Your dad really does mean well. I can tell."

"Deep down I know that, but—" Brooklyn leaned down and kissed my forehead. "It's okay. I'll only be a few minutes, I promise."

I nodded, watching Brooklyn turn and walk out, shutting the door behind him. A heavy breath escaped my lips as I lay back on Brooklyn's bed, watching the ceiling fan cast shadows on the walls. This hadn't been the first time—and wouldn't be the last—I'd be left alone in Brooklyn's room, and the logical side of me knew this was all part of what I'd signed up for, but I still watched the clock on his bedside table turn minutes into hours. At least, that was what it felt like.

I swung my legs over the side of the bed and thumbed through a few DVDs we had, plucked *Reality Bites* out of the stack, and loaded it into Brooklyn's Xbox.

As I was about to sit back down on the bed and resign myself to whatever the night was going to bring, my foot collided with something hard sticking out from under the bed.

Wincing in pain, I dropped to the floor, rubbing the bruise that had already begun to develop on the top of my foot. I glanced under the bed at whatever I had kicked, seeing the corner of a wooden box peeking out from behind the comforter.

I could have just pushed it back under the bed, and maybe I should have, but my body betrayed me. I was still trying to figure out where the lines blurred between being trustworthy and being cautious, and I guess I'd decided cautious was the better option, since I pulled the box out in front of me and ran my hands over the smooth, dark wood. It was heavy in my hands, but the top of the box slid off with ease, and I was instantly greeted with a heavy, musky scent.

Relief washed over me when I realized what was actually in the box. About a dozen cigars were stacked neatly inside, some wrapped in plastic while others were covered in intricate paper labels. I picked up a more expensive-looking one, with a big gold foil label that read ROMEO Y JULIETA.

"You're worried for nothing," I muttered to myself, cringing inwardly for letting some kind of unfounded worry get the best of me, because I knew better. I knew *him* better.

I was about to put the box back when I noticed a white envelope pressed underneath the cigars. My body and my desperate need to know everything betrayed me again as I ran my fingers over the bumps and grooves of the envelope's contents, picking it up and spilling it onto the floor.

Two tiny plastic bags sat on the floor in front of me, and a sickening, nauseated feeling rolled through me as I picked them up and surveyed their contents. One contained a handful of tiny blue pills and three larger white bars, and the other was filled with white powder. I clenched my eyes shut, but when I opened them again, the bags were still in my shaking hands. I'd never had my heart broken before, but I imagined it felt something like this, as my whole body seized up from the impact.

I didn't know how long I sat on the floor of Brooklyn's bedroom, half in shock and half completely dumbfounded, but it was long enough that the heavy, sick feeling that filled my stomach bubbled and festered until it turned into rage. I was like an active volcano.

Eventually I heard the door open behind me, but I didn't turn around.

"Nat? Why are you on the floor?" Brooklyn asked.

I blinked away the tears that stung the corners of my eyes before shakily rising to my feet and turning to face him. Looking at him, his blue eyes still filled with a haze of lust from earlier, made my heart break even more.

"What is this?" I choked out, shaking the bags at him. Every time I tried to swallow, it was like there was glass in my throat. I clenched my other hand into a fist, hoping the stinging pain from my nails in my palm would wake me up from whatever nightmare I was having.

Brooklyn's voice dropped to a low whisper. "Where did you get that?"

"This box was sticking out from under your bed." I kicked the box toward him. The color from his cheeks drained, and he made a move to grab the bags out of my hand, but I jerked back.

"Nat, come on, are you serious?" He chuckled dryly, trying to hide the panic in his voice. "It's a humidor for cigars, it keeps them from going bad. I probably haven't opened that in months. That stuff could have been from—"

"Bullshit," I snapped before he could finish. My voice began to crack. "You literally just got through telling me how fine you were. After everything you said to me that was all so meaningful and I thought . . ." I choked back a sob, my head heavy and spinning. "Brooklyn, you *promised*."

"Nat, I swear," Brooklyn pleaded. "I didn't even know I had any of that."

"I don't care." I shoved the bags in his hands. "Get rid of it. Now."

He slowly crept toward the bathroom door, holding his hands up as if he was under fire. "I'll get rid of it."

I followed him into the bathroom and watched him dump

the bags' contents into the toilet. I wanted to keel over and vomit, but I swallowed it back. He threw the bags in the trash can and moved back toward me, but I pulled away. I wrapped my arms tightly around my torso, as if that could somehow keep everything in me intact.

"Natalie." Brooklyn moved toward me again, but I backed up.

"Take me home." I turned on my heel and made a beeline for the stairs. I heard Brooklyn's hurried footsteps behind me, but I kept my quick pace straight for his car.

We drove home in silence with the windows cracked open. The wind was cool and dried the sweat on the back of my neck. When we pulled up to my house, Brooklyn killed the engine.

"Natalie, please." He reached for my hand, but I pulled it away again.

"Don't," I snapped. I pushed the car door open and slammed it behind me. I thought I heard Brooklyn call my name again, but he sounded far, far away. Maybe in another life I would have turned around, but I kept my head down and disappeared into the house.

How did that saying go? Fool me once, shame on you, fool me twice and shame on me for completely tricking myself into thinking I knew better. I obviously didn't know anything.

I sat on the edge of my bed and hung my head between my knees. I felt ill, and even in the dark my room spun around me. I stayed in that position and waited for the engine on Brooklyn's car to turn. After a deadly silent few minutes, I heard the Jeep rumble as it drove away from my street. I lay in bed and stared at the ceiling, not even bothering to change out of my clothes. My sweater still smelled like him. I rolled over, buried my face into my pillow, and screamed.

July 12

Dad,

I'm mad. I'm mad at me, I'm mad at Brooklyn, I'm mad at Nikki, and I'm mad at you.

I know that sounds childish, but I don't care. You left, and now every time someone starts to leave, I lose my mind trying to stop it. It's like my brain hits some panic switch that screams not again, not again, and suddenly I'm holding on so tight I start to hurt myself.

I don't know what to believe anymore about Brooklyn.

You'd think I'd consider walking away now. Any rational person probably would. But I can't. I won't. Because every time he comes apart, I see that same grief I've been dragging around since you died. The kind that settles in your bones and makes everything heavy. I can't abandon him in it. Not when I know what that kind of aching bullshit feels like.

Maybe that's my punishment for still missing you. I find pieces of you in broken people and call it caring about someone. I tell myself I'm saving them, but maybe I'm just trying to save myself from feeling all these awful things. I'm self-fulfilling prophecies that aren't even mine.

I feel like I'm being torn in two. Half of me knows I should leave before it gets worse, but the other half firmly believes that I can hold someone together if I never let go.

So I'm staying. For now. Because I still believe, deep down, that if I keep holding on, maybe one day someone will stay for good.

Nat

Twenty-two

"Hello? Earth to Nat! Are you even paying attention?"

Nikki's voice pulled me from my daze. I shook my head and blinked a few times, letting my eyes adjust to the bright fluorescent lighting of Reformation. A sweet lavender and vanilla scent wafted through the air, and it was enough to put me to sleep. I rubbed at my tired eyes, feeling my head sit heavy on my neck. The image of Brooklyn's plastic bag of little pills flashed in my mind every time I tried to close my eyes, and my stomach ached even at the thought of it. It had had me tossing and turning for the past few days, my head swimming like a small boat lost at sea.

"Do you like this or not?" Nikki waved a mustard-yellow sundress embroidered with flowers in my face.

"Um." I scrunched my nose up. "I think that would look better on you."

Nikki frowned and tossed the dress back on a rack. "We're supposed to be shopping for *you*, remember? You're the one who needs more cute clothes."

"I'm fine, I can borrow some of *your* very cute clothes," I said as she shuffled through racks of more dresses, occasionally picking one up only to put it back.

"No, you need your own clothes, so you can look good for your boyfriend," Nikki said with a nonchalant shrug. She pursed her lips and waited for my response. After a moment of my silence, she groaned and shoved my arm.

"Come on, you've barely told me anything about your date and stuff," she prodded. "This is the first time I've seen you all weekend."

I put on a thin smile, feeling the very act of trying to keep it together stretching me thin too. "We had a nice time this weekend. He took me for tacos one night, and we ate dinner at his house with his parents. That's all."

I felt words I couldn't say well up in my throat, and they stung hard as they scratched against my insides. I wanted to tell Nikki that he'd taken me to a secluded beach to watch the sunset, and that the way he held me set fire to my insides, and that he smiled at me with his gleaming white teeth like I was the only person in the room. Like I was the only person who even mattered.

But something so literally small—six little blue pills no bigger than my pinkie nail—loomed figuratively large over my head, like dark clouds about to unleash a hurricane.

"Natalie Ray Owens, my goodness gracious," Nikki called out in singsong, causing me to drop the dress I had picked off the rack. "What is your problem?"

"I don't have a problem," I said, hyperaware of how hard I had to try to keep my hands steady. "I'm fine. Everything's fine."

I kept it all in, realized exposing the good also meant exposing the bad. It was better to pretend none of it had happened at all. For both of our sakes.

"Fine." Nikki groaned. "I need you to focus. I refuse to leave this store with nothing."

"So, then *you* get a dress," I quipped. "And I'll borrow it later."

After a beat, we laughed at each other. I finally studied the dress I had pulled from the rack. It was floor-length and a silky pale green, with a high neckline and splashes of white flowers that looked like they were painted in watercolors directly on the fabric. It felt like almost nothing in my hands.

"Wow," Nikki chirped. "You have to get that. You'd give Brooklyn a heart attack in that dress."

I bit down on my lip hard. I felt dizzy and was just about ready to reveal everything to Nikki in the middle of our shopping trip when my phone buzzed in my pocket.

BROOKLYN KELLER (like the bridge): Nat please talk to me

BROOKLYN KELLER (like the bridge): I'm begging you

BROOKLYN KELLER (like the bridge): I'll do anything

I scowled, quickly hit Delete, and shoved my phone back in my pocket. Every few hours it had been another desperate plea from him, and despite the cracking I felt in my heart, I had ignored every single one of them. The day after dinner at his house, he had called me ten times, but gave up and resorted to texting when I refused to answer. I couldn't figure out if I was sad, frustrated, angry, or some sickening combination of the three. I rubbed at my eyes again to dissipate the stinging I felt from holding back tears.

"You should get that dress," Nikki piped up. I looked down and realized I was still clutching the long dress tightly in my hands.

I ran my fingers over the silky fabric again. It felt new and exciting—things I was desperate to feel. "I think I will."

>> <<

When we returned home Nikki retreated to her bedroom with several shopping bags in hand, claiming she was exhausted and needed a nap.

I sighed and felt a pang of remorse radiate through me. It was easy to let Brooklyn's turmoil and shortcomings overshadow everything else in my life, but that didn't mean I could let my sister's recovery take a back seat, no matter how well it appeared she was doing. As I had recently learned, I am nowhere near as keyed in to the people in my life as I thought I was, and that stung.

I lay back on my bed and squeezed my eyes shut. An image of Brooklyn's guilt-stricken face flashed in front of me, his cheeks blotchy and his eyes glassy, and my eyes shot back open. My phone buzzed against my stomach.

BROOKLYN KELLER (like the bridge): I'm outside. Please come talk to me. Just for five minutes

I clenched my jaw, hovering my thumb over the Delete button. Another text came through.

BROOKLYN KELLER (like the bridge): Please. I'll stay here all day if I have to

I inhaled as much air as my lungs would allow before heaving myself out of bed and quietly making my way outside. Even after everything, there was something in me that wanted to keep giving him chances. I wanted to keep believing in something, even if it wasn't necessarily him. Maybe just something tangible.

Brooklyn leaned against the door of his car with a bundle of flowers under his arm, larger and more impressive than the previous ones he had given me, and his tired eyes lit up as I approached him. His hair was unkempt and it was obvious he hadn't shaved in a few days. I fought the urge to fling myself at him, to wrap my arms around his broad figure and nuzzle myself into his chest, feeling his warmth surge through me. Instead I crossed my arms tightly over my torso and gave him a stony glare.

"You have five minutes," I told him.

Brooklyn gave me a quick nod and handed me the bouquet of flowers. "They don't suck as much as the last ones."

I took the bundle gingerly in my hand and ran my fingers over the colorful array of roses. I looked up at him, and he gave me a weak smile, letting a small dimple pop up in the corner of his cheek. If he was trying to completely unravel me, it was working.

"Look, Natalie." Brooklyn rubbed at his neck, and I cringed hearing him say my full name. I had gotten so used to hearing him say *Nat* that *Natalie* sounded foreign and far away, almost like it didn't even belong to me.

"I cannot thank you enough for how supportive you've been these last few months. You make me want to do the right thing. You're good, way too good for me, and I know it. But I *am* trying, and I don't know what else I can do to get you to believe that." He paused and sucked in a shaky breath. "I need someone on my side."

I clutched the stems of the flowers tightly in my hands until my knuckles turned white. "Brooklyn, I *am* on your side. But what am I supposed to think when I find bags of drugs in your room not even two weeks after you relapsed and promised me it wouldn't happen again?"

"You're supposed to trust that I kept my promise!" Brooklyn's voice cracked. "Nat, I swear I have no idea where those pills came from. I didn't even know that box was still under my bed. I'm trying to move on from all this, but I can't do that if you're going to assume I'm lying all the time."

The backs of my eyes prickled with unshed tears. My chest burned, and I felt like someone was trying to rip me in half right down the middle; one half ruled by my heart and soul, and the other half ruled by logical judgment. My head spun. "Brooklyn, I don't know what you want me to say."

"I don't, either, and I'm sorry for even letting it get to this point."

Brooklyn reached down and wiped away a tear that had fallen down my cheek with his thumb. "Please don't cry. Not for me. Whatever I have to do to not ruin this, I'll do it. You mean so much to me."

I swallowed the lump that had formed in my throat from holding back tears. The honesty in his voice was jarring and raw, and the side of me ruled by my aching heart took over. I nodded and gave in, wrapping my arms around his neck and kissing his cheek. I felt his arms around me, protecting me from all the bad. But I knew I could protect him too. At this point, I had to.

"Now what?" I asked as I pulled away and wiped my eyes with my hand.

"Now"—Brooklyn produced an envelope from his back pocket and handed it to me—"say you'll be my date to this."

"You're not asking me to prom, are you?" I shot him a deadpan look.

"Open it," he said with a slight chuckle.

Inside the envelope was a thick, glossy piece of paper, and in embossed script, it read KAYLEIGH MAE AND JACKSON PHILLIP INVITE YOU TO CELEBRATE THEIR WEDDING SATURDAY THE EIGHTH

OF AUGUST, TWO-THOUSAND AND TWENTY-FOUR AT SIX O'CLOCK IN THE EVENING. THE GRAND ISLAND ESTATE, HILTON HEAD, SC.

"Who's getting married?" I asked.

"Childhood friends," Brooklyn replied. "Me, Alec, Stella, my parents, we're all going. We're renting a beach house for the weekend, and I got a plus-one."

He took the envelope from me and flipped it over. In script it read MR. BROOKLYN KELLER & GUEST.

He pouted and clasped his hands in front of him. "Please."

I smiled and shook my head. "I can't say no to that face."

Brooklyn returned my smile and kissed me on the cheek. "You're amazing. I really don't deserve you. I have to go home, but I'll call you later, okay?"

I nodded and watched him get back into his car, smiling at me the entire time until he drove away down my street. I made my way back into the house and closed the door softly behind me, smiling as I looked down at the flowers again.

"What was that all about?"

I jumped out of my skin when I saw Nikki emerge from the living room. I clutched the flowers to my chest.

"Brooklyn asked me to go with him to their friend's wedding," I replied with a faint smile, suddenly aware of the sense of unease in the room. "Seems like it'll be fun."

"That's a little dramatic for the occasion, isn't it?" Nikki gestured to the flowers.

I couldn't hide the redness in my cheeks, and looked down at my sandals.

"Nat, what did he do this time?"

I heaved out a groan. "Why do you assume that? That's not fair."

"Natalie." The sternness in Nikki's voice was jarring. "You're the worst liar I know. What did he do? Is he doing drugs again?"

Hearing Nikki say it out loud felt like a stab in the chest. I shook my head at her again. "No. He's fine."

"You know this is exactly what addicts do, right? They beg and they apologize and they make promises they have no intention of keeping."

"You don't know him."

"He has such a hold over you, Nat," Nikki said sharply. "You're so blinded by your infatuation with him that you can't even see what's going on. You barely make time to write anymore, you don't hang out with me or Mom, you're so wrapped up in him that if it doesn't involve him, you don't want a part of it. So, what, are you going to forgive him every time he comes over here with flowers and a cute apology?"

"You have no idea what you're talking about." The words stung as they left my throat. "You don't know *anything* about him."

"You obviously don't either." Nikki's voice had dropped to a harsh whisper. "You think that the more you involve yourself with people, the more you can mitigate the damage they've done to themselves."

"Who's this really about?" I narrowed my eyes on her. "Him, or you?"

"Does it matter?" she snapped. As if there was kickback from her own words, she took a step backward up the stairs. "You're not a solution. You're a fucking bandage."

"And you're a shallow little girl who wants everyone around her to be as miserable as she is."

I barely recognized my own voice, harsh and cold and completely detached from the rest of me. But this time, I did mean it, and she knew it too. With tears trickling down her face, she turned to head up the steps, but spun back around in a flurry to face me.

"You know what? Do what you want. But when whatever this is blows up in your face, I'm not helping you pick up the pieces."

Nikki turned back around and stormed up the steps, then slammed her bedroom door. I looked back down at the flowers. One of them had already wilted and died.

Twenty-three

I stood over my blue suitcase, wide open with its contents strewn across my bed. It was as if it had gotten sick—food poisoning from being stuffed with too many unnecessary outfit options.

I groaned and pulled at my hair, letting chunks of blond locks fall flat over my face. I gazed past my open door and to my sister's room. The door was shut.

Two weeks had gone by since our fight, and we were decidedly not doing any tiptoeing this time. It was as if we didn't even live in the same house. If I was down in the kitchen or the living room, she'd wait until I'd left or gone back upstairs to go downstairs.

Mom had tried to intervene at the beginning, but there was no hope for us. We'd never had a fight like this before—so pointed and personal and mean—so we didn't know how to make up or get over it either. This was all dark, uncharted waters, and it was impossible trying to navigate it.

There were nights I'd sit at my desk, looking dead-eyed at my laptop screen begging and willing the creative block to clear. But Nikki had been right about one thing: I'd been so distracted by everything going on (both her and Brooklyn included) that that only added to the blockage. What was once a small pile of dirt and muck had evolved into this heaping mountain of bullshit, and I did not have a shovel.

However, that could not be a *now* problem, as I still had to pack for this trip.

My phone buzzed somewhere underneath a pile of shirts, and I tossed them to the side over my bed until I found it, smiling to myself at Brooklyn on the caller ID. It was a photo I had snuck while we were at the beach. His back was to me but his head was turned around, and he was smiling that big dorky smile of his, with his cheeks tinged pink from the sun and the heat. Water glistened on his hair and sand dusted his shoulders. I had never been a great photographer, but I'd be lying if I said he didn't make it easy for me.

"I'm outside. Are you almost ready?" His voice came through the phone as soon as I swiped to answer.

I eyed my suitcase. "Define ready."

I heard a groan from the other end of the phone. "Nat, we're only going for a weekend, and it's a two-hour drive away."

After a few moments of silence, he sighed. "You were definitely in bed reading all morning instead of getting ready. Admit it."

"You know me so well." I couldn't help but chuckle. I held up a lime-green tank top, scrunched my nose at it, and tossed it to the floor. "I'm trying to be strategic about the clothes I'm bringing. That's all."

Brooklyn groaned into the phone again. "It doesn't matter what you bring. You'll look great anyway. You always look great."

I saw a flash of blond hair in the corner of my eye. "I'll be down in five minutes," I said hurriedly, and hung up the phone before he could answer. I stalked into the hallway to see Nikki ready to disappear back into the void of her bedroom.

"Hey, wait," I called to her.

She stopped, but kept her back to me for a few moments, and I held my breath for what felt like *way* more than just a few moments. Finally, she sighed and turned around, leaning against the door frame in an oversized pink hoodie that almost covered her tiny running shorts. "What?"

I realized I was sorely unprepared for if she'd actually turned around. "I just wanted to let you know I'm leaving in a few."

She pinched her lips together and nodded tersely. She took one step to turn back into her room, but froze in the way people do in suspended animation and they won't move until you activate them again.

"You should bring that silk dress you bought from Reformation," she said. "It complements your eyes."

Then she turned and shut the bedroom door behind her, and I let out a long exhale. The dress she was referring to was on my bed, unpacked and in the "questionable" pile. I had a long baby-blue halter dress I'd worn to a few formals in school neatly folded beside my suitcase, but as if touched by some kind of divine intervention, sunlight came through my window and shone directly onto the Reformation dress. There were little iridescent glints in the threading of the dress, and I could almost *hear* the dress saying *Pick me, I'm perfect.*

Now I guess I was taking advice from a dress.

>> <<

The Grand Island Estate definitely lived up to its name—it was actually its own private island, and the entire estate was on acres of open land, with little inlets of water that spilled in from the ocean running through the open fields. The entranceway was well manicured, and the lengthy driveway leading up to the estate was lined with rows of colorful flowers that swayed gently in the breeze. It was dusk by the time Brooklyn and I arrived, and the sun was barely visible as it sank behind the horizon of the ocean, darkening the sky and turning it a grayish-purple color.

Brooklyn refused to let me carry my own suitcase as we trekked from the gravel parking lot through the property, passing the main pool deck and an extravagant garden where I was sure the wedding would take place. Farther off in the distance, a dock jutted into the bay. The property was quiet and empty, with most of the hotel's patrons either enjoying a luxurious seafood dinner on the water or prepping for whatever nightlife was around in the area.

Another section of the estate stretched far past the main building, which looked more like a row of condos, in the same slate-gray color. It had its own smaller gated-off pool, and strings of lights hung low between the trees.

"My parents rented a suite here," Brooklyn said as he swiped the key card into the room. "They're finishing up a few things at home so they'll be here tomorrow. Stella is *supposed* to be here already, and Alec's also coming tomorrow since he's got some work thing."

"Wow," I said as we made it through the front door. "I'd *live* here."

The entire floor plan of the suite was open, with all the bedrooms and bathrooms to the left, and a small eat-in kitchen that blended into the common area to the right. Large sliding glass doors that opened onto the balcony covered the far side of the room. The bay was barely visible in the dark, but I could hear the faint sloshing of the waves in the distance.

"I'm here," Stella called from the room closest to the balcony. "I've already claimed this room. And I don't want to hear any thumping, humping, moaning, or groaning from you two. I need my beauty sleep."

I smirked through my cheeks, flushing a brilliant shade of red. After giving his sister a disgusted look, Brooklyn slung his arm around my shoulder and guided me into the bedroom closest to the front door. A queen-sized bed adorned with plain white sheets and pale-blue accent pillows was pushed against the far wall. I took my time unpacking, and realized when I ran out of space in the small dresser by the bed how excessive I had been with choosing how much to bring. I delicately hung my dress bag in the closet, brushing over Brooklyn's eccentric patterned suit jacket. It definitely suited him.

"Well, it's still early." Brooklyn sat on the edge of the bed and beckoned me over. I stood over him, my hands on his shoulders to steady myself as he gently ran his hand up my thigh. He looked up at me, and his blue eyes had a devious glint to them.

"We have the whole night to ourselves." Brooklyn took my hands off his shoulders and held them gently in his. "You want to explore a little?"

I glanced at the bed, neatly made and so inviting, and then back at Brooklyn, still grinning and glowing and everything that made my stomach flutter.

"Lead the way," I told him.

"I have an idea." He gave me a wink, then quickly pulled me out of the suite and down to the courtyard below. Tiny lights twinkled above us in the trees, and a cool breeze cut through me and sent goose bumps prickling up my skin.

"Where are we going?" I asked.

Brooklyn stayed silent and raised his eyebrows. He led me through the courtyard and out to the empty pool deck. The surface of the pool was calm and clear, like a sheet of glass had been laid over it. The lights above the pool reflected glowing pale-yellow dots on the water.

"Up for a late-night swim?" he asked with a grin as he pushed the gate to the pool open.

"Of course, the one item I didn't pack was a bathing suit." I chuckled, my arms still wrapped around my shivering body.

Brooklyn shot me a knowing glance. He grabbed the hem of his faded Carolina Panthers T-shirt and pulled it over his head, exposing his freckled chest. Goose bumps continued to run along my skin as I watched him with the intent of tackling him where he stood.

"You've never gone skinny dipping before, have you?" he asked, but he knew the answer.

"I intend on keeping it that way. Someone could totally see us here."

"Come on," Brooklyn pleaded. He slid his shorts off so that he was only in his boxers. "Live a little, babe."

Suddenly I wasn't so cold anymore. He motioned for me to come over to him, and with every step I took I heard my heart throb in my ears.

"What if someone catches us?" I whispered.

Brooklyn reached down and tenderly pulled my loose cotton dress over my head. I silently thanked past me for picking out a lacy matching bra and panties set. He discarded the dress next to his own clothes. "Look around. Nobody's here. We're out of sight. I promise it'll be fine."

"Okay, but—"

Before I could even finish my sentence, my whole body jerked forward and hit the surface of the water. I sank to the bottom, letting the cold chill my heated nerves. When I came back up for air, I felt Brooklyn pull me up into his chest. I smacked him on the arm.

"Not funny," I snapped. "I wasn't ready!"

"That's the whole point." He grinned and reached into the water and wiggled me out of my bra and underwear, tossing them and his boxers onto the side of the pool.

"That's not so bad, is it?"

"No." I sighed, giving him a faint smile. "It's great, actually."

Brooklyn smoothed my wet hair back and kissed my forehead. "You're beautiful."

"No, *you're* beautiful," I teased him, sending a gentle splash his way.

"Stop it." Brooklyn splashed me back. "I mean it. I don't know what I've done to deserve you. You're so fucking great."

He looked down at me, and I swore that the moon had come down from the sky and made a home in his eyes. My heart swelled, and I leaned my head into Brooklyn's so our foreheads were touching. Water dripped off our hair and onto each other's cheeks.

"I'm so glad I met you, Brooklyn Keller," I said in a breathy whisper. "You make me feel so seen and so understood. I don't take that for granted." Our noses rubbed against each other. Brooklyn brought his lips gently to mine, and I felt him smiling against my mouth.

"Me too," he whispered between kisses. "You make me want to be a better person, better than I ever thought I could be."

"You *are* a good person." I held his face in my hands and stroked his cheeks with my thumbs. "I promise."

Brooklyn pulled away from me and his smile faded. I ran my fingers along his jaw, stopping at his mouth and letting them brush over his lips.

"Nat," he mumbled against my hand. "I have to tell you something."

"Tell me what?" I jerked back, feeling my heart jump into my throat. That combination of words was usually never good.

He must have sensed the uneasiness in my voice, because he offered me a faint smile. "It's nothing bad. I've just had a hard time figuring out how to tell you."

"What is it?" I asked, feeling my heartbeat slow.

He closed his eyes and dunked his head under the water, then came back to the surface and pushed his wet hair out of his face.

I splashed him again. "Come on, spit it out."

Brooklyn splashed me back, and when I closed my eyes, he wrapped his arms around my waist and pulled me into him. His warmth engulfed me.

"Natalie," he said in a breathy voice. "I think that I, um . . ."

He closed his eyes and sighed, and every nerve I had shuddered in anticipation.

Suddenly a group of raised voices penetrated the night air, growing louder as they came closer.

"Shit," Brooklyn hissed as he pulled me to the edge of the pool. He hoisted himself out, and then reached down and lifted me out of the water with ease. Scrambling to wrap me in a towel he pulled from a chair with one hand, he grabbed our clothes with his other hand and yanked me toward the gate. We ducked behind a row of bushes as we bolted back to the hotel suite in only those stolen towels.

We made it back to our room, laughing and chests heaving as we tried to catch our breath.

"Well, trying not to get caught is half the fun," Brooklyn said. He fumbled around the pockets of his shorts for his wallet.

"Hey." I bit my lip. "What were you going to tell me before?"

Brooklyn cleared his throat. “Nothing. It wasn’t that important.”

He gave me a weak smile before turning around and retreating into the suite. A shiver ran through me as water dripped off my body. Maybe it wasn’t that important, but when it came to him, something made everything feel important.

Twenty-four

Morning crept up slowly on me as I stirred awake, blinking a hazy sleep out of my eyes. Light filtered into the room through the blinds on the window, sending streaks of dusty sunlight onto the bed, and I needed a moment to remember where I was waking up. I rolled over to see an empty space beside me, only an imprint where Brooklyn's body had lain so close beside me. The sheets still radiated with his warm scent.

I made my way out to the common area and felt a gust of cool, salty air. The doors to the balcony were open, and Brooklyn leaned on the railing, looking out at the ocean.

"Hey, you," I said as I approached him.

"Hey, yourself." Brooklyn snaked his arm around my waist and pulled me in close to him. It was amazing how at home I had become in his arms, letting his warmth and his fresh, clean scent consume me.

The sun hung high over the ocean, decorating the waves with glints of gold and white. A comfortable quiet consumed the space, with nothing to hear but the faint sloshing of the ocean.

"It's so pretty out here," I said.

"It is." He gently kissed the top of my head. "Not as pretty as you, though."

I nuzzled in closer to his chest, and felt a smile pull at my lips.

I wondered for a moment if this was really how it was going to be. Mornings on the ocean, coffee and soft kisses, warm bodies and the fluttering sensation I got in my stomach every time he smiled at me.

Or maybe it was all an illusion. A trick my mind was playing on me to deflect me from the inevitable crash. I tried not to give it credence, but that didn't mean it wasn't *there*—the constant threat of his relapse crept in the shadows of my mind, only exposing small bits of itself and making me wonder if he could handle another collapse, or if we'd collapse too. I shook my head, desperate to expel it all from my mind. It had no place here, and I wouldn't let it stay.

A knock at the door of the suite disrupted the brief lull of peace.

"I got it!" Stella burst from her room in yoga pants and a sports bra. Brooklyn whipped his head around when he heard Alec's voice at the door.

"Brooklyn, you need to learn to pick up your phone." Alec strode into the common area of the suite, head up and posture rigid like a machine. He slid a bag of golf clubs off his shoulder and let them clatter to the floor. "Our tee time is in a half hour."

"Shit," Brooklyn hissed.

Alec's lips twitched downward into a slight frown, which was about as much emotion as he could muster. He raked a chunk of curly hair off his forehead. "You forgot, didn't you?"

"Give me five minutes," Brooklyn replied hurriedly. "I swear I'll be ready."

Brooklyn groaned and retreated to our room, leaving me alone with Alec. I'd never actually been alone with him the few times we'd all hung out, and the tension of things unsaid was so thick it was almost physically tangible. Alec cleared his throat.

"Nice to see you again, Nat." He nodded cordially.

"Likewise," I replied. I looked down at my newly manicured nails and fought the urge to rip the gel right off.

"You can come to the golf course if you want," Alec offered.

"Oh no, that's okay." I shook my head. "I don't golf. I can't golf."

Stella reemerged from her room and slung her arm around my shoulder. "You don't *actually* golf. You sit in the golf cart with me, drink Bloody Marys, and watch *them* golf."

I cocked an eyebrow at her. "Really?"

Stella nodded with enthusiasm. "Would I steer you wrong?" She paused and tapped her chin. "Actually, don't answer that."

>> <<

The golf course was within walking distance of the estate, and while the walk was pleasant, it was at least ten degrees hotter on the golf course. Thankfully Stella and I sat in the shaded confines of the golf cart with icy Bloody Marys in our hands. The boys unloaded their golf clubs and set them down in the tee box. Brooklyn looked out of place in his loud jellyfish-patterned shirt and blue-tinted sunglasses. Older men in conservative colors with graying beards and cigars in hand strode past their group, eyeing Brooklyn with furrowed brows and noses turned up.

"I didn't even know you golfed, Brooklyn," I said.

"He doesn't," Alec chimed in. "He has more of a Happy Gilmore approach."

"I'm an *athlete*, that's good enough." He pulled a golf club out of his bag to swing it a few times. I took a sip of my Bloody Mary, letting the tangy frigidness of the drink cool my throat. Stella nudged me.

"I'm not trying to be blunt or anything but did you ever figure out what they argued about on my birthday?" she asked.

I couldn't see her eyes through the thick frames of her cat-eyed sunglasses, but I could hear the tinge of hurt in her voice.

I looked down at my half-finished drink, watching the droplets of condensation drip to the bottom of the cup. "No, have you?"

Stella shook her head.

I had an inkling (more like a very large inky smudge) of an idea, but Brooklyn and I didn't talk about it. Almost as if it hadn't even happened.

She took a long gulp of her drink before answering me. "It doesn't really matter. I'm over it and everything. I was only wondering."

Or wondering what the other knew—or didn't know. But that was the problem, wasn't it? It wasn't our thing to tell, and neither of us wanted to violate the sister/girlfriend code.

"You're a good sister, you know," I said softly. I felt a pang of guilt thinking about how much of a *bad* sister I'd been lately, but it was nice at least one of us could be the good one.

"Well, I try." She gave me a pinched smile. "I'm going to get another drink. Do you want one?"

I hadn't even realized how quickly I had finished my drink, leaving only the olives rolling on the bottom of the cup. "Sure."

She hopped out of the golf cart, and my gaze wandered over to the two boys. Their sunglasses hid most of the emotion in their eyes, but Alec talked with his hands, and Brooklyn kept his gaze away from him. He was fidgeting with his gloves, or taking swings with his putter.

I tried to fish out an olive with my finger, but only managed to succeed in spilling ice in my lap. As I dumped the rest of the ice into a nearby bush, my ears perked up when I realized I could hear Brooklyn and Alec's conversation. Alec's voice was even toned and calculated as ever, a distinct difference from Brooklyn's, which was rough and deep.

"All I'm saying is that you can tell me," Alec said. "I'm not *insinuating* anything."

"I know you're not. Neither am I." Brooklyn reached down to the green and placed his marker next to the ball. He swung his putter back and forth a few times, keeping his gaze away from Alec. "Can we just drop it, please?"

"Fine." Alec clicked his tongue. "Things are getting pretty serious with Natalie, huh?"

I bit down on my lip, tilting my head slightly to see if I could hear them more clearly.

"Smooth subject change," Brooklyn muttered.

It was one of the first times I'd actually heard Alec laugh. "Oh wow. I know that look. That's your I'm-in-deep-shit look."

"Yeah, Alec, I'm in deep shit," Brooklyn scoffed. He stepped up to the ball and swung his putter a few more times. "I'm in so fucking deep that I'm drowning."

Alec whipped his sunglasses off and let them dangle around his neck. "Wait, are you serious?"

Brooklyn stepped away from the ball and put his hands on his hips. "What do you think?"

"Well, do you love her?"

I almost lurched forward. Did he love me? And even if he did, would he tell Alec? Would he tell *me*? Or would he hesitate and then pretend it was "nothing important"?

Brooklyn met Alec's question (and mine) with silence. He licked his lips before lining back up with the ball, swinging his club back, and hitting the ball farther up the green.

"Oh good lord," Alec continued. "You do. You love her."

After a long pause, Brooklyn sighed. "It's fucking terrible, isn't it?"

Fucking terrible. The words echoed in my head like a broken record. I tried to keep my head steady to keep myself tuned into their conversation.

"Terrible?" Alec asked. "How so?"

"Because I'm terrible for her," Brooklyn answered. "But I can't stay away. It's like even when I'm not getting high I'm still fiending like a junkie."

He took another absent-minded swing of the golf club and scraped the ground, sending a chunk of grass and soil flying into the air.

"That's kind of insane." Alec scrunched his nose. "Have you told her?"

"I tried to last night. But I got nervous, and I couldn't get it out."

Of fucking course.

"You better tell her," Alec said with a shrug. "Before you fuck something else up."

"Yeah," Brooklyn replied and clicked his tongue. "I know."

My heart jumped into my throat. I didn't know how to feel; some fuzzy mixture of confusion and happiness and a little bit of nausea, though the latter was probably from the alcohol and the heat.

"Here." Stella reappeared with drinks in hand, sticking another Bloody Mary under my nose. She squinted her eyes at me. "You good?"

I let out a heavy exhale. "Yeah. A little hot, that's all."

I looked back at Brooklyn, still lost in his conversation with Alec. He glanced in my direction and smiled at me.

I realized the fuzzy, sickening feeling that rattled my stomach was whatever feelings I had for Brooklyn, taking a form and shape I could finally recognize. It took the air from my lungs until I was just about ready to pass out.

Because I did. I loved him too.

>> <<

"Oh wow. That dress is insane. In a good way, of course."

Stella had come into the bedroom to borrow a spritz of perfume when she saw me crouched in front of the mirror in the corner of the room, finishing up my makeup. I'd tied my hair into a slicked-back bun, leaving the entire open back of the dress exposed.

"Thanks," I replied. "You don't think it's too much?"

"Oh please," Stella replied with a nonchalant wave. "You're going to give my brother a heart attack, and I can't wait to see that."

She echoed Nikki's words from when I bought the dress, and I couldn't pretend that didn't sting a little. I wished Nikki was here to see it herself, and I wished I didn't feel so guilty that she wasn't.

"Are you two ready yet?" Brooklyn's voice came from the other side of the bedroom door.

"You can't rush perfection," Stella snapped back.

"I'm not rushing perfection, I'm rushing *you*," he retorted.

I tried to stifle a laugh as Stella huffed out a sigh. "I guess we have to go now."

Stella strode into the common area of the suite, the chunky six-inch heels of her fuchsia satin shoes clacking against the tile floor. I followed her, in my less impressive three-inch gold sandals that I had borrowed from my sister (because I'd learned the hard way that size did *not* always matter).

Brooklyn was leaning against the back of the couch in the living room of the suite, wearing gray pants and the navy paisley patterned jacket I had seen in the closet earlier. Anyone else could have worn that and looked ridiculous, but he looked amazing in all his wild, unkempt glory. I smiled so wide I felt my cheeks ache. His face flushed, and he ran his tongue over his bottom lip. He kept opening and closing his mouth, as if the words were on the tip of his tongue but wouldn't come out. We drank each other in for what seemed like hours.

"Wow," he whispered. "Wow. I, uh—" He reached down and brushed his fingers over my cheek. "For once in my life, I'm at a loss for words."

"I consider that an achievement in and of itself," I said with a soft smile.

He smelled like a sweet mixture of vanilla and sandalwood, and I wanted to bathe in it. Even in heels, I had to lean forward on my toes to kiss his cheek.

Stella made a gagging noise in the background.

"Oh my god, I'm gonna be drowning in this today, aren't I?" Stella groaned.

"I'm sorry, were you not aware that we're going to a wedding?" Alec asked, and there was enough upward pitch in his tone to distinguish that he was in fact trying to make some kind of joke.

"You know what? You're *almost* funny," she huffed, and she and Alec made their way outside.

Brooklyn offered his arm to me. "My lady."

I took his arm, feeling my heart continue to swell in my chest.

The wedding was held down in the extravagant gardens by the main estate, and most of the sun had set behind us, keeping the crowd cool between the shade and the salty breeze. Rows of white chairs were lined up in front of an altar draped in white tulle and vines of red and orange azalea flowers. The bay served as the backdrop, calm and quiet as night approached.

It reminded me of something my sister would rave about on Pinterest, or something that should be photographed in those wedding magazines that sat in dentist's offices.

"Weddings are so boring," Brooklyn muttered as he unbuttoned his suit jacket and lowered himself into a chair. "At least the wedding ceremonies are."

"Guess it's a good thing it's not your wedding," a deep voice behind us said.

Brooklyn's parents sat in the seats behind us. His father wore all black and large sunglasses even though it was almost dusk. Brooklyn's mother put her hand on my shoulder.

"You look fabulous, Natalie," she offered.

"Thank you." I tucked a strand of hair behind my ear. "So do you."

She tilted her head in Brooklyn's direction. "Keeping him out of trouble?"

For a moment, I caught myself wondering how much Brooklyn's mother really knew, and if she was good at masking her worry. "Of course."

She gave my shoulder an affectionate squeeze before sitting back in her chair.

The wedding ceremony couldn't have been longer than fifteen minutes. Their friend Kayleigh's gown was fully adorned with lace, and the train that draped off of her dress was probably five feet long. The officiate was a gangly, quirky kid who tried to crack jokes, but wasn't very funny. I exhaled, and felt at ease as I leaned into Brooklyn's shoulder.

I was never one of those girls who fantasized about their wedding when they were fifteen. I didn't have Pinterest boards of all the dresses and rings I liked, and I never really had any friends I swore would be in my bridal party. But sitting there listening to Kayleigh and Jackson exchange vows, and the smell of the flower petals as they danced through the air filling my nose, I thought maybe I could see myself doing it all. I'd wear a dress, and I'd carry lilacs in my bouquet, and I'd exchange vows with someone I wanted to be with for the rest of my life. Without thinking, I reached down and laced my fingers between Brooklyn's.

The reception was held a few feet away from the ceremony gardens, up on the main deck of the estate. We were seated at long white tables that were dotted with candles and the same azalea flowers from the altar. Stella and Alec sat across from us, and I lost track of how many *Oh my god I haven't seen you since middle school* people came up to Brooklyn, or how many people he proudly introduced me as his girlfriend to.

"Are you going to sit there and nurse your vodka tonic or are you going to dance with me?" Stella called to me over the table. I opened my mouth to protest, but Stella darted around the table and pulled me up, nearly yanking my arms out of their sockets. I looked back at Brooklyn and mouthed *Save me*, but he chuckled and shook his head. Stella took me to the center of the deck, which served as the dance floor. Lights danced across the tiles, and upbeat pop music I didn't recognize thrummed through the speakers. Every so often I glanced back to the table, where Brooklyn and Alec sat alone, talking with their heads almost pressed together so they didn't have to shout above the noise and commotion.

Song after song played, and every time I tried to sneak to my seat to give my feet a break, Stella pulled me back in. She finally let me go after retreating to the bar to get another margarita.

I teetered back to my seat with shaky legs. Brooklyn laughed as I slumped into my chair, still trying to catch my breath.

"Where does your sister get her energy from?" I asked, fanning my face.

"Who knows? Sometimes I think she has caffeine instead of blood in her veins."

I laughed, and felt my cheeks start to ache from smiling so much.

"I'm going to get another soda, do you want anything?" Brooklyn asked as he got up from his chair.

"I'm good. Thanks, though."

He leaned down and kissed my cheek, and I watched him disappear into the sea of people. My heart jumped when Brooklyn's father lowered himself into Brooklyn's chair.

"Having a good time?" he asked, taking a sip of water. Although I'd only been around him a few times, I'd never seen him drink, and I wondered how personal of a choice that was.

"Yes, definitely," I replied. "It's beautiful here. The hotel, the wedding, everything. Thank you for including me."

He nodded intently. I followed his line of sight over my shoulder. He had centered in on Brooklyn, who spoke to an elderly gentleman in a gray suit. The two shared a laugh, and it made me smile.

"He's happy, you know," Charlie said. "Happier than I've seen him in a long time. Maybe I'm the one who should be thanking you."

I turned back to him. "Really?"

Charlie said nothing, but pointed to the shadow hovering over my shoulder. I turned to face Brooklyn, who held his hand out to me. A light strum of guitar played through the speakers.

"Will you do me the honor?"

His blue eyes gleamed even in the dim streaks of flickering gold light cast over the darkness of the deck. It was like all of the air had been sucked out of the room and then whooshed back in like a punch to the chest. Just like the day we had met.

Except now, it was more than spilled coffee and hot morning sun and worrying about whether or not any of us would have the summer we wanted. Now, he was everything I never even knew I wanted, in all his grinning, charming, larger-than-life glory.

"I'd like that," I replied as I slipped my hand into his. He gently pulled me to my feet and onto the dance floor. With his arms around my waist, he swayed me back and forth, like a tiny ship on the vast ocean, feeling every ebb and flow, every dip and curve. Everything else around us faded away.

"I've never told you this," Brooklyn said, brushing a strand of hair away from my face. "But I'm really glad I crashed into you that day at Otter House."

"Me too. Although I'm sure my tailbone and my T-shirt weren't too happy at the time," I added with a soft grin. I sighed and rested my head on his chest, his arms still draped around me like a layer of armor.

The song ended, but I found it hard to pull away from him. I realized I had been gripping his suit jacket like my life depended on it, and my knuckles were turning white. He tilted my chin up with his hand, brushing his thumb over my lips. My insides fluttered like a caged butterfly, begging to be set free.

"Wanna get out of here?" His voice was low. He jerked his head toward Stella, who'd coerced Alec into being her dance partner, smiling and laughing as they nearly tripped over each other. "We could have some time to ourselves before those two idiots come back."

I didn't even care about how quickly I answered. "Yeah. Let's go."

Without another word we darted back to the suite, kicking up dirt as we trekked down to the docks and ducked in and out of the streams of light that came from the courtyard.

Brooklyn pulled me through the front door, immediately bringing his lips to mine. He kicked the door shut with his foot, and his hands kept me steady as he pulled me farther into the suite without separating from me. My hands roamed up his chest and rested on his jaw, pulling him closer into me and eliciting a deep moan from him.

I kissed him like his lips were oxygen, and I was suffocating. He touched me like every inch of my skin was an antidote to his poisoned hands. Even when he spoke he kept his lips to mine, breathing life into me so that we didn't have to come up for air.

"Make love to me," he whispered, his voice rough as his lips brushed against my ear.

He pulled away from me for a moment, just far enough so that our noses still brushed against one another. His eyes were like a storm, as dark and vast and deep as the ocean, and I was sure I was drowning, but I didn't care. I'd be content lying at the bottom of his ocean forever. I had to tell him.

"Brooklyn, I—" I whispered, but he put a finger to my lips.

"I know," he said softly, his breaths heavy on my cheek. His lips grazed against mine. "Me too."

He moved his lips down to my neck, and hoisted me into his arms, wrapping my legs around his waist. My entire body was engulfed in ferocious emotion, something that set every nerve ending on fire and ran wild throughout my body. It was like my soul had left my physical being, and I was watching us from above. It was love—real love—as pure and as passionate as I could only ever dream of.

"Tell me in the morning." My voice was raspy as I whispered into his neck.

"I will."

We retreated to the bedroom, slamming the door behind us.

Twenty-five

Sometimes when you're asleep, you wake up for no reason at all other than your body's will, as if it knows something you don't. I blinked my eyes open, adjusting to the dim light of the moon that filtered through the window. The space beside me was empty, and I felt a shiver rip through me as I'd kicked off all the blankets sometime in the middle of the night.

Hushed voices came from outside the door. In my half-asleep trance I could barely decipher words, only emotions. Anger. Hurt. I pulled myself out of bed, my body still trying to shake sleep out of me, and pushed the bedroom door open slowly. The common area of the suite was empty, but the door to the balcony had been left wide open, filling the room with a cool salty breeze. I shivered again and slid the door shut.

Out of the corner of my eye I saw the bathroom door cracked open, with little streams of light spilling through the bottom. I moved closer to the door and was about to push it open when Stella's voice rang clear.

"I don't know." Her voice cracked when she spoke.

"Stella, I need more help," Alec replied, more calm and collected than Stella, but it wasn't hard to pinpoint that something was wrong. "Can you please go wake them? *Please.*"

I couldn't breathe. Alec's words were like a string tethered to my body, pulling me closer until I pushed the door open slowly. Part of me was convinced none of this was even real, and my sleeping mind had been playing *Inception*-like tricks on me, still dreaming but making me think I was awake.

Stella stood with her back to the door, and Alec was crouched over a body leaning against the wall between the glass shower doors and the toilet. Bloody towels were strewn across the bathroom floor, lying in puddles stained red. The water in the sink was running. When Brooklyn came into view, my body went numb. His face was pale, and I couldn't tell if it was tears or sweat that rolled down his cheeks like tiny rivers, mixing with the blood that caked around his nose. A mix of blood and sweat and bile stained the front of his T-shirt, and all the smells hit me like a freight train. It smelled like death. My stomach churned, and I felt like I was going to be sick. I went to step backward but my legs felt too heavy to lift and grounded me where I stood.

"Stella." Alec's voice remained steady. "Please. You're only making things worse."

She exhaled sharply. "Worse? How much worse do you think things could possibly get?"

Alec finally noticed me standing petrified in the doorway, his eyes wide and bloodshot and absolutely filled with panic.

"Much worse."

Stella turned around to face me. Locks of her hair stuck to her forehead in sweaty clumps, and mascara streaked her cheeks in harsh, shadowy lines. "Nat . . ."

"What's going on?"

It took me a moment to realize I was the one who had spoken. A knot made its home in my throat, and I was worried if I tried to speak again I'd choke on my own words. Silence bogged down the air. It seemed like time had stopped entirely.

"I got back a little while ago. I came into the bathroom to take my makeup off." Stella choked back a sob. "I don't know. I found him like this. I don't know what he's taken, or—"

She sniffed and turned away, like despite all of this she was still terrified of looking like she cared. That really was the problem, wasn't it? We all cared too much, and it was killing us.

I stumbled forward into the bathroom and looked down at Brooklyn, his blue eyes wide and glassy, pleading and beckoning me closer. The bathroom felt like it was getting hotter, the air stale and heavy. I squeezed my eyes shut, hoping with every ounce of my being that when I opened them I'd be back in bed. I balled my hands into fists, letting my fingernails dig into my palms.

But when I opened my eyes, Stella was still crying, Alec was still trying to catch his breath, and Brooklyn was still sitting on the bathroom floor, shaking and sweating and high. My palms stung as I released my shaking hands.

"Something's wrong." Alec's voice penetrated the silence. "He's cold. He's really cold."

Brooklyn's body trembled, and his lips began to turn a sickly shade of blue. I tried to move forward but I had lost all feeling in my legs, in my arms, in my face. My head was spinning.

"What are you guys doing?" My voice shook as my nerves kicked into overdrive. "We have to take him to a hospital."

Nobody would say the words, but I knew. Murphy's Law—that anything that can go wrong will go wrong, and *everything* was going wrong.

"Stella," Alec said with panic rising in his voice. "Stella, stop trying to protect him. Go wake up your parents. *Now.*"

Stella nodded and exhaled a shaky breath. Without a word she backed out of the bathroom and bolted out of the suite.

Alec moved his gaze to me. "Call 911."

I gasped for air. "I don't have my phone."

Silently, Alec slipped his phone out of the pocket of his sweats and handed it to me.

"Nine-one-one, what's your emergency?" the operator answered immediately.

I hadn't been there when my mom had found my sister passed out in the bathroom because she hadn't eaten in days and was continuously purging. I never thought about that moment, and all the things my mom must have had to do and feel and suffer through on her own. We never talked about it, but I realized it must have felt like this. No matter what you do, there is some nagging feeling in the back of your mind that it might not be enough.

"Hello? Are you there?" the operator's voice brought me back down to earth, the one place I didn't want to be.

"Sorry, yes. My boyfriend, he's unconscious. I—" I could barely breathe. There was no point in denying it, as much as every neuron in my body wanted to. There was still some sane, logical part of me that knew the longer I hesitated, the worse it was going to get. "I think he is overdosing. Has overdosed. I'm not sure."

Alec had put a wet towel to Brooklyn's head, whose mouth was now hanging open and his whole face going ashen, as if someone was sucking the life right out of him. I had to turn away, otherwise I might have never gotten the words I needed to get out.

"Okay, honey, paramedics are on their way." Her voice was kind, and I swallowed my tears down. "Do you know what he's taken?"

"I don't," I told her. "His nose was bleeding, and now his lips are turning blue. His whole face, it's . . . please help."

"Is he breathing?"

I looked wide-eyed at Alec, who shook his head.

"No," I squeaked.

"Okay, you're going to need to give him chest compressions. Can you lay him on his back?"

I nodded, completely unable to register the fact that she couldn't see me. "Lay him down," I told Alec.

As he lowered him to the bathroom floor, a deep, guttural wheezing sound came from Brooklyn's mouth—the kind of sound you thought the monsters under your bed made.

"Oh god," I choked the words out. I wondered if this was what drowning felt like. "Please, are they close?"

"A few minutes out," she told me. "Are you with someone who can help?"

"Yes."

"Have them do the chest compressions while you're on the phone with me. They should be hard and fast but allow the chest to rise completely in between compressions. I can count them for you."

I counted while she counted, and Alec pushed down on Brooklyn's chest with his palms in time with the counting. Brooklyn made another one of those guttural wheezing sounds, like he was begging us to keep him alive.

You never think this kind of thing could happen to you. That's why nobody's ever really prepared. Who ever *really* assumes the worst? Nobody, until the worst happens.

I'd blacked out by the time the paramedics arrived, and things only started coming back to me in flashes as I drove with Stella and Alec to the hospital. I remembered Brooklyn's father lifting me up off the floor (but not how I ended up on the floor), I remembered seeing the table in the living room of the suite moved all the way to the wall by the television, and I remembered getting defensive with a police officer who showed up, as if somehow, nobody had done anything wrong. That wasn't true, but I must have thought that it was.

I'd curled myself up into a ball in the back seat of Stella's car, watching the flashing of passing streetlights with bleary eyes. I didn't realize we'd even gotten to the hospital until I'd somewhat come to my senses in the cushy chair of the emergency room lobby. It was almost 2 a.m., and we seemed to be the only people in the area with any kind of emergency, our various stages of distress and disarray only on display for each other.

Stella's updo had fallen out, and streaks of makeup still decorated her face. I was in my pajama shorts and one of Brooklyn's hoodies. Alec's shirt was on inside out. Brooklyn's parents had managed to get somewhat dressed, but the worse for wear showed the most on their faces.

We all sat in unbearable silence, because what could any of us have said that would have mattered? It felt like an eternity before a nurse came out from behind the stark-white swinging double doors.

"All right, I can only take family back to see him right now."

"Are you serious?" Stella snapped with a kind of viciousness that came from somewhere deep and hurting.

Charlie put a hand to Stella's forearm. "It's okay."

Stella squeaked out a sob as she clung to her father, dotting his gray T-shirt with wet spots. Then Annie looked back at me and Alec with tired eyes before following them back.

For the short period of time I'd known Alec, he hadn't been very emotive—almost robotic in nature (as those kinds of engineering people were). But when I glanced over at him, he seemed like a completely different person than the one I'd come to know. His whole face was red and puffy, his eyes were bloodshot, and he seemed younger somehow. Someone too young to take on these kinds of burdens.

He must have felt me looking at him, because he glanced over at me, and his features softened.

"Are you all right?" he asked me.

I let out a humorless chuckle. "Are any of us?"

Alec sighed deeply. "No."

Maybe it was just because we were all too tired and too vulnerable to bother with niceties, which was why I didn't feel bad asking, "You've known this whole time, haven't you?"

"Knowing things isn't as objective as you think," he replied. "But I had a *feeling*. I—" His voice cracked and he paused, pressing his hands hard into his thighs. "I could say I wish I'd done more, but there's nothing any of us could have done. Not really."

The truth of Alec's statement hurt more than it should have, and maybe that's what finally allowed my tears to flow freely. I leaned my head on his shoulder, and he gave me a gentle pat on my arm.

"I'm sorry about you and my sister," I said to him.

I felt Alec's body shift underneath me as he let out a sigh. "Me too. I liked her."

"She liked you too." I sat back up and looked at Alec head-on, seeing so much human vulnerability in his bloodshot eyes and his pale cheeks. "I don't think she was as ready as she thought she was for someone to see her. I mean *really* see her, like you did."

Alec nodded, pinching his lips together. "Sounds familiar, doesn't it?"

"Yeah." And I wished it didn't.

Another eternity went by before the same nurse came back out to us.

"I can take one of you back there now."

Without hesitation, Alec motioned for me to go. I got up shakily, my body almost numb as she walked me through a long, sterile hallway.

"He's okay," she said softly.

"Oh." I had to tell myself to actually breathe. "Thanks."

She led me through another set of doors to the emergency room bays sectioned off with plastic curtains. Outside one of the bays Brooklyn's parents were talking with another nurse. I exchanged a sympathetic glance with Annie before the nurse brought me into the bay.

Brooklyn was mostly upright in the hospital bed, his shirt torn off and draped over the side of the bed. There were breathing tubes up his nose and an IV in his arm, and although the color was starting to come back to his face, his eyes were dull and lifeless as he noticed me walk in. He barely looked human, and it scared the shit out of me.

"Hey," he croaked.

My body moved on its own again, lowering into the lone plastic chair beside the bed.

I sighed and rubbed the corners of my eyes, blinking back the tears that threatened to fall. I thought back to last night, and felt sick to my stomach as I replayed every word he had said to me. Every single perfect word that made me feel like I could fly. That guy was long gone. The boy who lay in front of me now felt like a stranger, and I was no longer flying. I was falling—hard.

"Hi." I put whatever energy I had left into keeping my voice steady.

"I feel real sick." He groaned.

"Do you want me to get the nurse?" I asked.

He moaned and shook his head.

The exhaustion seemed to hit me all at once now that all the adrenaline had worn off, and I could have fallen asleep in that stiff plastic chair. I wasn't sure how to decipher the feeling that was left. It was murky and sad.

"Nat, do you hate me?" He spoke up again, his voice scratchy and raw like someone had rubbed sandpaper on his throat.

I clenched my jaw, feeling tears sting the corners of my eyes. "Why would you even ask me that?"

"Because I hate me."

I opened my mouth to say something—I wasn't even sure *what*—but nothing came out. It was my body interfering again, desperate to keep me out of harm's way.

"Please." Brooklyn's words were barely audible through his heaving breaths. "Help me."

Somewhere deep in the back of my mind, I must have known. It was there, buried under movie nights and singing in the car with the roof off and laughing over chips and salsa. I just couldn't have borne to face the truth, because despite all of that, I really did love him. But I only truly knew that now, because nothing but love could hurt this fucking much.

I stood up, scraping the chair back against the linoleum floor. Alec was right. What could any of us have done? What could I have done? Brooklyn wasn't ready, either, but I wasn't sure he'd ever admit that. So I had to.

"I can't." My chest ached as every word I said made my heart crack into tiny pieces. "How am I supposed to help you when you can't help yourself?"

He reached out to me with a trembling hand, but I backed away from him until my back was pressed against the wall. Brooklyn choked back sobs, gasping like a fish out of water, tears streaming down his blotchy red cheeks. The machines he'd been hooked up began beeping, and a few nurses came scrambling in, giving me a way to slip out of the bay.

I found an empty spot to lean against the wall, heaving to catch my breath while all the emotion in me came rushing in like a landslide. Stella appeared beside me from seemingly out of the void, and she put a hand to my back.

"You knew, too, didn't you?" I barely recognized my own voice, muddled under all of the tears and the hurt. "You knew he was using, and you didn't tell me."

"I don't know," Stella said haltingly. "I didn't know what to do. I guessed maybe he was getting high again, but I couldn't accept it. I thought maybe he'd change. That his feelings for you would have made a difference. He loves you so much. I know he does."

I struggled to find my words. I wanted to scream, I wanted to throw up, I wanted to unravel, but I didn't. I kept it together, because that was what I did, and that was what I'd always do. But this wasn't for anyone else; this was just for me, because for once, I had to think about myself.

"It doesn't matter, does it? He loves drugs more."

Stella led me out to the emergency room lobby to Alec, rubbing at her tear-stained cheeks as she hugged me goodbye. She might have said sorry, but it sounded far, far away.

Alec and I took Stella's car back to the estate complex, and I threw anything of mine that I could find into my suitcase. I took Brooklyn's car keys, and I drove home.

As I sped down the empty back roads along the bay, I blasted the radio to his stupid grungy rock music and let the wind from the open windows tear through the car. He had promised me he would tell me in the morning. He would tell me that he loved me, and we'd wake up happy to the sound of the ocean and a beautiful sunrise.

It was almost 5 a.m. by the time I got home. I parked Brooklyn's car in front of my house but I didn't go inside. I walked down the street shoeless, willing myself forward until I got to the beach. The sun rose over the ocean, calm and tepid, lined with streaks of orange and gold. It was morning, and it was beautiful. But he didn't love me, and I didn't really feel happy, or sad. I felt nothing.

Twenty-six

It had been raining all day. Water poured off the broken gutters on the side of my house, and even though I was under the porch, droplets still plopped onto my arms and head. Stella stood in front of me, rocking back and forth on the heels of her sandals. She wore no makeup, her face pale and her eyes tired. She must have noticed the disdain on my face, because she huffed out a breath and looked down. Thunder rumbled the porch.

"I promise I'm only here to give you your makeup bag." She handed it to me gently. "And to get Brooklyn's car."

Over her shoulder, Charlie waited in Stella's car. When he noticed my glance, he lifted his hand to give me a small wave.

"Thank you," I muttered, dropping the keys to the Jeep in Stella's hand. I was about to go back inside when she stopped me.

"Wait." She put her hand on my arm. I turned to face her, crossing my arms over my chest. I didn't know if I should feel angry or sad or some combination of both, but it unsettled me either way.

"I want to say how sorry I am about everything. I really should have told you my suspicions. I know you're angry, and I'll take full responsibility for it. You should have never had to see what happened the other night." She paused and let out a sharp exhale. "I don't want you to think that he didn't love you. He did. He does."

I wanted to not care. I wanted to rip Brooklyn out of my system, even if that meant ripping out my own heart, for my own self-preservation.

But I couldn't help myself. I had to ask. "Where is he?"

"I can't tell you. He didn't want me to. But—" She produced an envelope from the pocket of her sweatshirt. "He wanted me to give you this."

I quickly took the envelope from her, trying to hide my trembling hands.

"Anyway, that's all. I'll let you go now. Goodbye." Stella turned and walked back to her car, handing the keys to the Jeep to Charlie. I stood on my porch and watched them drive away, realizing that was probably the last time I'd ever see them.

I darted back up to my room and shut the door behind me, clutching the envelope to my chest. All it had was my name on it, and that was all I could seem to focus on. *Nat*, the way he'd say it with that self-assured smile.

I don't know how long I sat on the floor of my bedroom, running my fingers over the black ink of my name in Brooklyn's scratchy handwriting. I put the envelope on my bedside table before grabbing my phone. My thumb hovered over my favorites list in my contacts for a few moments before shakily hitting Brooklyn's number. It only rang once before the chirpy automated message came through.

"*I'm sorry, this number has been disconnected or is no longer in service. Please try—*"

I hung up the phone and threw it onto my bed. Tears that had been begging to come out spilled down my cheeks, staining my pillow. My head ached and throbbed as every raw and ridiculous emotion surged through me like the dam I'd been so desperate to keep constructed had finally given. I cried and cried and cried until I had no more tears left. Things from the other night I thought I'd forgotten came to the forefront of my memory, and every time I closed my eyes, I saw Brooklyn in that hospital bed. I was sure it would haunt me for a long time.

At some point (though I wasn't sure exactly when) I stopped, and took deep, heaving breaths in some kind of attempt to land back in the safety of my bedroom and not all the dark places my mind was wandering through. I lay in my bed quietly for what felt like hours, until the darkness of the night crept through my bedroom window. It was still raining.

I blotted my face with the sleeves of my shirt before turning back to face my room. What was normally a clean haven for me had become a crime scene. Shoes had piled up in the corner by my dresser, and various articles of clothes strewn across the floor had seemed to multiply, turning small piles into mountains. My desk chair was barely visible underneath another pile of clothes. I shakily got up from bed and poked at a stray shirt with my foot. When I bent down to pick it up, my chest tightened and more tears threatened to well up in my throat. The bright-blue Clayton baseball T-shirt Brooklyn had given me still smelled like him.

I gingerly folded it and set it down on my bed, swallowing the lump that had formed in my throat. I picked up another shirt that sat at my feet, folding it the same way and setting it down in a new pile.

Soon enough I began shuffling along the floor of my room, picking through piles of shirts and adding them to the folded pile on my bed. Eventually I did the same for my sweaters, grabbing bunches of hangers and placing them back in my closet. I stacked my shoes in pairs against the wall by my dresser, finding sandals I thought I had misplaced at the beach and a pair of chunky heels Nikki had been looking for weeks ago.

A pile of Brooklyn's clothes had its own place on my bed, from a teal Clayton University hoodie he had given me after a night on the beach to an old Montgomery Prep Football long-sleeve shirt that had thumb holes cut out at the ends of the sleeves. I scowled at the pile before shoving it on the top shelf of my closet.

"You're up."

I whipped around to see Nikki standing in the doorway. It was so easy to forget that we were technically still in a fight, and suddenly all of that seemed so meaningless and inconsequential.

"How long have you been standing there?" I asked.

"Long enough."

She made her way over to my bed and sat on the edge, patting the space beside her and beckoning me to join her. "How are you?"

I blew a piece of hair out of my face and made my way to my sister. The bed squeaked as I sat down. I leaned on my knees and rubbed my face with my hands. "Terrible." I almost wanted to laugh. "It's amazing how someone can do something awful and still make you feel like you're the one who did something awful."

Nikki chewed on her bottom lip before she spoke. "Are you sure you don't want to talk about what happened?"

"No," I replied quickly. "I mean, yes, I'm sure. No, I don't want to talk about it. It's exhausting to even think about."

"We don't have to, then." Nikki pulled at the sleeves of her colorful knit cardigan. "You can talk to me when you're ready. But can I say something?"

"Even if I say no, you're going to anyway. So go ahead."

"I'm sorry about the way I've acted the past few weeks. I overstepped. A lot. I shouldn't have said those things to Brooklyn, and I shouldn't have tried to manipulate you or the way you felt. Part of me wanted to protect you, but the other part . . . there was probably some kind of mixture of pettiness and jealousy."

I lifted my face from my hands, my cheeks still hot and sore from rubbing at them. Unshed tears in the corners of my eyes blurred my vision every time I blinked. "You don't have to apologize. You *were* right, all things considered."

"Well, I am surprisingly *way* above saying *I told you* so here."

We shared a soft, genuine laugh—the kind that lets you know all has been forgiven even without saying it—and she leaned her head on my shoulder like she did when we were kids on long drives.

"You were really jealous?" I asked her.

She'd been crying, and I only realized that now when she reached up to blot the corners of her eyes with the sleeves of her sweater. "Yeah, I was. Not only that you had somebody to love, but that somebody loved you. Because for all the people I've kissed and dated and done whatever with, I never found that with anyone. I push people away—Alec, case in point—and you do the opposite. You make people feel so loved, even without expecting it in return."

I shook my head, letting a stray tear run down my face. "Maybe that's the worst part about all of this. All the love in the world still couldn't have saved him."

"You couldn't have saved him no matter what you did, and I know you know that."

"Didn't stop me from trying." I sighed, and felt something leave my body when I did. I wasn't sure what it was, but I felt lighter.

"Maybe it's finally time you started thinking about saving yourself. You're the only one who can do that." Nikki gave me a hug, one of those long, lasting ones where you feel like you could eventually melt into the person, before leaving my room.

Without allowing myself even a moment to have second thoughts, I finally ripped the envelope open.

Nat-

I don't even know where to begin, but I'll start with I'm sorry, even though I know I won't be able to say it enough. I'm sorry for lying to you, and for putting you in a situation you never should have been in. I'm sorry for letting you down. I'm sorry for not telling you how I felt about you when I should have. I'm sorry for so many things but I don't have the space to write them all. Most importantly, I'm sorry that I couldn't be everything you deserve, because you deserve the world. You deserve the world and the moon and the stars and everything in between. You were the peace that I craved in my fucked-up life, and like a true addict, I became completely addicted to you and the way you made me feel. You made me feel invincible. But it was selfish of me to hold on to you when I knew I was doing all the wrong things. The time I spent with you will never have been enough for me, but you're enough. You're more than enough. You're everything.

Love, Brooklyn

Twenty-seven

The month of August went by in a blur. Days between Sunday and Thursday came and went, much as they had before that day I ran into Brooklyn at Otter House. It was almost like hitting a reset button. I went to painting classes that Mom taught. I ran every morning. I started a part-time job as an English tutor at a private elementary school in the next town over.

And with any free time I had, I was writing my new novel—a story told through a collection of letters to and from a girl who signs up to be a pen pal to a boy in rehab. I'd recently sent it off to a few agents, and although it was crickets as usual on that end, I felt good about it. It finally felt like the story I wanted to tell.

"So, you know my friend Raquel, right?" Nikki asked as she bit into a carrot. A gust of wind blew by us, sending sand swirling in every direction, including onto our paisley beach blanket.

"Is she the one who has, like, four pet snakes?" I replied.

Nikki pressed her lips together. "I'm pretty sure she's down to three. I think one of them escaped."

I felt my skin crawl as I imagined lifting up the toilet seat and seeing a thick spotted snake curled up in the water, like in those videos people post online about finding wild animals in their house.

"Anyway, that's not the point," Nikki continued. "The point

is, Raquel invited us to Oakridge Farms for some rosé festival thing, and you're coming. You're the only person I trust to take photos for my Instagram anyway."

"I don't know, Nikki. They're your friends, not my friends, and I wouldn't want to impose or anything."

Nikki rolled her eyes. "Ridiculous that you'd even think such a thing. They can be your friends too."

"Okay, okay, I get it." I sighed and started drawing circles in the sand with a twig that had been lying beside our blanket. "But it's fine. Really, I'm fine."

Nikki slung her arm around me. "I know you're *fine*. But I want you to be *happy*. There's a difference, you know."

I glanced out at the ocean in front of us, calm and glistening with rays of the afternoon sun. The salty air filled my lungs, and I felt a strange relief wash over me. I couldn't help but smile faintly to myself, because as much as I hated to admit it, everyone was right about one thing: salt water truly was the cure to everything. I had done enough crying, letting all my sadness and anger and frustration melt away with my tears, and now the spray of the ocean cleared my head. It was as if I was being rejuvenated here.

"I know. I will be. I just need some time."

"Well, we've got *plenty* of that." Nikki heaved out a sigh and sat back on her hands. "Speaking of Instagram pictures, what are we supposed to be wearing to this cooking class later? I'll want a few pics, obviously."

"Whatever you want," I told her. "Except maybe things without strings or big sleeves or dangly things, because I can foresee that stuff catching on fire."

"Of course you can," she drawled, rolling her eyes behind her purple heart-shaped sunglasses.

We'd booked a cooking class for Mom's birthday, partially as a joke since *she* was always cooking for *us* and partially because it was finally something the three of us could do for fun without worrying about the aftermath.

It was almost easy to forget that not everyone made a recovery, because my sister was a perfect example of someone who finally did. The class was *her* idea, and we didn't question it. She still went to group therapy once a week, because there was something to be said about continuity and consistency and learning how to move forward and let go of the past.

But Nikki wasn't the only one who had learned a thing or two about letting go. I was definitely trying. But sometimes when it was quiet and I would close my eyes, I could still hear Brooklyn's laugh in my head and still smell his warm scent in the air around me. So I had learned *how* to let go, but there were little things that I kept, just like his sweatshirts in the back of my closet, which I wasn't quite ready to let go of.

>> <<

"I cannot believe you *burned* it."

"I am obviously not meant to be confined to the walls of domesticity," Nikki said as she skipped out of our cooking class with our takeaway boxes in her hand (obviously *not* including the tarte Tatin she burned).

"Or a kitchen," I grumbled, and Mom laughed.

"Not everyone has the gift."

The sun was starting to set earlier and earlier as autumn quickly approached, and we were bathed in golden, dusky light as we walked down the street to the car.

I wasn't sure if it was just a trick of the time of day, but my mom and my sister looked a bit brighter, as if the sun had lent them some of its light. As we rounded a corner to the side street where we had parked, a guy in a suit collided directly with my mom, spilling her leftover coffee all over the front of her green sundress.

"Oh my goodness, I am so sorry," he hurriedly apologized, handing Mom a pocket square from his blue button-up shirt. He looked to be in his forties, with hair neatly styled back and faintly peppered gray. He swung his messenger bag on his shoulder behind him, and I could barely make out the name on the ID tag hanging from his pocket, but *Dr.* in bold letters was hard to miss.

"Oh, don't worry, this coffee was no good anyway." Mom blotted at her dress, still smiling that same smile that gave her eyes a bit of glow.

"Can I at least buy you another one?" he asked.

I felt Nikki nudging me with her elbow. "Take your time, we're gonna get a drink at Ru Ru anyway," she called, and pulled me away quickly, before my mom had a chance to say otherwise. We cackled as we made our way down the street to Ru Ru, a small place we'd grown to like that served tapas and drinks. After catching my breath when we made it to the restaurant, I felt an odd pang in my chest, and it reminded me about Brooklyn and the day we first met. Was he off in another rehab, running away from nurses and spilling coffee all over someone else?

I looked back down the street, where my mom was still chatting with the man. She laughed at something he said, and the sight of it lifted my heart in my chest. She deserved to move forward, too, like Nikki and I were.

Twenty-eight

I wasn't sure how I had initially gotten roped into Sunday brunch with Nikki and her friends, but by now bottomless mimosas and French toast with strawberries and bananas at a place downtown called Tides had become a staple in my weekend plans. I wasn't complaining, but feeling like you really belonged somewhere took some getting used to. I was *almost* there.

Nikki returned to our table with more mimosas from the bar, and Raquel eagerly grabbed two. Fallen leaves danced across the patio deck in the crisp autumn air. I pulled my cream sweater tighter over my chest as I reached for my drink. Raquel nudged me, almost spilling my mimosa on my jeans.

"Listen, babe, all I'm saying is my brother is very single and you are very much his type." Raquel didn't slur her words, but I could tell she'd had one mimosa too many as she pulled on the sleeve of my cardigan.

"Raquel, I appreciate it, but I already told you I'm not interested in dating anybody." I wiggled out from under her grip. Nikki giggled from the other side of the table and shook her head.

My phone buzzed beside her, and an unknown number with a New York City area code popped up on the screen.

"I should take this," I said before sliding out of my chair and walking to an empty corner of the patio.

"Hello?"

"Hi, I'm looking to speak to Natalie Owens," a woman's voice responded on the other end.

"Yes, this is her," I responded. I started to pace around an empty table.

"Hi, Natalie, this is Marlene Hunt from the Hunt Agency, how are you today?"

I stopped pacing and felt my heart seize in my chest.

"Oh, um, I'm great, thank you. What can I do for you?" I tried to keep my voice steady, but my nerves were firing on overdrive. I'd submitted my manuscript to over fifteen agents in the last couple of weeks, but Marlene Hunt was at the top of my list. I hadn't been expecting to hear back from *anyone* so quickly; publishing notoriously moved at a glacial pace.

"I've just finished reading through your manuscript, and I have to say I'm enthralled with your epistolary novel. The voices of the characters absolutely shine, and you've artfully crafted a story and a romance that is both sweet but so heartbreaking in a very clever way. I had to reach out to you."

I couldn't breathe, although I had to do *something* before she thought I was brain dead.

"Thank you," I finally blurted. "Wow. Thanks. That really means a lot to me."

"The story feels incredibly personal," she continued.

"It is. Some of it is fictional, but, yes, it's very personal."

"I especially liked JD." There was a pause—one I wasn't sure was intentional. "Too often people like him are portrayed negatively in fiction, but you know that's not true. You made him someone to root for."

Then and there, I knew she *really* understood, in the way that I did. "I agree, and I'm glad you think so."

"Yes, well, I'd love to represent you and champion this novel for you. We can set up a Zoom call to go over it in more detail, and then I'll give you some time to think on it."

"Oh, of course, absolutely," I replied, not bothering to hide the excitement in my voice. Why should I? I was getting something I wanted—something I'd worked hard for—and I was so over playing it chill and put-together. I had earned this. I knew I had. "I'm available anytime."

"Perfect, my assistant will email you and we'll be in touch."

I hung up and clutched my phone tightly in my hands. I looked back at the table of Nikki and her friends cackling like crazy hyenas. I decided I would wait until I was alone with Nikki to tell her. I didn't want to share the moment with anyone else.

>> <<

When I finally told Nikki during the car ride home about my call from Marlene Hunt, Nikki squealed so loudly that I thought I had burst an eardrum.

"Well, *obviously* she liked the characters, one of them is based on me after all." Nikki held her head up.

But what I didn't tell Nikki was that JD was her favorite character in the story, because despite all of his problems and struggles with addiction, he tried so hard to be a good guy, and it made her want to root for him. It made me want to root for him too—the real version of him.

I turned onto our street and slammed on the brakes when I saw a red Jeep Wrangler parked at the curb in front of our house. My breath hitched in my throat, and I felt like someone had stomped on my chest. I wasn't sure how long I sat in the middle of the street, but a loud horn honked behind me and shook me out of my initial shock.

"Jeez, Nat, just drive," Nikki said, tugging on my arm.

I tried to swallow the lump that formed in my throat as I slowly maneuvered past the car and into the driveway, doing everything in my power to avoid looking at the tall figure slumped in the swing on the front porch. I turned the car off but sat still and rigid in my seat.

"Nat, you need to get out of the car," Nikki said.

"I don't want to talk to him." I could barely speak past the knot in my throat. "Tell him to go away."

Nikki put her hand on my shoulder. "You need to."

I looked at my sister with wide eyes, and shook my head adamantly. I opened my mouth to protest, but Nikki stopped me.

"Don't fight me on this," she continued. "Forget everything I've said to you about him and people like him. All I know now is that you shouldn't deny yourself what could possibly be love and happiness for maybe even the rest of your life, but you're not gonna know unless you hear what he has to say."

I bit down on my lip as I stole a glance in his direction. He crossed his arms over his chest and slowly rocked back and forth on the hanging swing.

"Look, if you want to tell him to go fuck himself afterward, then fine, but maybe give him a chance." Nikki didn't give me time to respond before getting out of the car. She walked up the porch, and I watched them exchange a few words before Nikki disappeared into the house.

My heart throbbed in my ears as I shakily got out of the car and walked up to the porch. He jumped out of the swing when I approached him and brushed off his green camo-patterned hoodie.

"Hey, Nat."

His voice was exactly how I remembered it, and the light of his presence was like a thousand suns—bright and burning.

"Hi, Brooklyn."

He smiled when I said his name, and *that* was exactly as I remembered it too. I avoided his eyes, blowing out a heavy breath and leaning against the railing of the porch.

"You look nice." He kept smiling at me, and part of me wanted to smack it clear off his face, but the other part of me wanted to fling my arms around him and feel the warmth that radiated from his body.

"Thank you." The cold air stung my chest as I struggled to find my words. "What are you doing here, Brooklyn?"

He cleared his throat and rubbed at his face with shaking hands. He looked raw and unguarded, like he'd reverted to the same vulnerable guy I had met back when the air was warmer and I was more naive than I'd known.

"Can we, uh . . . can we go for a walk?" he asked.

I gave him a curt nod, and followed him in silence down the front steps and out to the street toward the beach. I kept my arms crossed and my head down, doing anything I could to shield myself from him. When we got to the edge of the street where the beach met the concrete, I felt like I could breathe. We sat down in the sand, a breeze blowing through us as we looked out at the ocean.

"I practiced what I was going to say like ten times in the mirror this morning," he began. "But it's not coming out. Not coming out the way I want it to, anyway."

I kept my arms crossed tightly over my chest in an attempt to keep myself from unraveling in front of him. But he'd tugged at the little frayed edges of me, and I felt myself start to come undone. "Take your time."

The silence between us dragged on until finally he let out a heavy breath before he spoke. "I know that I won't be able to tell you enough times how sorry I am. For everything."

"I want to accept your apology, but—" I sighed, keeping my gaze on the water and its choppy waves. I felt so small, like one drop in that whole ocean, but I didn't want to be now. I had to be bigger. "You can't just show up unannounced like this, you know?"

I didn't know if I'd *ever* be ready for this conversation, but I also didn't think I'd ever needed to be. I was fine with ending this chapter of my life—it was short but big and blinding, like a supernova. Like him.

"I know." He paused, and I couldn't bring myself to look at him yet. "Let me get this off my chest, and then if you never want to see me or talk to me ever again afterward, that's totally fine. I get it."

"Fine. You have two minutes."

"When I met you, I wasn't taking my rehab or any of that shit seriously. That's the truth. I thought I didn't have a problem, that I was just a party kid in college who got a little out of control and everyone was being so dramatic about it. That wasn't true, obviously, but that's what I thought."

I finally willed my gaze up to him, and it didn't feel like the sight of him was about to burn every nerve ending I had, so that was a start.

"Okay," I said. "Go on."

"Well, then I met you, and it was easy to lean on the way I felt. Not just about you, but about how I was okay and normal and didn't need to put in any work to *stay* okay. I took advantage of the kind of person you are. I'm sorry for that too."

"It's not like I knew any better," I grumbled. "I'm so used to being the person who fixes everything, I never stopped to think about how that was probably hurting you and not helping you."

"Right, because even now you're trying to take on blame that's not yours."

I hugged my knees to my chest. "I'm working on it."

His breaths were shaky, and he rubbed his eyes before continuing. "But I want you to understand something. No matter what I did or the lies I told, the way I felt about you was never a lie. It was more real than anything else I had in my life."

The air whooshed back into my chest, and even though it hurt, I felt like I could breathe normally again. "I'm not even going to bother asking about what you've done or what you lied about, because it does nothing for me now. But that night after the wedding, it haunted me for weeks. Still does sometimes, but not as much as it used to. I want to understand how or why it even happened. We were happy. At least, I thought we were."

"You can be happy and still do the wrong thing," he said. "I'd bought some oxy before we left, and . . . I don't know. I'm not gonna try and justify it. I did it because I was in active addiction again. That's all. I wish there was more to it, but there's not."

"I get it. It's not personal."

"Of course not," he blurted. "It's *me* and *my* shit."

I nodded.

"So, at the hospital they found out what I'd taken had been laced with fentanyl. I hadn't even taken enough of it to OD, not that that's an excuse or anything. But fentanyl poisons you. It's scary shit."

I scoffed. "You think?"

I wasn't sure anything in my life would ever scare me as much as that night, and maybe I should have told him that, but it was no longer my place to direct his feelings. That was on him now.

"I can't tell you enough times how sorry I am, Nat. No matter what was going on with *me*, all I really wanted was for *you* to be happy. I still want that. Even if you hate me, even if you want nothing to do with me, I'll still do everything I can to make sure you're happy."

"What makes this time different?" I asked. "How do I know that won't happen again? How do any of us know?"

Brooklyn sighed again, pursing his lips together like every time he went to speak, the words weren't right. "The reason rehab doesn't work for people the first or second time they go is because they go when they're not ready. I sure as hell wasn't. They're not prepared to give up that part of their life, mostly because they have nothing to move on to. But I did a lot of work in rehab this time to come to terms with all that, and I realized I have a lot more than most people do. I have my sister, my mom, and my dad. And I have you."

"Me?" I could barely choke the word out.

"Yeah, you." He looked at me, and the gleam in his eyes matched the ocean. "I love you, Nat. I'm not asking you to love me back, even if you maybe did once, and I'm not asking you to save me, because I know now I have to do that myself. But if I let you go without at least trying, I'll regret it for the rest of my life."

I could feel him reach out for me, but something in me seized up. Maybe I wasn't ready for this. Or maybe for once in my life I had no idea what I was supposed to do. Who really *does* at twenty-two?

I pulled away from his gaze and looked back at the ocean. Lately I had come to realize how much life was like the waves. The water comes in fast and heavy, and the moment you think you're about to drown, it pulls back. The hardest lessons in life teach us the most. They come at you like a wave, crashing down on you and threatening to pull you under with the tide, and sometimes you think you're not going to make it, but then you do. You come up for air, you see the sky, and you move on. You're okay.

"You know, when you left I finally started writing again," I said softly, as if I was speaking to the ocean, not him. "I wrote a book about you."

"I bet it's great." He paused. "And not because it's about me."

I drew a heart in the sand with my finger. "Yeah, well, I got an offer for representation earlier. I'm going to accept it."

He put his hand on my shoulder, and even though it was a simple and subtle gesture, it felt right. "I'm proud of you. Really, I am."

"Thanks, Brooklyn."

"I have one question, though. Your book, how does it end?"

I shrugged and finally looked over at him, and in that moment I knew. I knew despite the heartbreak and turmoil, he was exactly as I'd written him to be. Someone you wanted to root for. Someone you wanted to love.

"Guess we'll have to find out, won't we?"

September 13

Hi Dad,

It's been a while. I guess that's sort of the point, isn't it?

For the first time in a long time, I didn't know what to say to you. Not because I didn't WANT to write, but because I needed to find out what it felt like to write for myself again. To let the words belong to me, not to my grief.

I've been good. Not perfect, not fixed, but good.

Nikki's thriving, Mom's painting a gorgeous new collection of portraits, and I'm finally learning how to be part of the world instead of just orbiting around it. I got an offer from an agent for my new novel—the one that was inspired by all these letters I write to you. I decided to start writing letters to someone else, too, and the book kind of wrote itself from there. It's strange, isn't it? I spent so long trying to avoid real stories about real life and real experiences, choosing to fall backward into fantasy worlds because that was easier than real life, but it turns out that was the story I needed to write all along.

I owe you an apology, though. I blamed you for a lot of things that were never yours to carry. It was easier to be angry at the ghost of someone I loved than to admit that I didn't know how to stop clinging to people who reminded me of you, or what you've left. But I finally understand now, you didn't leave ME. So, I've been learning how to stay.

I still miss you every day. I still want to talk with you, so this isn't goodbye. It'll just be different. I've got something that finally feels like mine.

You once told me that life doesn't stop for anyone (even though I'm pretty sure that was about soccer), but for a long time, I thought that meant I'd always be running to catch up. But now I understand it means it's okay to keep moving. Even when it hurts. Even when you're scared. It's how we become what we're supposed to be.

Love, Nat

Acknowledgments

Of all the things I've had to do to this book and for this book, this is the part I was dreading. Not because I was dreading thanking people, but because like Nat, I am an eldest daughter who dreads forgetting people, coming off as insincere, or saying things that are funny in my head and realizing too late that nobody else will get the inside joke I have with myself.

I also never had anything prewritten, like the person who unexpectedly wins at an award show but doesn't have a speech prepared because they didn't think they'd be standing up there. Despite my love for my craft and my dream to be published, there was definitely a part of me that never thought it would happen.

In keeping with the award show theme (and the fact that I just watched the Heisman Trophy ceremony), it's sort of an unwritten rule that when you accept the Heisman as a quarterback, the first people you thank are your offensive line, for protecting you and getting dirty so you can perform your best.

So, to my own offensive line, I would not have been able to navigate publishing my debut novel without any of you. To Anna, the first person to see the potential in *Crash Into Me*, and to my editor, Deanna, who steadied me while I rewrote the entire book in a span of two months and endured my gross overuse of the words *well* and *just*. And to everyone else at Wattpad and Frayed

Pages: Fiona, Delaney, Monica, Rebecca, Erin, and Douglas. Thank you!

To my husband, Greg, this book simply would not exist without you. In 2018, we had just moved almost 800 miles away from where we grew up in New Jersey, down to South Carolina. We were dealing with grief and loss and trauma, and I had all this time and all these feelings with nowhere to put them. So I started writing stories again for the first time since I was sixteen. *Crash Into Me* was eventually born from all that. You listen to me rant and rave and cry and complain, turning into a logical compass when I am lost in emotions. Even when you don't know what exactly it is I'm going on about (which was often when I was neck-deep in these manuscript edits), you never fail to support me. I am so thankful for your constant reassurance (even when I've asked five times already) and for bragging about this crazy achievement of mine to all of your friends, your parents' friends, and your coworkers. You are not just my husband, you are my partner in life through every storm, sunny day, and bad Clemson football season. You have taught me things about myself without even realizing it, and I am better because of you. And Hudson, of course.

Mom and Dad, you are literally my north stars, and I am so thankful for the relationship I have with both of you. I mean, what other daughter can say they've emotionally damaged their father by getting him into Formula 1, and turned their mother into a metalhead? But hey, that was *your* fault for following me down to Charleston. I am what I am because of both of you—anxiety-ridden, loudly opinionated, independent to a fault, and constantly thinking I need more than one dog—but I am also loved and supported in a way that I will never take for granted.

And to my little brother, Tyler (who is not only a whole foot taller than me, but is usually mistaken as my older sibling), you're not too bad, second favorite child. Not too bad at all.

My grandmother Renee, whose house was always a safe place for me, who read all the drafts of some of my earliest work, and who always reminded her granddaughter how special she was and how special she is going to be. I remember showing her the cover of this book when I'd first received it; she got so emotional, and I wasn't sure why since it was only the cover, but maybe she just knew. She passed a couple of months later, in July of 2025. I miss you all the time, Grammie.

Sarah, my writing soulmate. The yin to my yang, the sun to my moon, the push to my pull, the . . . you get it. You are the creative mind I trust the most. I'd drop one hundred more inside jokes if I could, but instead, I'll say something uncharacteristically serious. I am not only a better writer because of you, but a better person too. You are the younger sister I never had but always wanted.

Bri and Angie, who, even though I have to get on planes to see them in person, remain my closest allies, confidants, and yapping partners (from Pokémon to football to *Lord of the Rings*). I'm pretty sure we were separated by a higher spirit because they knew we'd be too powerful if we all lived close together. I think the little Montclair State college girlies we were would be very proud of how far we've all come.

To the rest of my family and friends, thank you for always being in my corner, on my team, and a whole bunch of other sports analogies.

And finally, thank *you* for reading this little story of mine. To everyone who's read it on Wattpad over the last eight years or if you've read it for the first time today. Thank you for helping me realize I had a light to shine.

It's humbling in the best way to know how many people have contributed to making the publication of my debut novel happen, and it's something I have to remind myself of often—you do not need to do things alone.

About the Author

Taylor Romagnoli started on Wattpad in 2018, and after just a few months on the platform, won a coveted Watty Award with her first draft of *Crash Into Me*. Having grown to amass millions of reads across her six completed novels, Taylor focuses on slow-burn romances with complex characters and the raw vulnerability of what it means to be human. There are pieces of herself in everything she writes, and she hopes you see pieces of yourself too.

When not plotting her next trope-twisting novel, she is an avid playlist maker (including everything from Sabrina Carpenter to Metallica), football and Formula 1 watcher, and designer handbag aficionado. Born and raised in New Jersey, she now lives in Charleston, South Carolina, with her husband, Greg, and much more famous rescue pup, Hudson (who once was called beautiful by Jesse Palmer himself).

Behind the Book

People who have been with me on Wattpad know my closing author's notes to any book I write tend to be a long-winded, semi-coherent stream of consciousness. I've been informed I have a word count limit for this, so we're going to try (being the key word) really hard to keep the yapping to a minimum.

I wrote the very first draft of *Crash Into Me* over the summer of 2018, during a period of upheaval in my life. I was moving 800 miles away from my hometown and my parents. My boyfriend's mother had just passed away after a long battle with cancer. I was twenty-six years old, had just bought a house, accepted that I was never going to work in the field of my college degree, and was truly just starting to figure out what it was like to be a real adult.

Suddenly, without friends close by and with a lot of free time, I revisited a hobby I had in high school (similarly when I was without friends and with a lot of free time). I'd found Wattpad on a whim, like I'd blinked and there it was, without even realizing at the time that it was exactly what I'd needed. I'd never written anything that wasn't fanfiction, and I'd never finished anything, but I figured, why not try. So I started posting chapters of this . . . thing. Let's be serious, it was barely a story at the time—it was a concept. And the first draft was in third person . . . *yikes*. Even so, I won my first Watty Award for it a few months after joining the platform. Even though there are still times I think it was a fluke, it gave me the confidence to keep going and say, "Hey, maybe I'm good at this writing thing." I've written six more books since this, and won two more Wattys.

The inspiration for this book came from my own experiences as someone who has friends and loved ones struggling with addiction and substance abuse. I didn't like seeing addicts portrayed with all these negative, often incorrect stereotypes and clichés in a lot of modern media, because I knew it wasn't reflective of the people I knew. I realized I could use my own experiences to tell a different story. There's been four full rewrites of this book since that first one in 2018, mostly because I always felt the need to tweak and change things over the years as I gained new knowledge and experiences (both good and bad), but the core of the story has always been the same.

Addiction still has horrible stigmas attached to it, including what people assume a typical person struggling with addiction should be, but here's a reality check for you—a good majority of addicts are like Brooklyn. They're probably your friend or your next-door neighbor. People who society deems as "normal" are the ones who are more afraid to get help, for fear of how their peers and acquaintances—who are also "normal"—will view them. I didn't write the book to be a "cautionary tale," but rather a way to view this subject matter through a different lens.

I don't like to overdramatize my experiences, because 1) I'm an eldest daughter (like Nat) and have this deep-seeded need to be thought of as independent and tough, and 2) I have a jarringly self-aware sense of perspective that someone *always* has it worse than I do, and people are always fighting their own battles. Why should I burden them with mine? Instead, I found my outlet in writing stories, and here we are.

My life has changed a lot (as it does when you go from twenty-six to thirty-three). Nat has changed a lot as well over the years, from this meek, listless girl to a woman who is almost desperate to show how together and how strong she is—sometimes to her own detriment. Both of those versions of Nat have been versions of me at various points in my life, and I'd be lying if I said I have figured it all out.

For people in my shoes, I want you to feel seen, and I want you to know that you are far more capable than you might realize. I've needed to hear that over the years, and still do sometimes. For people with this disease, who have anywhere from twenty days to twenty years of sobriety, I want you to know that you are more than your addiction, and you are always deserving of help and support. We as people contain multitudes. Never forget that.

Reading Group Guide

1. *Crash Into Me* details the experiences of a recovering drug addict in rehab; do you think Brooklyn's character is an accurate depiction of people going through this journey?

2. How did Brooklyn's addiction impact the way you viewed the love story?

3. In what ways do you think Natalie best supported Nikki and Brooklyn through their recovery journeys? Which decisions do you think were less helpful?

4. Do you think it was right for Natalie to not heed Nikki's warning about Brooklyn after she finds out he is in rehab? Do you think Nikki had a reason to be concerned about Brooklyn?

5. Aunt Mel tells Natalie, "You can put an exorbitant amount of effort into fixing someone who maybe doesn't want it or isn't ready for it, and you end up just damaging yourself in the process." How did you feel when she said this? Did this change your perspective of Natalie's relationship with Brooklyn?

6. To what degree do you think Natalie and Brooklyn might be using sex to ignore the growing flaws in their relationship?

7. After a heated argument with Alec, Brooklyn tells Natalie that he feels like a virus to those around him, and that he doesn't deserve her help. If you were Natalie at this moment, what would you say to Brooklyn? Would it be better to give him space?

8. Natalie's family warns her that she has a bad habit of "fixing" people and that it would end up hurting her. Do you think her relationship with Brooklyn is a result of this, or is their love worth the effort she is putting in?

9. Natalie finds a bag of pills under Brooklyn's bed and, feeling betrayed, storms out of his room. She spends the next day ignoring the calls and texts Brooklyn sends, pleading for her to speak with him. What would you do if you were in Natalie's shoes? Do you think she was right to become distant from Brooklyn?

10. This book covers various sensitive topics. How do you think the author handled them?